THE ARK OF LIGHT

The Ark of Light

KATHERINE GARDNER

Illustrated by: Maria Lyons, Kassandra Jordan, and Rowan Kirk

Lester Beacon & Co.

DEDICATION

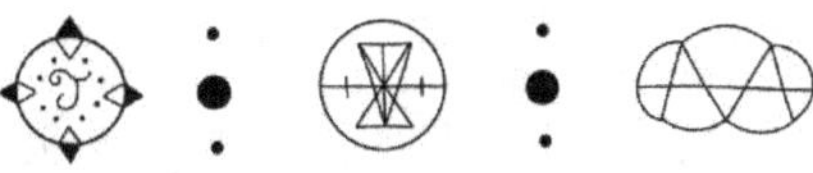

For Pop-Pop, who helped me tell my very first story.
I wrote this on your typewriter.

And for Beth, the first adult I shared this story with.
I know you would have loved what it's become.

CONTENTS

PROLOGUE: A MEETING OF THE COUNCIL OF BLIGHT

"I want them dead."

Her husband's astringent voice seemed to wind through the room like a boa constrictor, capturing the attention of all and quelling every side conversation with the force of a snake crushing the life from a rat. Caeda's head immediately snapped up, hazel eyes wide like a deer in the headlights of a semi-truck.

Who is he talking about?

All members of the Council of Blight immediately took their seats in the basement of the only hotel in the town of Dufferton. Their placement denoted their rank, and some of the more reckless recruits whispered in the back of the room. Roger Callsworth silenced them with a glare so abrasive it put a dragon's scales to shame.

From her seat in the third row, Caeda could see that Roger held a large piece of paper in his hands as he stood in front of the assembled members of the council. When the room was silent, he began to speak again, his dark vibrato echoing through the room.

"This council was created with one purpose in mind: to put magic users in power, who would restore order to the Hell these... heretics have created. They, who use their magic to grow pretty flowers and make coins disappear. They pose a threat to all who understand the true purpose of magic. They want the naked apes who run this realm, who have no magic or ability or importance, to know our power. To enter into our world. These inglorious bastards do not understand our place. They think we are equal to the scum that lives here, the useless filth who walk on mortal legs and use magic not."

Roger paced back and forth before the council, gesturing as he spoke.

"We have put up with it for *too long*. It is time to fulfill our promises and answer to the oaths we swore. We must obliterate all who stand against us and wipe out everyone who would dare defy our will. *We,* who understand the true power and importance of magicians and sorcerers and all else who control the mythical arts, must show the...*ordinaries* all around us who is *really* in control. Every member of this council must step up to fill the role they were assigned so that the leaders of our council may soon become the rulers of this world. All will tremble before the might of the Blight."

Cheers erupted throughout the room. Uproarious applause shook the building's foundations, and Caeda felt as if the room was falling down on top of her. She managed to keep her calm, to keep up appearances and not arouse suspicion by joining in the clapping, though she barely felt her arms moving as she stared at her husband's back. He was, thankfully, looking away from her. He would have noticed her distress if he had seen the look in her eyes. As she continued to pretend to be elated, the weight of Roger's words wove around her body and squeezed the air from her lungs, and it felt as if they had stopped the flow of the blood in her veins entirely.

No. No, no no, this wasn't supposed to happen. I have to make sure they don't go through with this; I can't let them-

All noises around her stopped, and Caeda sat back down in a daze as Roger cleared his throat for silence again. He now held up the paper in his hands as if to let everyone in the room read it. Caeda could barely make anything out, but from what she could see, it seemed to be a list of names. A very *long* list of names.

"With these ultimate goals in mind," he began again, "we must begin to take action. A list of traitors' names has been drawn up. These loathsome imbeciles all side with the quotidians; they will pay for this mistake in blood. We must destroy them, but we must do it in a way that will not attract the attention of our true prey. I think," he said as he took a few slow steps across the front of the room. There was a contemplative swagger to his voice that told Caeda he'd been *thinking* for a long time.

"We should capture and imprison them all!" he revealed with a flourish of his hands. the other elders behind him, over whom he presided, each had a sickening smile on their face.

"Every group of opposing magic users must be rounded up and taught a lesson. There is a large compound outside of town which I know is owned by a man of our own ideals. Before the assembled now, I ask that he allow us to use this place, let us convert it to a prison to house these mortal-loving lunatics. We will place members of our own at the head of it, and those who we can, we will convert. Let the others meet a grisly fate." He looked out into the crowd and singled out a man in one of the farther-back rows, locking eyes with him as he asked, "Sir, will you allow the council to use your property for the greater good of all magic users?"

The man, who looked like he did not at all belong at a meeting of so many devotees, stood up quickly, fear in his eyes at the prospect of having to speak actual words, out loud, to *Roger Callsworth.* He nodded far too vigorously as he said, "O-Of course, Elder Callsworth!" He beamed as Roger's perfected, almost-false smile fell upon him and Roger exclaimed in an overly-enthusiastic tone of voice, "A round of applause for the councilman!"

The applause lasted nearly ten minutes. When the crowd finally stopped clapping, an uneasy silence fell over the room.

Who will be the one to oversee this hell? Caeda found herself thinking.

Roger must have thought the same thing, as he broke the silence by asking, "Who will volunteer to play chief warder for our exiles? It must be someone strong of mind, who will not be influenced by the sinful whispering of our prisoners."

For once, the crowd remained silent, waiting in breathless anticipation for someone to answer the call. Caeda would have been grateful for the momentary peace and quiet, had her mind not been swimming with dread at all of the possibilities. She looked around her, just as everyone else did, and just like everyone else she searched the faces of the people near her for any sign that they would be the ones who would break the silence.

Who will it be? Helen McDreedie, the middle school librarian who once had a student expelled for making a pencil levitate in front of a friend? Or perhaps it will be David Winslow, the only man I've ever had the displeasure of knowing who could gut, clean, and cook a phoenix faster than a farmer could a chicken. Oh, gods, I hope that it isn't-

Caeda was torn from her thoughts by a sudden flurry of motion that came from the back of the room, catching everyone's attention. All turned in their seats to see a gaggle of the more advanced novices- those who were apprentices and clerks for the council's more distinguished members- shuffling. From the center of the group rose a blonde head, then a torso, as one novice stood tall, pulling some of her peers up with her.

"We volunteer."

Shocked gasps and harsh laughs of incredulity escaped the throats of the assembled, and Roger looked with glinting eyes at the young newcomers who stood before their elders with devoted pride.

"You? You think that you are devoted enough to our cause to be so instrumental in our schemes?" Roger looked...unimpressed.

Voices started to overlap as everyone began to say their opinions on the matter.

"They're too new. Too young."

"How could a woman lead such an integral venture?"

"How do we know they aren't spies?"

The crowd fell silent as the blonde spoke once more, her voice even and confident.

"We *are* worthy of this role, Elder Callsworth. I vow, should I be chosen as warden, to bring these traitors to their knees and show them our *power*. Show them what the council stands for. Should I be chosen, I would assess the powers, abilities, and skills of those in the prison, and I would turn them toward the council's goals and teach them that our way is what is right."

She seemed to notice the skeptical looks which were garnered by her opening statements and was quick to continue, "Think about it. A powerful pack of werewolves and their trained-wolf packmates, all fighting for us? A ferrokinetic on our side who can destroy human infrastructure and defenses? Sirens and animal talkers and pyrokinetics who can infiltrate and capture the enemy? Don't try to tell me that you all don't want to convert the *goddamn openly-magical photokinetic* to our side. Those would all be huge, *huge* assets for our army. They could tip the scales, be foot soldiers in our war against the quotidian imbeciles we seek to rule over."

People were starting to nod their heads as she spoke, and the elder council members seemed much more interested in the proposal than they had at the beginning. Caeda felt a glimmer of hope, because this meant those she was really loyal to in the Marmara would stay alive to see her dethrone her husband.

"I know you think me unworthy. You think I'm too young, too inexperienced, you think myself and my fellow recruits are too new to be trusted, but please, let us prove ourselves. Does anyone else here really want to just sit in a warehouse all day and night, watching over prisoners you're going to kill anyway unless they convert on their own? We are *more* than happy to play guards and warden to a group we think we can convert to the powerful army of Blight," the woman finished, still standing tall and confident.

Another of her compatriots began to speak. "We are all warriors. We've won wars for them before, and each time, all we got for thanks was the bitter taste of blood in our mouths and a lashing for back talking to our 'superiors'. They truly believe themselves superior to us, and we're sick of it! We want to win this war for the council. It is a war that we all truly *want* to fight. We understand the importance of going into battle with the biggest army possible, and that is why we want to turn our enemies into allies to the council. All who use magic should come together against the real enemy- those who have no power, but act as though they own the universe."

When the volunteers were done speaking, the hush of the room disintegrated as the elders of the council sat, huddling together to hurriedly discuss the situation. Many liked the proposition, but other, more tenured members were still skeptical as to whether or not it would work. Roger kept glancing out at the crowd and watching the reactions of the volunteers to the pandemonium that had broken loose upon their suggestions.

Caeda, for her part, had been silent the entire time that the volunteers spoke. As soon as she had opened her mouth, Caeda recognized the one who wished to lead the prison. She knew the blue eyes, the blonde hair pulled back into a tight updo, the ramrod spine. She looked so different from the lost young elf she'd been when Caeda had last seen her.

She's gotten so much older, changed so much.

Roger's words were icy and sharp, like a dagger made of frost, and they instantly cut through the hubbub of the room when he asked, "What is your name, novice?"

"I am Linda Bernard, sir. I'm an elf who was born over seven centuries ago, and for every moment of every day that I have been alive, I've wished the mortals around me were not."

The elders looked at one another and murmured some things, and then Roger leaned back in his chair, seemingly at ease with whatever verdict they'd reached. "Well, *Linda Bernard*," he squinted at her, "You had best hope your plan to win over the weaklings is successful, and that your friends over there are strong enough to thoroughly guard those who can't be converted. The council will be monitoring your progress closely, and elder members will drop in *often* to ensure that you're up to the task of being warden." He turned his attention back to the entire crowd after nodding to the volunteers and allowing them time to take their seats once more.

"Now that we have chosen our guards, does anyone have any suggestions as to how exactly we go about imprisoning them all?"

After that, the meeting returned to its usual, humdrum atmosphere. People raised their hands and the higher ranking members were always chosen first to speak (they were the best at stealing the novices' ideas without giving them credit). Caeda slipped back into her own headspace and chose to largely ignore the people and goings-on around her, turning her attention instead to the moral dilemma she was now presented with.

Though she'd never seen her at a council meeting before, Caeda knew this…"Linda Bernard." She'd known her for centuries. Caeda was very young, for a demigoddess, but she was still old enough to remember this elf by her real name, Aemenora. She was old enough to remember taking care of her when she was too young and new to the world to understand how to hunt or use magic. She had sung her into creation, brought her up as her daughter in more than blood. When they'd been separated, she'd gone into a century of mourning that made the skies turn black as pitch, with not a star to be seen at night.

Seeing Aemenora now, siding with the council, broke Caeda's heart. She always was a better actress than Caeda, and because of this it was sometimes hard to judge her true intentions. Caeda hoped by all the Gods and Goddesses of creation that Aemenora hadn't lost herself to the cynicism that so many other ancients had. She hoped she had raised her elfin daughter well enough that she could remember who she was without letting the council corrupt her.

*Why would Aemenora fight for the council? Does she know that I'm here? Does she think **this** is what I would want for her?*

CHAPTER 1: MIDNIGHTS LIKE THESE

When the meeting finally adjourned for the night, Roger and the other elders stayed behind, talking at the front of the room. Roger told Caeda that he would be home before midnight- she doubted it. She knew he was disloyal, but frankly she didn't care. They'd been married for only a few years, and though he knew she had elven blood and knew a lot of powerful magic, he never bothered to get to know her. She let him sense that she was an elf (which was as close to the truth as it was safe to get) and told him that she knew some powerful healing magic. This cover story kept her useful to the council and their plans to create their "new society free from quotidian influence," as her husband loved to phrase it, but not relevant enough to have to actually *do* anything. He made it clear the night they married that he wanted her so he could learn and use her powers, and had married her to ensure her loyalty to the council, and nothing more.

He repulsed her, and anytime he tried to touch her she drew away or deflected his attempts. He soon turned to others, which was just fine. Let him find a mistress who would be willing to give him what he wanted. Caeda would feel nothing but sorry for her.

Roger's "late-night revels" were actually proving quite help-ful now.

They got him out of the house long enough for her to get in-formation to her contacts outside the council. The Council of Blight was not the only group of magic users in Kacapa county, but it *was* the only one that was obsessed with magical supremacy. She vehemently opposed everything the council stood for on a fundamental level, so she did everything in her power to dethrone Roger Callsworth.

Practically, this meant making friends with the mayor of Dufferton, who also led the Marmara, another of the magic groups in the area. She relayed information to Marlene as often as she could, though that was usually only after council meetings when she could get to a payphone. Tonight, she had to sacrifice that time to talk to someone else, and hope that she'd be able to contact Marlene before the council got to her.

Caeda left the hotel and walked out into the cold late-autumn air, hoping to find Linda before she went home. She wasn't disappointed.

"It's been a very, very long time since I last saw you, *Linda,*" she said as she approached the younger woman from behind. The blonde was standing beside a beat-up sedan that was probably twenty years old, speaking to someone inside. She looked up in astonishment when she heard Caeda's voice.

"Wh-what? My god, you're..?" Linda cleared her throat to try and hide her disbelief at seeing Caeda standing before her. The older woman didn't seem to hear her, and continued,

"That's what you're calling yourself now? You've changed so much..." She started to drift into her own memories before shaking her head to get back on topic. "But I suppose I have too. Do you even recognize me after all these years?"

"I...you...you're- ahem. Yes. I recognize you. I know who you are. You're a member of the council?" Linda cleared her throat to try and hide her disbelief at seeing Caeda standing before her. She cautiously continued, "I wouldn't have pegged you as a member, but I'm...glad it's brought us back together." Caeda could see a cloud of something lurking behind Linda's eyes, more than just the confusion that both women seemed to feel at their reunion. Caeda's curiosity, fear, and hope for an explanation beyond what lay on the surface got the better of her, and she spoke again.

"I would never have thought I'd see you fighting for these demonic pigs. What's become of you, my daughter?" Caeda asked in the German-elvish dialect they'd developed together long ago, when they lived in what humanity now called the Black Forest. Linda seemed surprised to hear it, and as she stared at Caeda, a look of elation came over her face. Caeda could feel a mind reaching out to hers. The sensation felt like, as best she could describe it, someone were knocking on the door inside her consciousness. She answered and let them in, standing perfectly still as

She knew the young elf had found the confirmation she was looking for when Linda launched herself at her.

"It's you! It's really you! I was worried one of the elders had touched my mind without my knowledge and was using glamor magic to trick me," she said, her face muffled in the crook of her mother's neck. "Oh, Caeda, I'm so glad to see you. I thought you were dead! I left to assassinate *one* tyrranical king and when I came back you were just... nowhere. Your house was abandoned and there were scuff marks and bloodstains on things and I just thought.."

Caeda held her tighter and laughed, interrupting her.

"Oh gods no, I wasn't dead. I got into a little... disagreement with someone and had to flee, or risk being found with his corpse. I thought you were dead- that's actually what he and I were fighting over. He was a suitor sent to 'persuade the beautiful widow of the wood to forget her dead child and marry him instead'." She shuddered dramatically at the memory of him. Linda laughed at her mentor's dramatics, and Caeda playfully pushed her.

"I'm so glad that something good- that is, seeing you again, has come out of my council recruitment. Speaking of which, why are you here?" She fixed Linda with a stern and slightly disappointed look.

"I heard there's a $50,000 bounty on Roger's head," her daughter replied simply. Caeda looked shocked, and a small part of Linda was momentarily worried that she'd tipped off a loyal council member and screwed herself over.

"Damn, I wish I'd heard of that sooner. I married him to get dirt on the council, but I'd much rather have fifty thousand than work as a spy."

It was Linda's turn to look shocked, but her wide eyes soon turned into the bellowing laugh that Caeda hadn't heard in ages. They laughed and joked with each other, happy to know that neither had gone mad in the time between their last encounters.

"Gods, I'm so happy to see you again, and that we're on the same side. I was so worried I was going to have to fight you like I'm fighting the council." Caeda switched back to English and spared a glance toward the back seat as she spoke, feeling suddenly uneasy again. "Your friend here, do they feel the same way that we do?"

Linda's thin brows furrowed in bewilderment. "My friend? There's no one...Oh!" she laughed when she realized who Caeda was talking about.

"Yes, I would hope my friends hate your husband as much as we do. Here, come and meet them!" She motioned for Caeda to come to her side as she moved to open the door to the back seat.

Caeda cautiously came around to the back door, nearly falling over as two large, energetic dogs bounded out to greet her. She exclaimed happily, letting the dogs (who's enchanted fur miraculously didn't seem to shed much) jump up on her and lick all over her face. She spent a good five minutes like that, then the dogs calmed some and jumped back in the car, watching her fondly from the blanket-covered vinyl seat.

Caeda talked to Linda for almost an hour, catching up and reminiscing. Before they knew it, it was almost midnight, and she was watching Roger leave the basement of the hotel, a black-haired woman on his arm. She knew who she was: as the only female elder of the council, Felicia Hemsleigh, was quite easy to recognize.

Before they were spotted, Caeda and Linda ducked into the car and Linda started it. A few hotel patrons had left to head to their cars, so the women weren't noticed as they slipped out of the parking lot.

"So, where to now?" Linda asked, not bothering to watch the midnight road in front of her.

Caeda was displeased with this, and her voice stuttered and cut off a few times as she bounced around the front seat of the car and replied, "The house is -oof- about -ow- ten minutes away..."

You'd think she'd know how to drive a car after 100 years of holding a license. After the 4th time Linda almost hit something (in the first two and a half minutes of the car ride), Caeda couldn't take it anymore.

"Can you *please* pay attention to the road?" She asked, sounding like a mother scolding her child. Linda scoffed, then gave an exaggerated sigh and took as much time as she possibly could to face front again, swerving back onto her side of the road as she did so.

The rest of the ride to the Callsworth residence was uneventful. They made it to the door at ten to midnight.

"You should make it look like you cleaned up the house while he was gone. It's a mess," Linda commented. Caeda shuddered at the thought of the fight that caused it as she watched her daughter notice, one by one, the fist-sized holes in the walls and the broken vase of dying flowers which lay on the floor.

Linda bent, slowly, and picked up one of the flowers from the ground. She continued to collect as many as she could salvage and brought them to Caeda.

"Caeda, go find a vase for these."

"Aem-*Linda*, you don't have to-" Caeda's protest was cut short by a look from the younger elf, something not quite angry but concerned enough that Caeda felt bad. She walked around the glass with the flowers and put them in a new vase, filling it with water and placing it in a less open and grab-able place. By the time she was done, Linda had thrown away all of the glass, wiped up the water, swept up any remaining shards, and taken out the garbage. The two worked frantically to get the rest of the house clean with Linda even using her elven speed to her advantage as she vacuumed. They were done with the whole house by 12:02, and Linda said her goodbyes to Caeda.

"I'm glad to know I've got an ally," she said, pulling Caeda in for a slightly sweaty hug. "If you ever need anything, just make the Ox Bow. I'll be there as quick as I can."

Yes, Caeda thought, her fingertips tingling at the memory of her power. *Because rearranging the stars into a new constellation won't arouse **any** suspicion.*

"Or," she suggested, "I could scry you?" Caeda almost laughed at Linda's deadpan expression. She always had been fascinated by her mother's ability to manipulate the sky. "Now, go! Before Roger gets home and sees you. Oh, and you should know, I go by Cindy now. He doesn't know what I really am, and I intend to keep it that way."

Linda laughed and a mischievous smile spread across her lips. "Oh, I don't think he will. Bye, *Cindy.*" With that, she slipped out the door and disappeared around the corner of the block, where she'd parked the car just to be safe.

Roger got home ten minutes later, looking frustrated but pleasantly surprised at the unexpectedly clean state of the house. He came up to her and took her chin in his slender fingers, giving her a peck on the cheek as a formality. He then let her go so that he could put away his coat.

"I'm sorry it took me so long to get back, darling. I wish I had been here to help you clean up, but our meeting ran late, the car wouldn't start, and I hit *every red light* on the way home!"

CHAPTER 2: WELCOME TO THE POCKET WATCH

On the outskirts of Dufferton, just two miles from the highway, an old historical mansion sat on the edge of a forest. Mount Wapetona loomed in the distance past a thicket of trees and inside the mansion, which had been converted to a sort of trading post, a tall young man with dirty blonde hair was shelving paperbacks in the store's rather large book section. Suddenly, he heard someone clear their throat behind him, and he turned around on his bookshelf ladder to look through the doors that separated the tea room from the rest of his shop. There was a person standing just beyond the door, and Randy could tell who he was even without being able to see him.

"Everything alright, Ilya? You spill tea or something?"

The customer in question, a white-haired man with a curly beard and tired eyes, looked up at him sheepishly and cleared his throat. He motioned for Randy to come to him, and when the younger man did, he replied to the question.

"Mr. Jefferson, I'm so sorry, but I have forgotten the geodes I was going to pay for our bill with. I don't know if I have enough money with me to cover our bill, but my cane is made of fine rosewood, and the handle is genuine ivory. Perhaps we could-"

Randy raised a hand to stop the deal before it began. He placed it on the old man's shoulder and smiled at him kindly.

"*Mr. Ivanov*," he said with exaggerated formality, "You don't honestly think that I'm going to take your cane, a device which holds not only sentimental value but which you also *need* to be able to walk out of my shop tonight, in exchange for nothing more than some tea and spices? No, Ilya."

He began to lead the old man back to his table, where two other old men and an old woman were waiting. He smiled at them, then turned his attention back to Ilya.

"You and your friends have been loyal customers of this shop since I opened it two years ago, and you've all done so much to get the community to welcome Abigail and I. Tonight's tea is on me. Just remember your geodes next time, okay? Or, if you do forget again, just bring 'em by whenever it's most convenient for you. We'll get you a tab started here, then you can pay it anytime."

Ilya nodded, then Randy clapped the man good-naturedly on the back. He helped the others up from their seats, walking them to the door to say goodbye as they stepped out into the brisk autumn air and began to head back in the direction of the retirement community down the road. He watched them until they were out of sight, then he turned back to his shop. He walked back to the tea room and picked up the retirees' dishes, being careful not to let any of the delicate china fall as he balanced it in his hands. He placed the cups and saucers in the sink.

"Abigail, can you come down and help with the dishes?"

She came into the kitchen a few minutes later, griping about how sunny it had been all day. She stretched and yawned, making a point of seeming like she'd just woken up, even though Randy doubted it. She often went for days or even weeks without sleep, especially when she was in the middle of some project. She handled the money side of the store's business (which was good, because Randy was horrible at math) so she was always busy. She grabbed a towel and joined him at the sink.

"How was your day?" he asked, already beginning to wash the various cups from customers' tea orders. After each cup and saucer was washed, he handed them off to her and she gently dried them off.

"It was pretty good. I got a pretty good amount of sleep," she lied, unable to keep the smirk off her face. They both knew she was lying, and Randy snorted. The two laughed together.

"Pfft, yeah right," Randy said. "I definitely heard papers shuffling when I walked past the attic door at noon." He picked up a handful of suds and blew them at her.

"Gah!! Yeah, okay you caught me!" she laughed. "I was doing the paperwork to renew your business license and get myself fully registered as your partner for the upcoming year, then I got distracted by some old books. What about you? Did you get to talk to that one regular you were flirting with last weekend?"

Randy blushed and let his hair fall in front of his face to try to hide, but Abigail just reached over and tucked it behind his ear with a raise of her eyebrow. She'd clearly struck a nerve- from the way he wasn't smiling he knew she could tell it hadn't gone well.

"Damn, man, I'm sorry. He was really sweet."

Randy sniffed, wiping his nose and getting some suds on it in the process. He frowned and shook away the memory of the dusty blonde haired man who'd been coming in for tea every weekend for the last few months. The guy, who was a few years older than him, had been staying with his aunt while she recovered from surgery, but now that she was recovered he'd stopped by one last time to say goodbye as he went back to the city.

"Back to the drawing board, I guess. It's kinda hard to find someone in Dufferton, not gonna lie. 850 residents isn't a big dating pool, even when you swing both ways."

Abigail nodded along in agreement, and then Randy decided it would be best to change the subject. He told her about Ilya and they discussed how they might formalize the tab system they'd created for regulars as they finished up the dishes.

By the time they were done it was getting quite late, and darkness was falling outside. Through the kitchen window, he saw headlights cut through the twilight as a truck pulled around the side of the store to the back parking lot. He recognized the rusty blue thing, and he dried his hands immediately as he hurried out to greet the driver.

*Finally! I've called Marlene half a hundred times in the last two months, and now she's **finally** come to fix that damn timer problem in the greenhouse!*

Randy mentioned her to Abigail, who gave him nothing more than a nod in reply. She'd begun counting the number of herbs and spices that they were almost out of and this activity was keeping her full attention. Shaking his head, he made his way to the back door.

He stepped out into the evening air a few moments later, breathing in the scent of pine sap and car exhaust that lingered in the parking lot behind his shop. He made his way around the gnarled roots and rocks at the edge of the gravel lot until he reached the beginning of the woods. Following Marlene's footprints, he confidently made his way to his greenhouse.

He walked inside and navigated through the maze of copper piping and exotic plants that twisted through the building. Eventually, he found his friend standing in front of a large metal panel, trying not to harm the plants that had grown over the small door as she jimmied it open. She growled in exasperation when she looked inside at the web of vines and plants that were tangled up in the building's wiring.

Randy cleared his throat, and she jumped away from the panel.

"I told you to quit doing that to me!" she yelped, turning on him. "I might not keep fixing your things if you keep scaring me, you know." She said as she slapped him lightly on the arm. He just laughed and pushed her away.

"Yeah, well, maybe if you'd actually answer your phone once in a while and come fix my greenhouse when it breaks, I wouldn't have to scare you. This is vengeance for the deaths of almost a whole crop of Valerian root. If the greenhouse timer was working, my plants would have been watered properly," he snipped, pretending that he was incredibly mad at her, even though he knew that the Valerian root would've died no matter what because of an unfortunate squirrel-break-in incident.

"I found the problem. *Your plants* have begun to attack the integrity of *my* machine. Need I remind you that I'm the one that built this greenhouse, wiring and all." she shot back. "This thing is my technical masterpiece, and I'll not have you implying that it's my fault it isn't working. It'll only take me about five minutes to fix, but I have to kill your...whatever this plant is. Sorry, not sorry."

Randy let out a screech and stepped between Marlene and the plant, which was an extremely finicky moonflower he'd been trying to grow for months now. He motioned for her to step back, then muttered under his breath as he worked to get the plant untangled from the wiring. After a few minutes of tugging and a small amount of magic, he got the plant untangled and out of the panel. He then set it against an empty trellis nearby and wiggled his fingers so the vines would begin to wrap themselves around the structure and creep upward against it.

Marlene nodded to him in thanks, and raised her hand. The broken, jumbled mess of wires and gears inside the panel immediately began to shift, setting themselves right in a matter of minutes. She pulled a wrench out of her pocket and began tightening bolts and adjusting the dials and meters that kept the automatic sprinklers, lights, and humidifiers in running order. When she seemed satisfied, she looked back over to Randy, who was tending to his plants with a loving, vaguely paternal look in his eyes that almost made her laugh.

"Hey, uh, plant dad. You notice anything else off about the greenhouse? Nothing over-watered or under-watered or wilting?"

He shook his head, keeping his attention on the plants. She nodded to herself, then looked back at him with a cautious expression.

"You notice anything off in town lately? I've been hearing mutters around the county from various people that really don't sound too good."

He looked up at her, worry hardening in his eyes. He shook his head, then seemed to reconsider the question.

"You know what, yeah. I've noticed that more of the town's elders have been, like, *moodier* than usual? Does that make any sense? And I've seen large groups of cars driving by at night, heading toward the highway and hotel there. I figured maybe the Marmara had been having more meetings lately, and I was gonna ask you about it. If it isn't you all, what could it be? Do you think something more sinister could be going on?"

She nodded, checking her watch. "Yeah, I do. I know exactly what you mean, about the elders, and I know for a fact that none of them are Marmarans. Something's been up at the police station too- lots of new cops and a new police chief have come from up in the city to work on a case they wouldn't say anything about."

She paused in her speech to lead him to the door of the greenhouse, bringing him outside and pointing off into the woods toward the mountains in the distance.

"There was also a bunch of construction trucks up there the last time Konna and I went hunting, and a bunch of permits filed with the county for it too, mostly filed under the police chief's name, Roger Callsworth. That ringing any bells to you?"

Randy shook his head, looking toward the shop he called home. "You think it's connected?"

Marlene shrugged, following him as he led her back to the Pocket Watch. The cold autumn air was getting to him, and he didn't want to be in the woods at night any longer. He detested the dark, and Marlene knew it, too. She paused on the porch of the shop to flick the switch for the illuminated sign on the roof which glowed the words "The Pocket Watch Spice, Tea, and Curiosity Shop" into the night sky. She tried to change the subject and lighten the somber mood Randy had been thrown into.

"I'm pretty sure they can see that sign from space, Randy. What'd you do to it, shove the entire sun inside the light box?" She was relieved to see him laugh.

"No, but I *did* work a little magic on the bulbs inside of it. You can see it from city hall, if you look closely enough. Hey- that's an idea. Whenever something goes wrong with the greenhouse, or I happen to get a customer who wants a cuckoo clock, I'll turn on the sign. Even in broad daylight, that'll *definitely* get your attention."

She laughed as she followed him through the shop. He dusted various trinkets, rearranged some antique furniture, and finally stopped in front of the glass counter that held his cash register and all of the most valuable things the shop sold. Crystals and planchettes dotted the shelves, interspersed with various packs of incense and a rather intricately-carved set of knuckle bones. In the center of the bottom shelf was a heavy-looking leather bound book. He slipped behind the counter and unlocked the case, pulling the book off of the shelf and dropping it onto the counter top with a flourish. He pushed up his glasses and looked at Marlene with a grin.

"I believe, as payment, I owe you a spell. What'll it be, Ms. Fitzgerald? Pick your poison- card tricks or luck charms?" As he spoke, Randy turned the book towards him and cracked it open.

CHAPTER 3: THE WARNING

"You know what, make it a luck charm, the strongest you've got," Marlene said.

Randy grinned and snapped his fingers, hopping over the counter top to grab something from a jar on a nearby shelf. Bringing it back, he held it up to show Marlene that it was a section of antler.

"Three points from a newly killed buck," he explained, reading from the book as he dropped the bone into a large basin of water he'd prepared.

"Fern and heather, dill and thyme, bark of oak and columbine. Thrice a drop of blood to bond and now your bad luck will be gone."

As he spoke the incantation, Randy dropped each ingredient into the basin and swirled it with the bigger half of a wishbone. When it came time for him to add the drops of blood, he took one from himself, one from Abigail (who was very upset to have been interrupted from her counting), and then he let a drop of Marlene's blood fall into the water. This would make the charm stronger, or so his spell book claimed. When he was finally done creating the talisman, he pulled it out of the water and dried it with a large wad of cotton, then handed it to Marlene. It glowed gently and she took it, wrapping a length of cord around it and tying it onto one of the belt loops of the overalls she was wearing.

As Randy was making small talk and putting away his supplies, he heard another car pull into the parking lot. A moment later, the door to the shop was pulled open rather brusquely by a middle-aged man who looked like he lived in his parent's basement and showered once a month. Randy gave a bemused smile and looked at the clock, silently kicking himself for allowing the shop to close so late. The man looked as though he were there to do nothing but take his time and browse.

Marlene leaned over the counter and murmured, "I'd be careful about using that stuff in front of strangers, Randy. I know you Twalneres are all about being loud and proud about magic, but some don't like that very much." She nodded slightly to the man, who was coming their way, and gave him a knowing look.

"I do hope I'm not interrupting an important meeting with a constituent, Ms. Mayor," the man said, looking from Marlene to Randy as he stepped up to the counter. "I found this old ring in a trunk in my uncle's attic and I wanted to have it appraised. I believe it may be a...*ring of power*." He dropped his voice to a conspiratorial whisper, leaning in with a knowing look at Randy's magic cabinet.

Randy held out his hand for the ring, pushing his glasses up onto the top of his head so that he could see it better. He examined it for several minutes, humming occasionally and scribbling things on a small sheet of paper. When he finally looked up again, he passed the ring back to its owner.

"Well, sir, your ring is quite old, and it does seem to have a slight aura around it, but if it's a ring of power it hasn't been charged with energy in decades. As a ring by itself, it's lovely and probably worth two or three hundred bucks, but as for its magical value.... I can't really tell you how much power it could give you. In total, this ring is probably worth four or five hundred bucks, uncharged, to the right buyer. Try charging it with energy for a while and come back, then I'll be able to tell you how much it's really worth."

The man nodded to himself and sighed, muttering something under his breath that Randy didn't catch. Marlene turned to the man, steel hardening in her voice when she asked him what he meant by his comment.

"Wait, what did you say?" Randy asked, hoping to avoid a confrontation in his shop.

In a disturbingly calm voice, the man replied, "I simply said that it's a shame this place will be shutting down since it'll be impossible to find new management for such a peculiar place. I was hoping to trade in this ring for its full value before your shop shut down."

Randy's eyes widened, then narrowed. He opened his mouth to say something, but Marlene was quicker to respond.

"And what makes you say that?"

"Things are changing around here, and soon the new will usher out the old." The man's eyes turned to Marlene with a dark gleam as he looked her up and down. "The Marmara and the Twalnaverra are not the only societies of power around here, and they're too weak to keep the peace. New leadership will be taking over your position, mayor, and you'll no longer be...necessary. You should reevaluate your priorities, and decide whose side you're really playing for."

He took a step closer to her, and Randy saw a tattoo of a strange hourglass poking out of the top of the collar of his shirt.

He pushed between the man and his friend to cut their interaction off.

"I won't tolerate threats to my customers, sir. I don't know what you're implying, but I don't care. You need to leave. Now." He pointed to the door, and the man stepped back and raised his hands in surrender. He turned to leave, saying over his shoulder, "Fine. I'll leave. I tried to warn you, though. When we reach your names on our list, I hope you remember this interaction, and I hope you realize that you could have joined us."

Before either of them could ask him what he meant, he was gone, the door of the shop closing hard behind him. Marlene and Randy looked at each other uneasily, the silence of the room engulfing them. They both knew what he was talking about, but neither knew exactly who he was working for. As leaders of their respective communities, the Marmaran and the Twalnere were both quite put off by the stranger's words. After a minute that felt like a year, Marlene broke the silence.

"That was...unsettling."

"Downright creepy if you ask me."

"I agree. You think he was talking about what we were talking about before?"

"I think so," Randy replied, going through the shop to the back entrance and locking the door firmly. Marlene followed him, straightening a few books nearby. She kept most of her attention on him as she did.

They made their way back to the front entrance of the store, checking that all the windows were locked as they went. When they were confident the shop was secure, Randy turned to Marlene.

"You going home now, or you wanna stay for a drink?"

"I'm gonna head home," she answered, bending down to retie one of her boots. "Konna's gonna get back tonight and I want to make dinner for her. It's our anniversary next week and I wanna spoil her, especially since she's been gone for awhile on a business trip, you know? Hey, about that payment you owe me for the last time I worked on the greenhouse...you got anything she might like? As an anniversary present?"

Randy nodded, then motioned for her to wait where she was for a moment. He left her, then came back a few minutes later holding a small pink box. Inside, a flower carved from rose quartz was suspended on a thin silver chain. The bottom of the box was lined with satin and pink rose petals.

"Think she'd like something like this?"

Marlene gently picked up the necklace and began inspecting it, turning it over in her hands and seeing how the stone caught the light.

"She'll love it. Thanks man, you're a lifesaver." She put it in her coat pocket and allowed him to open the door for her. They stepped out onto the shop's front porch and Randy instinctively locked the door behind them.

"Oh, I'm an idiot. You parked in the back parking lot, didn't you? Oh well, you can just-"

Randy cut himself off and stared at something across the street. Marlene followed his gaze and cursed quietly. The stranger was standing across the street, his car nowhere in sight. He was just... watching them, and Randy grew more angry with each passing second.

"Hey you know what?" he asked loudly, his voice echoing across the street so he knew the man could hear him.

"Why don't I drive you home? That way I know you got there *safely.*"

He punctuated his words with a glare at the stranger (who, much to Randy's discomfort, seemed closer than he had a minute ago) and took Marlene by the arm, leading her around the side of the repurposed mansion. He listened carefully for any sign of anyone following them, and thankfully there was none. Marlene tugged on his sleeve a bit and leaned close to him.

"You don't have to drive me, Randy. He hasn't seen my truck, and the windows are tinted so he won't be able to tell who's driving it if I leave from the back parking lot."

"I know, I just wanted him to know I know he's there. I'll go in the back door once I've seen you drive off. Take the long way home, okay? And make sure Konna knows to keep an eye out if she's alone at night. Whoever he is, he's giving me *real* bad vibes and I wouldn't put it past whoever he's working for to go after people you care about, especially ones who don't have powers to defend themselves with. I'm gonna warn Abigail about it too."

They'd reached her truck uninterrupted and Randy helped her into the passenger seat. She nodded, saying goodbye as she pulled the car door shut and started the engine. Randy watched his friend pull out of the parking lot, then he waited until he saw her taillights disappear completely down the dark road before he went back inside through the back entrance, locking it once more behind him.

He called to Abigail, who came down the stairs with a concerned look on her face at the odd tremor in his voice.

"What's up Randy? Is everything alright?"

He sighed, rubbing his face and shaking his head. She followed him into the kitchen, where he put on a kettle for tea. She pulled the peppermint and chai out of the cabinet as he got out a couple mugs, then they waited for the water to boil. The silence in the room was tense, and Abigail couldn't help but notice how Randy jumped at every sound the old building made. She was about to ask him what was going on when the kettle whistled. Randy yelped and grabbed the nearest object to him (a teacup with a large chip in the bottom of it) and made to defend himself with it.

Abigail gave him a concerned look and walked over to the stove, making a big show of taking the kettle off of the burner, stopping the noise. Her business partner cleared his throat and put the cup back down, blushing and looking down in embarrassment. Abigail poured the tea and waited a moment for him to explain himself, but when no explanation was forthcoming, she let out an exasperated sigh and raised her voice.

"Okay, what the hell's going on? You're literally never this paranoid. Did something go down between you and Marlene? Is the Marmara trying to start shit again? I thought you all were finally getting along?"

Randy raised a hand, shaking his head at her questions.

"No, no, the Twalnaverra isn't fighting with the Marmara again. This is different and a hell of a lot more dangerous. Abigail...

someone just came in here actively threatening Marlene and I."
Abigail bit back a gasp as he continued,

"He said we weren't the only groups of magic users around here, and that 'new leadership' was coming and we should 'rethink which side we're on.' Something is going on in the shadows here in Dufferton, Abigail, and I don't like it."

Abigail immediately began to question Randy, asking for all the details he could remember of the evening. She knew if the stranger were threatening him, she'd have to protect her friend, no matter how much he told her not to. When he was done telling her about the night's events, Randy looked down into his teacup. He fidgeted with the cup's handle, turning his fingers around the ornate decoration there.

"He sounded almost like he was trying to recruit us, or scare us into joining whoever he works for. Look, I know I told you I would never pressure you into joining a side, but I'm worried these creeps are going to try and recruit you. I know you'd never side with people like this willingly, but I swear, the dude had an aura of pure malice around him. I could feel him trying to touch Marlene's mind, and if he's willing to try and control the thoughts of the mayor of Dufferton, he's sure as hell not gonna be afraid of attacking your mind. You're new, and you're young, and dammit you're my friend. They made it clear I'm on their list, and if I'm on it, they'll go after you to get to me. If you join the Marmara or the Twalnaverra, you'll have the protection of two hundred other magic users from both sides watching your back. I don't care what side you choose, Ab, but you have to choose one. The more members the Twalnaverra and Marmara have, the stronger and safer we'll be."

Abigail sat in silence for a few minutes when he finished speaking. To Randy, she seemed to be carefully considering all of the information she had been told, but in all honesty, Abigail was trying to remember the difference between the Twalnaverra and the Marmara.

Marmarans believe magic should be used for good and shared between magic users only, and Twalneres believe it should be celebrated openly and shared by all. Marlene's in charge of the Marmara, Randy's in charge of the Twalnaverra. Marlene's nice and all, but if her leadership of the Marmara is anything like her actions as our mayor, I won't know the difference between a Sunday school classroom and the actual magical society I'll be a part of. I like how Randy's open about magic and doesn't complain when I hunt live things. It's nice to not be forced into drinking nothing but donated blood...

Abigail was snapped out of her reverie by the sound of Randy clearing his throat, and she immediately became aware of his eyes on her.

"Oh, yeah, uh sorry. I mean, I work for you, don't I? And as long as I don't stay a rogue, I could always change my mind later. I guess I'll join the Twalnaverra."

Randy nodded, looking relieved that he didn't have to worry about Abigail betraying him and more than a little smug at the fact that he'd beaten Marlene yet again in their game of recruitment. He smiled openly, letting some of the tension of the night ease.

"Good," he said, "I don't have to worry about two people I know lecturing me about how I use my magic. Now, you can feel free to do whatever you want other than, say, cook meth in my living room, but I'm gonna head to bed."

Abigail was glad she'd chosen to chill with the Twalnaverra. She hated forced formality, which, coincidentally, was why she hated almost every other vampire she'd ever met. It was like everyone but her had been frozen in the Victorian era, which was a bad enough era when she'd been there the first time that she really didn't want to relive it. The fashion was gorgeous though, she had to admit.

Randy said goodnight to her and checked the windows and doors a few more times, then went upstairs to bed. She cleaned up the dishes from their late-night tea session, then decided she would do a bit of digging to try and find out who could possibly have something against her friends.

CHAPTER 4: STRANGE SCENTS

Paws pounded against forest floor, then grass, then a muscular body squeezed under some no-longer-sharp chain-link and the sound of tires on gravel stopped her. She crashed down a gully and into a stream to avoid being seen or hit, then leapt onto the small bank beside the water. Shaking herself dry, the wolf followed along the stream until she reached the edge of the trees. Breathing heavily, she dropped the leather pouch from between her teeth with a clink of coins, then stepped forward into the sun and up onto two legs.

The bell above the door of the Speed-E-Mart tinkled lightly as Quin Von Fer stepped inside. Her long brown hair was pulled into a messy, pine-scented braid and her damp black tank top revealed the black and gold wolf's paw tattooed on the dark skin of her left shoulder.

Quin was intimately familiar with the layout of the Dufferton Speed-E-Mart. Every aisle and row was etched into the back of her mind so well she knew the store better than she knew her own voice. This convenience store was one of the only stores she went to in town, as her family mostly grew its own food or hunted for the meat they ate. That was easier, for the most part, than lugging a whole bunch of groceries back to their homestead on Mt. Wapetona. Still, there were some things you just didn't make on your own when you could buy them for under a dollar fifty.

She waved to the twenty-something year old at the register and walked backwards down the snack aisle, casually surveying the new arrivals until she came to the section she was looking for.

She grabbed five of every dried-meat snack she found on the shelf (which was enough to make her go back to the front for a basket), then she moved on to the next items on her list.

Three cans of shaving cream, two jumbo bottles of overly-caffeinated fluorescent lime green gamer beverage™, four sticks of deodorant, a couple packs of toddler-sized snacks and several other nonperishable items later, Quin was almost done shopping for the month. She was standing in the aisle that held cans of soup, trying to decide which kind her younger siblings would hate the least, when she heard a car door slam.

She thought nothing of the sound and returned to her deliberations before deciding on a couple inoffensive soups she thought she could get her siblings to stomach when the weather turned bitter and their winter stock was running low. She started walking towards the counter, then stopped, remembering that they were out of coffee. She turned back around to grab some from the shelf and nearly ran into a tall, dark haired man wearing a hunting jacket and a scowl.

"Watch it, kid," he growled, pushing past her to get to the counter.

Quin looked at him quizzically, trying to smooth down the hairs on the back of her neck that were rising at the sight of him. Something about him seemed... off. He was bathed in the scent of cigarettes and cheap cologne, and maybe a little bit of alcohol too, but over all of that hung a curtain of a scent that was eerily familiar, and yet Quin couldn't quite place it. She watched him carefully out of the corner of her eye, grabbing two tins of coffee off of the shelf and adding them to her already-overflowing basket while keeping him in her blind spot. She stepped up behind the man, waiting for him to be done at the counter, listening in on his conversation.

"Yeah, I don't even know, man. It just ran out in front of me and I didn't have time to stop. Damn thing basically collapsed my bumper, and now the whole fuckin' windshield's smashed to hell. Mechanic said it'd be at least a week 'fore he is done with it. Man, and the weirdest thing? It got up and ran away! The thing smashed my truck's front end to hell and then got up and ran away like it was nothin'. Man, it was huge, too. I'm gonna go after it, once I've had a smoke and talked to Charlie again about the repairs. I'd heard about them things bein' out here, but I didn't really believe it until now. Yessir, I'm gonna go out there after it. That'd make a mighty fine trophy on my wall."

The cashier seemed quite enthralled by the man's story, taking longer than he needed to to give him the carton of Vipers he'd asked for. As the clerk handed the cigarette box over, Quin noticed a tattoo of a black widow that covered the man's forearm. The hourglass on its back had something inscribed in each of its halves, but before Quin could see what it was, the hunting camo of the man's coat sleeve hid the mark from view. As the hunter turned to leave, he caught her staring at him and he narrowed his eyes.

"What're you lookin' at, twerp?" he asked, malice in his tone. His sunburned face scrunched up in a strange expression as he got a closer look at her. He almost seemed to recognize her.

"Hey, you're one of them...huh. That thing must've been..." he trailed off, then laughed loudly in Quin's face. She shuddered, hackles threatening to rise on her shoulders as that strange scent surrounding him hit her in the face again, turning her stomach. Before she could stutter any kind of response, he turned and walked out of the store, still laughing. Slightly shaken, Quin stepped up to the counter and placed her items in front of the cashier.

After he gave her her change, she made her way out the door of the Dufferton Speed-E-Mart, arms full of shopping bags from shoulder to fingertip. She rounded the corner of the building, away from security cameras, ready to drop the bags in the grass and howl for some helpers to carry some of the groceries up the mountain. Before she could, however, she saw the mechanic, Charlie, standing by his tow truck and talking to the man with the spider tattoo.

She had to pass them to go home, but she hoped he wouldn't talk to her again. He had a sinister air around him, and that familiar scent whose name was on the tip of her tongue told her he was trouble with a capital "T". Nonetheless, the faster she passed by him, the faster she could go home. With much trepidation, she headed in his direction.

He noticed her walking towards him, and he cracked a nasty smile. He was taking things out of the bed of the truck, and as she got closer she realized that Charlie had gone back into the body shop to start setting up to begin the repairs. She was alone with him.

"Well would ya look at that. It's you again. That's a lot a groceries you got there, brat. I'd offer you a ride home so you don't have to carry 'em yourself, but as you can see, my truck's a little banged up. You really think you can carry all 'a that by yourself?"

She nodded, staying quiet. He continued taking things from the back of the truck and setting them on the ground beside him. He noticed the tattoo on her arm and raised an eyebrow.

"Your folks know about that paw print?"

She nodded again, inching around the truck. The smell was much more concentrated here, and as her eyes fell on its ruined front end, she realized where it was coming from.

A bloody mess of clumpy, grey fur was matted up into the grille and smears of still-fresh blood spread across the cracked windshield like bright red jam across a slice of toast. Her stomach lurched and threatened to rid itself of its contents. She'd hunted before, so she knew what dead prey should smell like, and this scent was *not* the smell of anything that should be hunted. She *knew* the smell, and yet she could not name it, and this fact was driving her insane.

The hunter noticed her staring and came around the side of the truck with something in his hands. He leaned close to her and pointed at the damage.

"You know what did that?" he asked, and she shook her head, too afraid to think of moving away from him.

"A wolf. A big, *nasty* wolf. I came out here to deal with a whole pack of 'em for my bosses. They're runnin' the construction up in the two peak area. They say they don't want any of them monsters runnin' around here anymore. It's bad for business, lettin' wolves run around and get in their way."

She gulped, coming out of her stupor a bit and leaning away from him. He seemed to get the message (and to realize that they were still close enough to other people for someone to come running if Quin screamed) and he stepped away from her, choosing instead to lean down into the truck bed and pick up one last item. She watched, terrified, as he pulled a hunting rifle and box of ammo out of the truck.

"Funny thing is," he continued, no longer paying her any attention and instead beginning to polish his gun a bit. "It had a mark on its back that was *real* similar lookin' to *that one.*"

He tipped the barrel of his gun toward her for a moment, pointing it at her tattoo, and she flinched involuntarily. Then the full weight of his words hit her, and she stepped away from him. There were *very* few wolves with *that* mark, and she knew them all. Had he hit a wolf from her pack? She could hardly bear to think of it. She ignored the man as he continued cleaning his gun and talking about what he would do if he found the wolf again, and without a second thought she tied several bags of less-important items shut, throwing them with all her might at the tree line 200 yards away. She held tight to the remaining ones and sprinted toward the forest, howling as she did so and not caring that the man could most definitely hear her. At the tree line she was greeted by four timber wolves, who looked up at her expectantly, then flattened their ears and growled in the direction of the hunter when they sensed the danger he posed. They took the remaining bags in their teeth and began running up the foothills of Mt. Wapetona, knowing that Quin wouldn't be far behind.

As she ran after them, she spared one last glance at the back of the Speed-E-Mart, and what she saw chilled her heart and told her they should take a different way home than usual. She saw the hunter smile his *disgusting smile* up into the woods after her, load his hunting rifle, and pull back the slide to bring the first bullet into the chamber.

By the time the wolves had taken their winding way up the mountain, away from the roads that criss-crossed up its sides, it was already getting dark and Quin had almost forgotten about the man with the spider tattoo. She barked past the plastic in her mouth to her packmates, whose paw print marks blazed across their backs in a uniform fashion, telling them to stop at the gates of the main property. The wind blew down the mountain at a steep angle, so from her place at the northern corner of the fenced-off yard she couldn't use her sense of smell to tell who was home and who was out hunting.

She dropped the bags from her mouth and shook herself, becoming bipedal once more and walking up to the gate to open it for her furry friends.

"I don't want you to jump the fence or go under the bottom slats when you have grocery bags in your mouths anymore. Not after last time." She almost laughed at the memory of her brother Maurice jumping the fence with a bag full of groceries that wasn't tied shut all the way. They'd had to wash everything off twice to get all of the dirt off of it after it fell in the mud.

The wolves snorted up at her, waiting until she'd picked up the bags she'd been carrying, then followed her in the direction of the house. They were almost there when the wind changed its course, and Quin stopped dead in her tracks. The familiar scents of her brothers and sister were drowned out by *that smell*. The smell of the ruined fender. The smell of death. The smell she found a name for as she stepped around the front of the house and gasped at the sight on her front porch.

The wolves whined and dropped their cargo, and she did the same as she ran up the wooden steps that were slick with blood and mud and covered in dark red footprints. The smell clung to the door like a drowning man to a life raft, dripping down the weathered oak in thick lines that spelled out a message Quin would never forget.

No time to explain, have to lead them away. Protect the pack, trust the Marmara. Take care of Theo, Titus, and Vasha. Hope I come back to you soon. Love you sis,

Maurice

She didn't hear herself scream, but she felt the sound tear its way out of her throat. Somewhere upstairs, she heard her two year old sister crying. She watched over her own shoulder as she quickly pushed her younger brothers back inside when they opened the door to find out what was happening. The timber wolves, those of her pack who could not walk on two legs but who accepted the Von Fer werewolves as their own, circled around the porch, growling and looking for clues as to where Maurice had gone. Whether or not he was okay.

She got the ten year old twins inside and calmed them down, trying to remember to breathe as she sent them up to the nursery to watch Vasha, then she picked up the landline phone.

"911, what is your emergency?"

"My name is Quin Von Fer, I'm seventeen and I live up on Mt. Wapetona on a ranch with my brothers and sister. I just got home from the store and there's blood everywhere and I can't find my big brother Maurice and he left a note and I.. c-can't..."

"Miss, hold on. Emergency personnel are on their way. Please stay on the phone with me. Are you and your other siblings okay? Do you know where they are?"

"They're upstairs in their rooms. They saw the blood but I don't know if they saw where he went or who was chasing him."

"You think someone was chasing him?"

"He said so in his note."

"Okay Quin. Everything's gonna be okay. Just stay on the phone until help arrives."

CHAPTER 5: VOICES IN THE DARK

Dang, it's lagging out again.

Mitchell O'Connell groaned, tipped back in his chair (nearly falling over in the process) and pulled off his headphones. Shivering, he looked at his alarm clock and saw that it was almost one in the morning.

I'll go get ready for bed, I guess.

He picked up the empty cereal bowl from the side of his desk (his dinner had been a midnight bowl of Rainbow Fruit Circle cereal) and went downstairs to put it in the sink. As he moved through the dark hallways of the house, he realized that several of the downstairs windows were still open from where he'd been airing out the first floor earlier. Now the wind was whistling eerily around the first floor, giving him the heebie-jeebies. He made a mental note to close them and moved on to the kitchen. After placing his bowl in the sink to be dealt with at a better time (next week, perhaps), he remarked to himself, *I guess there's one good thing about Aunt Edith's death. No one's gonna yell at me now for leaving dishes in the sink.*

He looked around the kitchen for other things to clean up, and noticed a mug with the words "world's okay-est firefighter" written on the side. He laughed as he remembered the day he'd earned it.

Aunt Edith always said I had a knack for screwing things up in the kitchen.

He'd been *trying* to make croissants from scratch for breakfast one day when he'd zoned out and spilled flour onto the stove. This normally wouldn't have been an issue, but the burner was on so it had created a small explosion. Nothing caught fire except for his hair and a recipe book, and Mitchell had a handle on the situation when Edith came in and saw him snap his fingers, extinguishing the flames. After that, he was never allowed to bake alone again.

He snapped out of the memory, picking up the mug to find it full of now-cold cocoa.

Ignis.

As soon as he thought the word, a small flame burst to life in the palm of one of his hands. He held the mug over it until it was warm, and then he let the flame die out. Sipping happily, he walked around the main floor, closing and bolting the windows as he did. When every window was locked tight, he returned to the kitchen to put his empty mug in the sink. All of a sudden, a breeze brushed past his shoulder and he heard a quiet voice in his ear.

"It's getting late."

At first, he was unconcerned. There were many times when Aunt Edith had come down in the middle of the night to get a drink of water and found him doing things in the kitchen, and on those nights she would pat him on the shoulder and tell him to go to bed. Mitchell was just about to apologize for leaving things in the sink when realization hit him like a punch in the face. He froze, then spun around, pulling a kitchen knife out of the knife block on the counter in front of him. The voice he'd heard stayed silent, and he didn't see anyone else there (especially not his dead guardian), but he wouldn't let his guard down yet. He walked around the first floor, holding the knife in front of him and turning on all of the lights he passed by. After he thoroughly searched every room and closet and was confident that no one else was in his house, he turned off the lights and decided to head upstairs.

Maybe watching Kill Die Slash Maul III earlier was a bad idea. Now I'm all anxious and paranoid...

He reached the top of the stairs and realized he was still holding the knife. Something about the main floor, and the pitch-black stairway leading to it, told him that he should just keep the knife with him until daylight.

No, shut up, I'm not scared. Everything's fine. There's probably nothing going on. It was probably just my imagination. Still, maybe I'll look around up here for a minute, just to be sure everything's the way it should be.

He walked down the upstairs hall, checking under guest beds and in his aunt's old room (which had been turned into a den with a TV and mini fridge) until he had checked every room except two: the bathroom and his own room.

Walking into the bathroom, he drew in a deep breath before flinging the shower curtain open and revealing nothing but shampoo dried to the wall and a handful of the hair he'd shed when he'd showered earlier. He sighed heavily in relief, then closed the shower curtain again and turned to face the bathroom mirror.

He pulled open the medicine cabinet and grabbed his toothbrush, brushing his teeth and washing his face. Past the sound of the water running in the sink, Mitchell slowly began to notice noises that seemed to come from the hallway outside the bathroom.

He rinsed his mouth quickly and turned off the water, hoping that it was just his imagination again. Much to his dismay, the sounds continued. It sounded like people were whispering to each other in the hallway, and he could very clearly hear footsteps. Mitchell grabbed the knife from the bathroom counter and stood back from the door, ready to defend himself from anyone who might be standing on the other side.

"GET OUT OF MY HOUSE!" He yelled, pulling the door open and slashing at... the empty air of the hallway. Where he expected there to be people -robbers, perhaps, who wanted to steal the valuables he'd inherited from his aunt- he found nothing but a cloud of eerie purple smoke swirling in the darkness. He looked around frantically to try to determine the source of the whispering and the smoke, but couldn't find anything. Deeply perturbed, he listened for several minutes, and when he didn't hear any other sounds, he took a deep breath and blew it out slowly in exasperation.

I really need to go to bed. I have to be dreaming! Clearly I have to stop staying up until- he checked his watch while he walked to his room- *3:45 in the morning.*

He came to his bedroom door and stopped, realizing that this was the only place he hadn't yet searched. It would be almost impossible for anyone to have gotten that far into his house without him noticing or hearing their footsteps, but still, he really wished he wasn't opening the door alone. He listened at the door for a minute, and to his horror, he heard the whispering start back up again. This time, they were right behind the door, and he could *just* make out a few of the things they were saying.

Someone's there.

He's weak. We can take control.

These phrases were overlapping with many other garbled mutters so badly that he wasn't even sure he'd heard them. He wished he hadn't left his phone inside his bedroom before he went downstairs. He peeked at the floor, where a pool of light shone from the crack under his door. There were shadows at the edges of the light that told him someone was *definitely* in his room.

A very large part of him wanted to get the heck out of dodge and run out of the house. He might be living in a two-story cabin in the woods, but it was a *very nice* two-story cabin in the woods and it was only about a mile outside of town. He could run to one of the bars on the outskirts of Dufferton and... call for help? No, he couldn't do that. If there were as many people as it sounded like there were, they would certainly have someone outside watching the house. No, the only way that Mitchell would be able to make it out of this unharmed would be to take them by surprise and hopefully somehow, drive them off his property. With this fact in mind, he took a deep, shaky breath, resigning himself to his impending doom, and flung his bedroom door open.

It loudly crashed against the wall, shaking the entire upstairs. There was no one in his room, but the curtains on his balcony window were moving slightly. He could see that the latch inside was locked, however, so he assumed it was just the wind from his grand entrance that stirred them.

Mitchell was exhausted. Actually, "exhausted" wasn't even a strong enough word to describe the state of utter *doneness* that the 17 year old was in. Not old enough to do anything, but too close to adulthood to be sent to live with a foster family, he'd petitioned the mayor to let him take ownership of the property a year early so that he could live in the house he'd grown up in. Mayor Fitzgerald had granted the request, but the last few months of meetings with banks and lawyers about his aunt's will had been too much. Clearly, he was so stressed that he was starting to have nightmares while he was still awake.

As he looked around the empty room, he searched for something, *anything*, that would explain the strange sounds he'd been hearing in the night. He closed his door cautiously after coming inside, then jumped nearly out of his skin when he heard a disembodied voice ask,

"Are you ready to fight for your life?"

Mitchell screamed in pure terror. He flailed around the room, kicking at shadows and slashing at moving curtains until he got to his computer desk, where the sound seemed to be coming from. He looked under it, then behind it, before he finally looked on top of it and screamed again, this time out of frustration.

"I'm a complete idiot!!!"

His computer screen was turned on and his gaming headphones were unplugged and lying where he'd left them on the desk. On the computer, the game he'd been playing earlier was still pulled up and open to the loading screen of the game. A message on the in-game display told him he'd just been kicked from the server he'd been on due to inactivity. He slapped himself on the forehead when he checked his settings and found that voice chat was not only on, but also on full volume.

That's it. I'm going to bed right frickin' now. I should have known that that was why I was hearing gosh darn voices all night.

He shut down his computer wearily and changed into his pajamas, turning off the lights and crawling under the covers. He gazed up at the glow in the dark stars on the plaster above his head, letting his eyelids droop and his muscles relax. He began to drift into the dead space between the conscious and the unconscious, the dream world and the world of reality, when he heard something outside his window.

His little balcony, which was connected to the back deck downstairs by a creaky wooden staircase, was only accessible from inside via a large window on the wall across the room from his bed. He kept it firmly locked at night, but the curtains were now somehow being blown open. As he looked on in horror, he saw through the shifting fabric a shape that was unmistakably, irrefutably, that of *something* trying to get into his room.

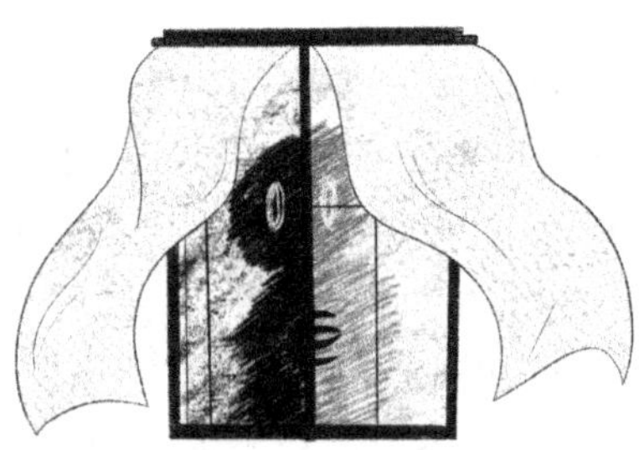

He let out a wordless cry and the black mass crawling in his window froze, then turned its terrifyingly white eyes to him and stared for a heartbeat at him before it abandoned his window and he heard the sounds of feet scuttling down the creaking outdoor staircase. He jumped out of bed and grabbed the knife that he'd left on his bedside table, along with a flashlight he kept by his bed for power outages, and pulled his jacket off of the back of his chair. He didn't bother finding a pair of shoes, instead running to the window barefoot. He stepped out onto the balcony and shined the flashlight down into the yard.

The fenced-in back part of the yard was completely empty. An uneasy stillness hung over the dark autumn night like a shroud, and Mitchell was hyper-aware of every sound around him. The barking of a fox in the forest nearby startled him, and he shined the flashlight wildly around his yard for a moment. He saw nothing, so he decided to go down to investigate.

I'm such an idiot. Why am I doing this? I would be the first one to die in a horror movie.

Mitchell didn't know why he was chasing after the monster of his worst nightmare, but at this point he didn't really think he needed to. When he got down to the deck, he stopped to shine his flashlight around the yard again. When he saw nothing, he moved down to the ground below and furiously began to circle the cabin. His patience for the supernatural crap he was dealing with was wearing very thin, and he could feel himself on the verge of losing control over his abilities.

As he circled the home, he began to hear the whispers again. Louder and louder they spoke gibberish at him, coming from every side and angle. He chased them around the sides of the house until he finally reached the deck once more and accidentally dropped his flashlight. The voices did not stop speaking, and with horrifying clarity they began to sound less and less as though they were around him and more and more as though they were *inside* his head.

Suddenly, he heard a twig snap in the dark tree line behind him. All at once the voices stopped. He didn't bother turning around or picking up his dropped flashlight, all he did was clutch the knife in his hands tightly and follow the direction of the voices inside his mind.

Run.

If he had turned back, he would've seen the purple smoke that came swirling out of the underbrush by his back porch. Instead, he kept his eyes forward on the darkness ahead of him while he crashed through brambles and branches. As he ran away, he didn't see the three men with hourglass tattoos that climbed the steps to his bedroom window once more.

Mitchell ran for almost two miles before he began to see the lights of the seedy bars that dotted the edge of Dufferton. He kept running, kept listening to the voices in his head as they told him where to go, until he ran straight into oncoming traffic.

Luckily for him, the car that he ran in front of happened to be driving relatively slowly. It was a cop car, and when it came to a screeching halt in front of him, he immediately dropped his knife and put his hands up.

"Oh my goodness! I'm so glad I ran into a police officer. Officer, I'm Mitchell O'Connell, I live back in the old Whittier cabin. Gosh, I'm so glad you're here."

The cop got out of the car, hand on his holster, and approached Mitchell slowly.

"Why were you running, son? What made you run around in the woods at three in the morning with a kitchen knife?"

Mitchell immediately launched into his story, telling the officer everything that had happened that night in minute detail. He emphasized the moving curtains and the shadows in his room, and shuddered with fear as he recalled the sight of the thing that had started to crawl in his window.

When he was finished, the officer nodded his head cautiously and said something that Mitchell couldn't hear into his radio.

"Why don't you ride back to the station with me," the officer offered next, "so that you have a safe place to stay while dispatch sends some people over to check on the house. How's that sound?" Mitchell agreed eagerly, sighing in relief as he got into the back of the squad car.

When he got to the station, they took his fingerprints. Mitchell was wary at first, so the officer who'd found him said, "Oh, just standard protocol, you know? They even fingerprint the chief every once in awhile. I think the clerk just wants something to do." That satisfied Mitchell enough, and he let his guard down and allowed the officers to take his prints.

They asked him to write down the night's events, then left him alone in a sort of conference-room looking area. Several minutes went by before an officer came back in holding a pair of handcuffs in his hand.

"Young man, you're under arrest for seven counts of arson. They've been trying to bring you in for almost a year now, Mitchell. You'd think you'd make up a better cover story when you're found by the cops than that crazy shit you told officer Davis."

Mitchell was at a loss for words. He tried to defend himself from the accusations, but none of the officers believed him when he told them that he'd never committed serial arson, nor had he ever even been to the counties he was supposedly an arsonist in. They took him down a long hallway to a holding cell, which they pushed him into hard enough to knock him to the floor. They closed the cell door a moment later, leaving him afraid, alone, and confused in the dark.

CHAPTER 6: WILD ACCUSATIONS

RING!

Abigail jumped, hitting her head on the beam above her head and dropping the handheld mirror out of her hand. She swore, looking down at the minefield of broken glass that now covered her floor.

The phone was still ringing, and the sound was grating on Abigail's eardrums. This was the fourth call tonight that had broken the pleasant silence of the sleepy house, and the eighth late-night call since Abigail had joined the Twalnaverra. Randy had answered all of the previous calls almost instantly, and the last call had been before dinner, so Abigail was very much not expecting another call so late at night.

Why is Marlene calling us so much? And what in the hell could possibly be so important that she has to tell us at three in the morning?

The phone *finally* stopped ringing, and Abigail heard the familiar click of the voicemail recorder playing its pre-recorded message. Notes of western, almost cowboy-ish music twanged lightly underneath a recording of Randy's voice.

"Thank you for calling The Pocket Watch. Unfortunately, we cannot come to the phone right now, but if you leave your name, number, and a

message, the owner of this little trading post will get back to you as soon as he can. Thank you!"

Abigail snorted when she heard the recording. She hadn't thought he'd actually go through with the dare. She stopped laughing when the cowboy music stopped and listened intently. She could just make out a few words of what Marlene was saying.

"...late, sorry... found..-tion...man...ring...coun-....building a ja-"

The call was fading and cutting out, almost as if the phone were in a tunnel. Abigail was about to go downstairs to pick up the phone when a huge crack of thunder echoed through the house. She heard the tell-tale sounds of Randy getting out of bed, and then the phone being pulled off of the hook. Assuming that Randy would deal with Marlene, Abigail tuned out everything in the house and chose, instead, to focus her hypersensitive hearing on the sounds outside.

Rain beating on the roof. Cars driving past on the highway. A radio two houses down playing classical music.

She counted the things she could hear, then focused harder.

The music of the Palaas nightclub. Damn, it must be loud enough to shake the walls of every bar on the block if I can hear it from this far away! I wonder who DJ's on weeknights when Randy's not there.

Abigail's thoughts were cut off by the bang of the attic access door and the pounding of Randy's feet on the steep old stairs. She had just enough time to pull the drawstring on the light bulb on the ceiling and to call out a warning about the glass shards before Randy came crashing into her room, babbling half to himself.

"Abigail! Ow-fuck why the hell is there glass all over your floor? No, never mind, I came up here because I knew you'd be awake and I wanted to know if you heard anything from Marlene's voicemail before I woke up? I couldn't get it to play back and the only thing she said before the call completely cut out was 'oh shit, what was that?' and then I heard a crash and the line went dead," Rady rambled, talking a mile a minute. He heaved for air as he finished,
"Did you hear her say anything?"

Abigail thought back to the tidbits she'd heard from the crackling phone.

"She was saying something about a man... the one who tried to sell you that ring two weeks ago? It sounded urgent. Maybe we should- dude are you gonna do anything about the cuts on your feet or...?"

Randy glanced down at his feet, then back up and Abigail.

"Do you honestly think I have time for that? If Marlene was trying to tell us something urgent and her call got interrupted, then she could be in danger! We need to help her, we need to-"

Suddenly, a howling wind and a huge clap of thunder shook the house, and the air seemed to crackle with energy. The lights flickered out and the whole house was plunged into darkness as the power completely went out.

Randy swore and clapped his hands, muttering a word. A blast of blue light emanated from his body and spread throughout the tar-black building, re-illuminating every room in the house as it stopped in various sconces along the walls. Thunder, lightning, and wind still raged outside, and Abigail had to cover her ears as she followed Randy down to the shop. He pulled a hoodie over his pajama top and a pair of fur-lined boots (that used to be Abigail's) onto his bare feet, then swept the front door open. He was immediately blown back by a huge gust of wind, and heavy drops of rain pummeled past the porch steps, ignoring the eaves and inviting themselves in to soak the welcome mat and interior rugs of the shop. It seemed that all the forces of nature were determined to keep Randy from helping Marlene.

Abigail came up behind him and put her hand on his shoulder, pushing the door closed.

"She'll be okay, Ran. Marlene's a ridiculously skilled magic user, and she knows how to defend herself. It's almost four in the morning and there's a fucking Typhoon going on outside. I know you're worried about her but there's nothing we can do tonight."

Randy nodded, sparing another glance at the tempest roaring on the other side of the window panes. He let himself be led gently upstairs to his bedroom, where Abigail left him to change into dry clothes and heal himself. Hopefully he would also get the blood out of her shoes, so she wouldn't have to throw them away.

She was getting tired herself, and though she, too, was worried about Marlene, she knew the mayor could handle herself. She fortified the spells that kept the house lit and then went to bed, leaving the broken glass to be cleaned up later.

The next morning they were both woken up by shouts and loud pounding below them on the front door. The power was back on, the sun was shining, and Abigail hurriedly got dressed and sprayed herself with an elixir to keep the sun from burning her alive, then walked down to the second floor just in time to watch through the banister at Randy opening the door for 2 police officers. Even from so far away, she could see a shimmering aura around them that indicated they had magic, and that they didn't have good intentions with it. She quickly retreated back into the hollow shadows of the upstairs hallway.

"Sir, do you know why we're here?"

A muscular man who looked like a detective flashed his badge, looking at Randy expectantly.

"No sir, I do not. May I ask why you're here?"

"Where were you last night, November 23rd?"

"I was at home all night last night. My housemate can confirm this. What's all this about?"

"Where is your housemate now, sir?"

Abigail stiffened, hoping they didn't come upstairs to find her. Her glamors weren't up at the moment, so she would draw attention with her pale skin and her own magic aura. Not to mention the collection of the rarer artifacts that Randy insisted on leaving in her room for safekeeping. She made her way up the stairs (thank the old ones that they were enchanted not to squeak) to her room just as Randy began his reply.

"That's none of your business. I'm not answering any more of your questions without a lawyer present. Now, unless you have a warrant-"

"Actually, we don't need one. We have probable cause. Randolph Jefferson, you're under arrest for the murder of Marlene Fitzgerald."

Abigail's jaw dropped. Marlene was dead? Tension knotted her stomach- she could hear Randy arguing with the officers, then there was a crash and some shouting, then a sound like something (or someone) being dragged across the floor. She concentrated hard, projecting a glamor on the whole upstairs which would hide the door to the attic and make every room but Randy's look like storage for antiques and books. She created a fake "bedroom" for herself and came out of it when the police knocked on the door, silently praying that they would be unable to detect her spell work.

Her prayers were answered, thankfully. Now that it was too late to stop them from taking Randy away, she was of course able to see that the aura the officers had been surrounded with was nothing more than a cheap glamor trick. They *did* have a little bit of power, but neither of them were particularly strong and they couldn't tell there were any spells on the house.

After a long time of tedious questioning where she repeated the same story over again-

"He and I were up last night fixing his telescope. It was storming so hard we lost power and had to use a backup generator. We were unable to leave to get telescope parts because of the storm, so there's no way he would've been able to go out and do anything to Marlene."

-the officers finally left. They hadn't found any evidence (because there wasn't any to find) and they wouldn't give her any information on Randy's situation. When the door shut behind them, she was left with a sinking feeling in her chest and rage flowing through her veins. She felt an unconscious urge to beat her fists into her legs as punishment for her failure to protect her friend.

She crushed the urge by putting her fist through some nearby drywall, deciding right then and there that she would make sure Randy got out of this mess.

They would *not* get away with this.

CHAPTER 7: A DISTANT HOWL

Quin sat at the Von Fer kitchen table, watching her brothers halfheartedly eat their breakfasts. She tried to get Vasha to eat, but her sister was refusing to do anything with the strawberries in front of her except push them onto the floor. Quin sighed and looked out the gauzy, sheer curtains at the muddy fields outside. Not even the flowers she'd embroidered on them with her mother were enough to cheer her up or take her mind off of Maurice's disappearance. By the edge of the property she could see several wolves pacing nervously, as though they were waiting for someone to arrive.

*They **are** waiting for someone. We're all waiting for him to come back.*

She was thankful that they were at home, for now, because it meant that she could watch out the kitchen window. It meant that she would be the first of the Von Fers to see him come home. They were being watched over by their "Aunt" from out of town. In actuality, she was a friend from Maurice's job. She was a Marmaran seer, and she'd known even before Quin had called her that something had gone horribly wrong. She'd taken as much time off as she could from work so that she could stay with the children while the police (who no one really trusted) "searched" for Maurice. She'd gone into town to pick up some extra clothes from her house, but Quin could see her coming up the driveway in an old green station wagon. The bare oak and elm trees groaned menacingly under the weight of the winter wind, almost blowing the door of the car shut as the Von Fer's new guardian tried to get out of her car.

When she finally got inside, Quin immediately noticed how pale she was. It looked as though she'd seen a ghost.

"What's wrong, Amy?"

Amy didn't respond, but she walked quickly over to the radio on the counter and switched it on to the news. A serious-sounding reporter was talking about the details of a news bulletin, and the whole house fell silent so that they could listen.

"The police have a suspect in custody, but the body has not yet been found. 27-year-old Randolph Jefferson, a Dufferton resident and owner of the Pocket Watch spice and curiosity shop, left DNA at the office of the late mayor Marlene Fitzgerald. Sources say that Jefferson was a close friend of the mayor, and many are questioning the motive for the killing. Security camera footage from the town hall was completely wiped. Statements have been collected from relevant parties, and Jefferson will face sentencing tomorrow, Monday November 26th."

When the announcer stopped speaking, Amy shut the radio off again. The whole house was silent- even little Vasha knew something was wrong. Quin could hear the timber wolves whining outside, as though they could smell the mayor's death on the wind. A pit opened in her stomach, stealing every bit of air before it could reach her lungs and swallowing all her tears before they could fall.

"Maurice knew her." She didn't even hear herself say it.

"We all did. She was the head of the Marmara, like an aunt to all of us."

Amy stared off into the distance, shock and dismay in her eyes.

"Randy would never do something like this-he's the leader of the Twalnaverra, but he's also the reason there is peace between our groups. His people believe that magic should be open and visible for all, magic users and quotidians alike. It is because of people like him and Marlene, who founded our groups as social clubs for the magically inclined, that we all work together and have a sense of community today. There have even, off and on, been talks of joining our two groups together into one big group for the benefit of all."

Amy smiled sadly, then suddenly got very quiet and still. Quin could see her wide-open eyes changing color from their usual vibrant green to a deep, dark violet. Her pupils clouded over and her body went rigid, and for a second, Quin thought that she might be having a seizure. Then, just as quickly as it came on, the fit subsided and her eyes cleared, and her eye color returned to normal. She relaxed back into her seat, closing her eyes in exhaustion for a moment.

Quin kept a wary eye on Amy as she helped her brothers clear their dishes and gather their books for school. They'd been home schooled until the start of this semester, but they'd begged Maurice to let them go to quotidian school in town. He'd agreed to it after some coaxing from Quin, who reminded him that he could pick up more hours at work if he wasn't watching the kids all day. She was far above her grade level anyway, so she chose to test and graduate early and help take care of her little brothers before she started college the following fall.

When Quin had seen her brothers safely board the only school bus that ever came up Mt. Wapetona, she came back to sit with Amy.

"So what happened to you at breakfast?"

Amy was silent.

"You had a vision, didn't you?"

She nodded almost imperceptibly.

"What did you see, Amy?"

The skies outside the window were getting darker and the wind was picking up. Quin hardly noticed the heavy raindrops beginning to fall, didn't see when the timber wolves retreated to their dens. She could pay attention to nothing but her guardian.

"There was nothing but an all-engulfing blackness, then I heard someone laughing. There was a gunshot. I felt myself falling. After that it changed, and I could see myself standing on Bigfire bridge, looking down into the Wapetona River. There was dark, red-tinged fog everywhere, and I could see people fighting on the far side of the bridge. I heard your brother shouting for someone to run, then the vision ended. I think it was happening sometime in the spring- there were new leaves and flower buds

on the trees on the banks of the river. There was an overwhelming sense of importance and feeling of urgency that filled me as I saw all of this.

I've only had a few of this kind of vision, Quin, but they've all come true."

Quin took in a shallow, sharp breath.

"That means that Maurice must be...."

There was a sudden, loud knock on the front door of the house, and Quin's hopeful thought was brushed aside by Amy's calls for whoever was at the door to "hold on a minute!"

When the door was opened, Quin saw two official-looking adults wearing suits and flashing badges. They quickly took Amy into another room, and she looked furious (and a bit sick to her stomach) when they all returned.

"They're separating you. I'm legally your godmother, so the boys and Vee will stay here with me, but they want to take you away and place you in witness protection. Alone."

Quin's heart stopped. She tried to protest, but the agents shut down her arguments with patronizing baby talk and repetition of the same phrase over and over again- "you're the only one that saw that man. You'll be safer with us and keep your family safe too." Before she knew it, she was in her bedroom, packing a backpack with things to take with her when they took her to her new, "all amenities provided" home. She stopped for a moment after she zipped her bag closed, looking wistfully at her room and feeling tears well up in her eyes.

The rosy pink curtains hanging in her window were still in spite of the rainstorm outside, and the tapestries on her walls hung limply. She looked at the ingredients laid out on her desk- the ones that Maurice had told her to get so he could teach her to make the enchanted dye that they would use to give her brothers their paw print marks that would show that they'd come of age.

I'm going to miss out on so much preparation time for the boys' change ceremony. She started tearing up. *I can't do this on my own, especially if I'm in 'witness protection'- if this could even be called that. These 'agents' don't even seem legit.*

She angrily picked up a ribbon from her desk and tied it around her wrist. The dark green satin was her favorite color, and it comforted her as she walked down the stairs. She paused for a moment when she reached the bottom, hidden by several walls from the adults' view, to listen in on their conversation.

"What do I tell her siblings? They're young, but they're not stupid. They're already traumatized by the loss of their parents, and now their brother. I don't know what losing their sister too will do to them."

A chill went up Quin's spine at the mention of her parents.

"Tell them that she had to leave for an internship program that she got accepted to. Tell them she didn't say anything because she didn't think she got in."

"Quin would never act like that! They'll know instantly that that's a lie."

"I don't know what to tell you. She's coming with us."

The hair on the back of Quin's neck stood up straight at the sudden threat in the agent's voice. As she slipped down the hallway towards the back door, she thanked god for the recently-fixed, creak-free stairs she'd just stepped off of. She slipped out into the rain and made a bee-line for the barn, darting between raindrops and around mud puddles until she reached the heavy wooden door and slowly pushed it open.

The inside of the barn smelled like motor oil and old wood and all the other familiar scents of her brother's workshop. Old root beer bottles and dog collars hung from the rafters like wind chimes, and she had to be careful not to hit her head on them as she entered.

Maurice was more than a casual acquaintance of the mayor- she trusted him to help her oversee meetings of the Marmara, and she was teaching him to be a mechanic. Though Quin was not allowed to go to meetings yet, she'd heard they were a pretty dynamic duo. She ran her hands over their latest project- something that looked like a baseball bat, if baseball bats were made of weighted gears and they electrocuted you if you got hit in the face with them.

Somewhere in the back of the barn, something began to shuffle towards her. A stranger might have been afraid, but she knew who was coming to greet her. An old, slow wolf shuffled toward her, wagging its tail a bit in greeting.

"Hi Rusty," she said, looking back to check that the barn door had closed behind her all the way. She closed the distance between them and placed a hand on his head, scratching between his ears. Though he was once a powerfully wild animal, Rusty was now more domesticated than anyone had expected him to be. He could no longer hunt for himself, so the werewolves and other, normal wolves all took turns bringing him food and water and keeping him company.

"First Maurice disappears, and now you're losing me too," she sighed into his greying red fur. He whined and nudged her when she said this, and then she felt a quiet "why?" from him. She let him continue to touch her mind, and she shared her memories of the agents with him. His ears flattened, and he pressed his thin body against her side. She comforted him, telling him that she'd be alright and that her siblings and Amelia would stay to take care of him. She knew that she should be getting back, that the agents would be looking for her soon. She told him to let the rest of the pack know where she would be, then said goodbye.

When Quin came back to the house, she walked straight to the bathroom where she washed her hands and grabbed a handful of bobby pins, a comb, and her 10-piece hair care routine. Shoving everything in a bag, she tied her favorite bandanna around the bouncy mess of curls on her head and went to join the adults in the living room.

She said her goodbyes to Vasha and Amelia while the agents looked through her bag and deemed everything in it acceptable to bring with her, then she climbed into a small bus that was waiting in the driveway. Inside, she saw a boy a few years older than her.

"I'm Quin," she said, once the bus had started driving away and the agents could no longer hear them.

"I'm Mitchell," he mumbled in reply. "What are you in for?"

She was stunned by the question, and as she looked down to formulate her reply, she noticed that Mitchell's hands were cuffed tightly.

"Wh-what? I'm supposed to be going to a witness protection facility up at Two Peaks. Why are you..."

She backed away from him, pressing herself into the seat across the aisle.

"I got framed for arson," Mitchell said, sounding absolutely crushed. He was looking down at his hands, but met her gaze and put them up as much as he could in a gesture of surrender.

"I didn't do it, I promise! But no one would believe me when I told them that. Sorry to be the bearer of bad news, dude, but the only 'facility' at Two Peaks is a prison."

Quin's breath caught in her throat, and she turned her face away from him to watch the passing landscape. The bus made its winding way up the mountain, then across a barely-legal bridge on its way across Mt. Wapetona to her smaller sister, Two Peaks Mountain. The rushing waters of the Wapetona River told her they were crossing 10 miles or so from the mouth of Lake Tamory, which stretched between the mountains above the Wapetona Valley. The ride seemed to last hours, but it couldn't have lasted more than an hour or two, tops.

Quin could tell they were getting close to their destination when the agents at the front of the bus began to sit up straighter and look out the window. Mitchell locked eyes with her when she looked in his direction, and he gave her a sympathetic half smile. She turned to face the window again, gazing at the world outside the bus.

The bus turned off the road they were on, and suddenly the dense pine forest disappeared, replaced by a sea of dying grass and a few construction trucks.

"Welcome to Hell," she whispered across the aisle to Mitchell. He looked at her, mildly terrified, before he noticed the sign at the side of the road that she'd read from 500 feet away: "Devil's Bed Plateau."

The altitude had been marked on the sign as well, but years of graffiti and dirt had rendered it illegible.

They rode across the plateau for a few minutes, passing several lookout points and public trail heads. When the bus reached the edge of the gravel parking lot of Quin's new "home," it felt as though someone had poured cement over her limbs. Mitchell seemed to feel the same way, as he slumped back against the vinyl behind him, eyes closed and expression pained. Even the agents at the front of the bus were affected by it. They were sluggish and slow when the bus pulled up to the building's metal-framed front doors.

The air was cold, and the sun was only just cresting over the peaks around the plateau. The grey-black brick of the building in front of them seemed to stretch a thousand stories above them, and as they were harshly pushed inside the unsecured front desk area of the prison, Quin felt that sluggish force hit her again.

They've put some kind of barrier on the door to keep us trapped here. I'd wager it's around the whole property, too.

Quin briefly considered sending this thought to the red-haired boy she'd shared a bus ride with, but something seemed very *off* about him. She didn't have much time to think about him, though, because a blonde woman in a jacket and pants that definitely didn't look like a uniform walked up to the agents and nodded to them. They stepped back from Quin and Mitchell and turned to walk back to the bus. The woman waited until the door loudly buzzed to show that it was closed before opening her mouth to speak.

"I'm Linda Bernard. I'm the warden here. Yes, my ears are pointed. Yes, I am an elf. No, I don't give a shit what your powers are. While you're here, you answer to me, am I clear?"

She didn't wait for a reply, leading the pair into a side room where they were gently patted down and Quin's things were taken away. She was given a new set of clothes to change into (and the privacy to do so, thank god), then the warden was back in front of them.

"I don't make a point of mistreating prisoners, but this isn't a kiddie fun-land, got it? This facility is called The Ark of Light. You are here to be guided from the darkness and destruction of the path you're on into the light of our founders' mission. We want you to work with us, to use your powers for what is truly good."

Her speech seemed very rehearsed, and even as she tried to look imposing, she seemed more bored than authoritarian. Quin would have found it amusing, if she wasn't so put off by the woman's words. Physically, Quin looked much stronger (and taller) than Linda did, but she knew better than to rely on appearances for such crucial information, especially where elves were involved. Elves were known for being stronger, faster, and fiercer than any human, and Quin had no doubt that the warden could crush her if she so desired. Still, she wasn't supposed to be here. She needed to go home. There had to have been some sort of misunderstanding. She stayed close behind Linda as the warden led them through another set of metal doors into the main body of the prison and down a hallway lined with cells.

Cautiously, she raised a timid hand to voice her questions, catching Linda's attention. She turned to face Quin, jaw set and arms crossed, managing to look down at her even though she was nearly two inches shorter than the werewolf. Quin tried not to let her voice shake.

"I'm sorry, m-miss Warden, ma'am, but I think there's been a mistake. I'm s'posed to be in witness protection, not jail. My big brother just disappeared and I was the last one to see the suspect, so they said they wanted to keep me safe by sending me here. I don't think this is where I was supposed to-"

Linda cut her off by raising a hand.

"I'm aware of your situation, Ms. Von Fer. There was a major miscommunication, and when you were taken into the custody of the state, they labeled you as a criminal. Stay here a moment please."

She turned away to unlock a cell in front of them.

"You. O'Connell. This is your cell. You'll be getting a roommate soon. His name's Randy Jefferson, his court date is in a few days. Get inside and get acquainted with your new room. I suggest picking your bed *before* you have to share a room with someone- it'll be easier to defend your territory if it's already established."

He didn't have time to say anything before she shut the door behind him. The wall was made of thick brick, and the metal door in it had a large, barred window set in it for guards to look through and check on inmates. When Mitchell was in his cell and the door was locked behind him, Linda turned back to Quin.

"Look, I know you're not supposed to be here. Honestly, no one is supposed to be here, but they are and that's not something I can change. I'm not as much of a hard ass as I have to appear to be. Don't make this place look bad by fighting with other people or trying to break out and I'll let you do whatever. You don't even have a roommate for now! Think of this as a very boring sleep away camp that isn't over in two weeks. You'll get out eventually, if you play the game right. For now, though, I have to lock you in a cell, because if I don't, they'll fire me. And if they fire me, they'll hire someone else who will do what they actually want, which is to kill all of you."

While she was talking, Linda had led Quin down another set of hallways to her own "room".

"Who are they? Why do they want us dead??" Quin was frantically trying to find answers in the confusing mess she'd just been thrown into.

"I wish I could tell you. I really do. But I can't, and it's really dangerous for both of us if you keep asking questions. So for everyone's sake, just try not to think about it. Give the Ark a chance. You might make a friend or two."

She opened the door and motioned for Quin to step inside. Quin did, but she couldn't help the frustrated, exhausted, terrified tears that were welling in her eyes as it fully sank in that she was an *inmate*, not a witness. She let a few fall when Linda closed the door, loathe to let any adult see her cry, even one as sympathetic as this. She didn't know if Linda was lying to her to gain her trust, or if she really cared.

"Hey, woah. Uh, please don't cry. There should be toilet paper over by the latrine in the corner of your cell- that's the only tissues we have at the moment. I need to put in an order for some to be shipped up here." Linda's half-laugh did nothing to lighten the mood. She awkwardly cleared her throat, obviously uncomfortable with such a strong display of emotion.

"Uh, later today during free time in the common room I'll be letting you guys meet my dogs. Well, they're technically the guard dogs, but they were my dogs before they were the guard dogs. I know that dogs and timber wolves aren't exactly alike, but I think they'd like meeting a werewolf..." Linda trailed off when she realized Quin wasn't really listening anymore.

The talk of dogs reminded her of her pack, and her home, and Rusty, and she started crying even harder. She didn't notice when Linda awkwardly cleared her throat again and walked away down the hall, leaving her alone with her backpack and her tears.

CHAPTER 8: LOCKED AWAY

Randy sat with his head in his hands, broad shoulders shaking with a barely-concealed mixture of fury and despair. His long curly hair was pulled back into as tight a bun as he could produce at the nape of his neck, and he was wearing a dark blue button down shirt. He had a set of tiny 4-leaf clover studs in his ears, but they really didn't seem that lucky. His suit jacket was draped over the back of his chair, though it was big enough to go nearly all the way to the ground as it hung there. His usually sun-tanned skin seemed pale in the overhead fluorescence of the courtroom lights. The court-appointed quack who was supposed to be representing him was doing an absolute horror of a job, and now the prosecutor was leaning smugly against the witness stand, having just said, "no further questions, your honor."

Randy just wanted to go home and mourn. Marlene had been like an older sister to him, and now he didn't know what to do without her. Not to mention the fact that her second-in-command was missing and members of both factions were being arrested at a concerning rate. Hell, even Edith O'Connell's nephew, the one with fire powers, had been arrested for arson. Someone was targeting them all. It made Randy sick to think about.

"Look at him, he's overcome with guilt and crying about what he did."

Randy sat bolt upright when he heard the prosecutor talking about him, opening his mouth to respond hotly, but his lawyer gave him a pointed look and motioned for him to let him speak.

"So my client may be crying. Whether or not he's crying from the guilt of murdering his friend in cold blood that lies on his conscience has yet to be proven."

The jury murmured angrily and Randy sunk back down again, furious now with how much his lawyer had screwed him over.

The court proceedings had been a joke from the start. There were almost no witnesses called to testify for or even *against* him, and though there were quite a few people who'd shown up to watch his "trial" on its last day, when the media had finally broke the news of Marlene's death, no one had been allowed to say much.

Now, on the final day of deliberations, the jury seemed to be just as decided as they had been from the beginning. They only took ten minutes to discuss the outcome, then they came back out to announce that they found the defendant, Randolph A. Jefferson, guilty of murder. He wasn't surprised. Many of the jurors had ignored or even actively and openly disagreed with evidence and (limited) testimony in his favor. He was sentenced to life in prison in a "specialized facility for those with magic who the county deemed 'unable to be rehabilitated'," before being ushered out of the courtroom in handcuffs. On his way out, he heard someone say that the press would just hear that he went to quotidian jail, instead.

He was allowed to have a single visitor come to see him before he was transported to "The Ark," whatever the hell that was, and Abigail was the only person he wanted to see. She'd been there in the courtroom throughout the whole trial, and she'd testified that he'd been home all night. She'd handed over the shards of broken glass he'd stepped on as evidence that he couldn't have been away from the house all night if his (recently spilled) blood was all over her mirror. When she came into the visitation room, she was fuming and looked ready to kill.

"That motherfucker! I told you we should have hired a real lawyer! I know there's at least three lawyers in the Marmara and they can't all hate you. Dammit, we need to find a way to-"

He stood up and stopped her ranting by wrapping his arms around her and leaning heavily on her shoulder. Stunned, she just held him for a few moments. He was much bigger than her, but she still held him all the same. She stroked his hair, rocking him back and forth and comforting him before he let her go. Just as he did, the officer stationed outside announced that they had two minutes left of the visit. Abigail grimaced, wiping away tears she saw forming in his eyes again.

"Hey," she said gently, forcing back her anger so she could focus on being there for him.

"I'm not letting them get away with this. I'm gonna find a way to clear your name."

He hugged her again, this time out of quick gratitude. There was shuffling at the door again and they finally parted, realizing their time together was up, for now.

"How am I going to do this?" Abigail muttered under her breath. She hadn't expected him to hear her, but he did, and he replied,"

"You'll find something to help you at my desk in the back office of the shop. Let the light guide you." He tapped the side of his nose, and then the officer came in to escort Abigail back out of the room, leaving her confused and curious as to what Randy could possibly mean.

A few minutes after Abigail left, Randy was brought to a waiting bus, handcuffed to the seat, and told to get ready for a *long* ride. The bus started to drive out to the edge of Dufferton's municipal limits, and Randy waved pessimistically to each familiar place they passed.

First they passed the Palaas nightclub, which looked sad and empty in the daylight. Then, a few side streets later, they rumbled past the Pocket Watch. He could see a few cars in the parking lot, and the neon red "open" sign was illuminated. He waved even harder, thankful for the fact that the bus guard was paying attention to a newspaper and not to him. He couldn't see anyone in the attic window, but he hoped, all the same, as he waved, that Abigail was waving back.

They turned off onto the highway and rode for a while around the basin-shaped wall of the back end of the Wapetona Valley, passing the base of Mount Wapetona, then crossing several small bridges as they traveled past the high plateau where Lake Tamory rested. Before he knew it, they were turning onto the dirt road that wound its way up Two Peak mountain.

The bus bumped and creaked, and there were several times that Randy, as he watched the free world of the mountain woods pass him by, was sure that they were going to go off the road. It was narrow and crumbling at the edges, and whoever was driving the bus seemed not to care whether or not they made it to their destination in one piece. Randy would have at least grown a barrier of roots or plants at the edge of the road to keep them from going clear off the face of the mountain, but when he tried to access the part of himself that was responsible for his abilities, he found himself utterly unable to touch it. He felt as though he were drowning in a combination of tar and molasses, every bone in his body weighed down by an invisible force.

*They're blocking me from using my powers. That means they know that I **have** powers. Which means that whoever or whatever is targeting us, they're connected to the bastard who threatened Marlene in my shop.*

His vision went blurry for a moment, and suddenly he realized that angry tears were falling down his face.

I'm such an idiot! I should have seen it! The man with the ring- he testified against me! He lied to the court! I should have fucking said something!

And the lawyer- he was appointed by the same people who were fucking prosecuting me!

His anger hardened and turned into an icy, hopeless knot of realization, which quickly turned to dread.

Oh my god. Marlene said that a bunch of new police, including a new police chief, had just joined the force to replace others who left. The law of Kacapa county has been set in stone for nearly a hundred years- oh my god. The police chief is now in charge of the county.

If he wanted to get control of all of Dufferton, all he had to do was fucking take her out. And then find someone else -willing or unwilling- to take the blame. I...

Fuck.

The forest was getting darker. The *bus itself* was getting darker. No matter how many spells they put him under to keep him from consciously using his powers, there was nothing that anyone, not even Randy himself, could do to stop his powers from being influenced by his emotions and subconscious. Vines and tree branches pushed at the sides of the bus, and vaguely, some part of the back of Randy's mind could hear the bus driver and guard swearing to each other.

"Son of a bitch, the wind must've picked up a lot," the guard said to the driver, setting his newspaper down on the seat beside him and standing up a little to look over the driver's shoulder at the road ahead of them.

"Yeah, and a storm must be coming in," the driver replied, keeping his eyes on the road and pulling the bus a little closer to the rock wall beside them. "The sky's gone darker than pitch. It's barely 3 PM!"

The guard checked the time on his watch, then the date on his newspaper.

"It's almost winter now, though. Maybe the dark's just coming faster than we thought. The forecast said it was s'posed to be clear and sunny today, with a high of almost 60. That's pretty good, for this time of year anyway. Leastwise it is up in these mountains."

Randy stopped paying attention to their conversation about the weather and focused on keeping his breathing even. He would get out of this. He *had* to get out of this. For Marlene. For Abigail. For the Pocket Watch. For the Twalnaverra and the Marmara and for every living thing in the Wapetona Valley. He *had* to get out of this and set things right.

At some point, he was torn from his thoughts by the feeling of the pavement evening out and becoming level, flat ground. He blinked rapidly several times and let his eyes refocus, seeing the infamous stretch of the Devil's Bed plateau laid out in front of him. He saw, at the far end of the plateau, pressed against one of the two peaks that gave the mountain it's unique name and shape, a U-shaped building made of...concrete? stone? ash? He couldn't quite tell. Whatever it was made of, it was rapidly approaching. The bus driver was going twice the speed he needed to in an effort to get home faster.

By now, what magic his subconscious could muster up had been spent, and the sky was dark because it really was nighttime. There were no birds, or pleasantly chittering bugs, or even howling coyotes. The only sounds that Randy could hear were the murmur of the conversation taking place in the front of the bus, and the rumbling of its tires, and the roar of the diesel engine that propelled them along the road. As they approached the U-shaped building, and the giant (environmentally unfriendly as fuck) mud pit and parking lot in front of it, Randy noticed something...odd.

Randy had been a practicing magician for many years, and even before that, he'd always had abilities. As such, he knew the signs of magic that rested in and around the everyday intricacies of life. He knew what the air looked like around a normal building just as much as he knew the way that it shimmered with something akin to a sweltering summer heat when there were walls of magic around a place. He could see, as they approached the prison, that starting from about 500 feet from the walls of the building, stretched a scintillating dome of magic. It was faint enough that he could barely see it, but he knew that it would be strong enough to keep even the most powerful beings inside.

It's probably another one like what's keeping me from using my powers now, mixed with some wards on the doors, windows, and gates to keep people from going through them. Magic is cheaper than an electric fence. Hopefully that barrier works both ways. I've heard tales of...unfriendly things crawling through the grasses up here at night. More than a few have been dragged beneath the bed and into the depths of Hell.

Less than five minutes later, the bus turned off the road and into the parking lot, before finally coming to a stop in front of the prison. The guard stood and stretched, then unlocked the chain that tethered Randy to his seat. He dragged him out by the hair, depositing him in front of a set of doors that were made of equal parts metal and bullet-proof glass. A symbol that looked like an arrow, or maybe a catfish, was painted on the glass.

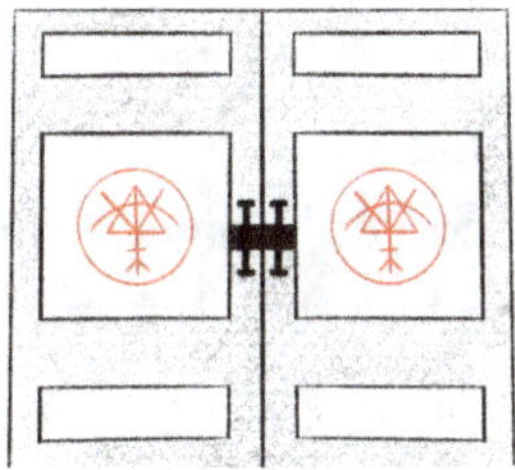

Randy didn't have much time to pay attention to what the door looked like, though, because as he knelt in the dirt, he watched a blonde woman with a pistol on her hip and a scowl on her face stalk across the front room of the prison to meet them at the door. She hit a button and the door opened, and she pulled him to his feet, motioning for the guard and bus driver to leave. They nodded to her and were gone before Randy could turn around.

"I'm Linda Bernard. I'm the warden here. Yes, my ears are pointed. Yes, I am an elf. No, I don't give a shit what your powers are. While you're here, you answer to me, am I clear? I don't make a point of mistreating prisoners, but this isn't a kiddie funland, got it? This facility is called The Ark of Light. You are here to be guided from the darkness and destruction of the path you're on into the light of our founders' mission. We want you to work with us, to use your powers for what is truly good."

Randy's head was swimming, and he barely paid attention to the deadpan speech given by the blonde lady as she patted him down and gave him a white t-shirt and pair of grey sweatpants to change into. He resisted the urge to outwardly grimace at the horribly unfashionable uniform, grateful that at least it wasn't an orange jumpsuit.

"Are you even fucking paying attention?"

A hand connected with his left ear and he winced, leaning away from the woman in front of him.

"I'm trying to be nice. I don't want to treat you like trash. But for this whole arrangement to work, for me to keep you here and off death row, you're gonna have to treat me with respect. You killed our dear Mayor Fitzgerald. She wasn't the one who cut my paychecks, but she was a good woman and a good magic user. You're gonna come with me, and you'll have a nice long time to rethink your life choices and convert to a better way of thinking, because once you step into this prison, you're never gonna leave."

With that, she dragged him (again, by the hair! Why was everyone always pulling his hair?) through a set of thicker, fully metallic doors and then down a hallway into a cell. There was a redheaded teenager sitting on the bed by the door, dangling his feet off of the side of it and watching him apprehensively. Linda's tone of voice softened considerably when she opened her mouth to address him.

"Mitchell, this is your new cellmate. Let me know if he gives you trouble so I can be sure that it's properly dealt with." She gestured to Randy, who stood awkwardly in the doorway, then pushed the older man in the door and shut it, looking through the bars at them.

"Randy, that's Mitchell. He's your cellmate. Treat him like shit and you will die in your sleep, got it?"

She didn't wait for a reply, instead locking the door and turning to walk back down the hallway.

A few seconds of awkward silence filled the room before Randy thrust out his right hand, trying to make a good first impression.

Mitchell tentatively looked at his hand, and then when Randy got closer to him so he could shake it without having to stand up, the teen shook it, hard and fast, and a faint orange halo surrounded their hands for a moment before Mitchell quickly let go, startled. Randy looked down at his hand, horrified to see burn blisters starting to bubble up across the back of it.

"Shoot, sorry, oh my god I'm sorry I didn't mean to burn you I'm an idiot please don't kill me! Aunt Edith always said I needed to control my powers more around people- it's just that I'm still learning how and now I'm rambling and-" He cut himself off to breathe, and Randy surprised him by laughing and sitting down on the other bed, one in the corner of the room.

"Oh, you're *that* Mitchell! I met your aunt a few times whenever I visited Marmaran meetings. Oh, and look. No harm no foul, OK kid? I wouldn't have killed you anyway, since I didn't kill Marlene and don't even like killing bugs and shit like that, but I guess I appreciate the apology."

As he spoke, he waved his hand and suddenly the burn disappeared. He was thankful that the inside of the prison didn't seem to suppress his powers as much as he thought it would. That fact, in the long run, would make it much easier to escape. He looked Mitchell up and down as he got settled in, and he could see from a mile away that the kid was terrified and still probably lost on the whole "almost an adult" thing, so he made a very easy decision.

He needs a role model, and I'm an adult, and I'm here, so that role model may as well be me. Randy thought to himself. Sure, Randy was only 8 years older than him, but he still knew more about life. Marlene had told him Mitchell's story once, and he'd donated to a community fund she'd set up to help the kid get groceries while he waited for the inheritance paperwork to go through.

The two got settled in across from one another, and Randy soon became lost in thoughts of his friends in the Marmara and Twalnaverra. The heaviness in his heart began to ease, just a little. He had faith that Abigail would know what to do, and now he had a friend to fight for while he waited for her to save them all.

CHAPTER 9: LOST LIGHT

Abigail furiously searched through every drawer and crevice of Randy's desk, looking for whatever the fuck he'd been talking about when they kicked her out of the visitation room. She mumbled angrily to herself as she did.

"Let the light guide you." What the fuck is that supposed to mean? If he's talking about sunlight then he must've been high on every kind of "herbal medicine" out there because this room HAS NO FUCKING WIN-DOWS. THERE'S NOT EVEN AN OVERHEAD LIGHT, JUST-

She cut herself off when her eyes hit the wooden base of a lamp that sat on Randy's desk. There was a tiny engraving on it, and when she brushed her fingers over it, it felt different than the rest of the lamp. Abigail leaned in to get a closer look.

The carving looked like a circle, and there were things that appeared to closely resemble the points of a compass around the circle's edge. The half of each diamond-shaped point that was out-side the edge of the circle was fully carved out, while the half inside the circle was just a thin outline. There was a dot on either side of each hollow triangle, just small and far enough apart to separate from one another. In the center of the circle, Abigail recognized the stylized "T" that looked just like the cursive capital ones that Randy drew when he wanted to use his best handwriting.

She touched the carving again, this time pressing down on it. Instead of being an on button like she expected it to be, she was surprised to hear a quiet *"click"*, then a square of wood popped out of place. A hollow compartment was revealed inside the lamp, and Abigail cautiously reached inside to investigate.

Inside the compartment, there was a tiny dodecahedron made of woven wire, with hexagonal holes on every face of the shape. When she picked it up and placed it in her palm, it began to glow and expand until it was roughly the size of a beach ball. Now, its outsides resembled hollow honeycombs, lit from the inside with a ball of yellowish orange light.

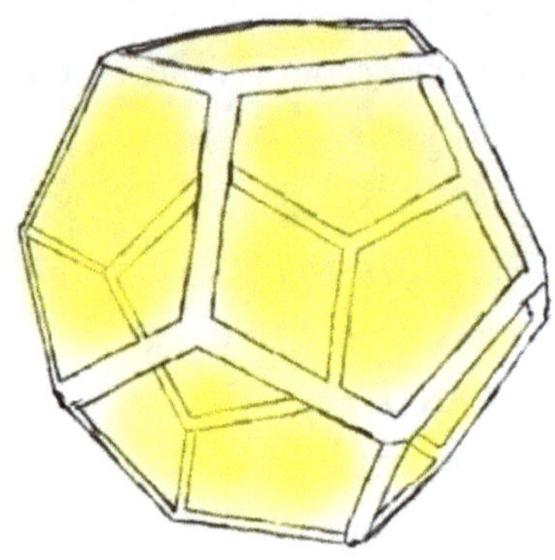

Huh. Cool, I guess? Randy, what am I supposed to do with this?

She looked at the thing in her hands, then at her surroundings. The shade on the lamp had a couple of small latches attached to its top rim, and on a hunch, she placed the prism on top of them. It locked perfectly into place, and then, much to her surprise, the lampshade began to spin.

It spun faster and faster, until all the spinning dots blurred together and became a solid aura of light. Then, the light began to change color, and as it streaked across the walls of the room, it gained an almost film-reel quality. Images flashed along the walls, first as stills and then as a moving picture. The light picked up speed again, and all of a sudden it drew in on itself, coming off of the walls and beaming down onto the floor in front of Abigail.

A ghostly, hollow voice echoed through the room, and the light condensed into its final form, and before her stood a hologram of Randy, looking at her apologetically.

"This recording was made three days after Marlene and I were threatened. If you're watching this, it means that something has happened to the two of us and you are to protect our allies in our stead."

The hologram gestured for its viewer to sit in the chair across from the desk, and when Abigail obliged, "Randy" began to speak again. As he spoke, he crossed the room and sat down in his place across from her.

"Magic runs in the veins of this town. Beneath every stone and atop every cloud, there is something ethereal, supernatural, or powerful lurking. Every industry, from the poorest farmer to the richest politician in Kacapa county, is affected by magic in some way. Now, why am I telling you things you already know?"

Here the spectre paused, whether for dramatic effect or simply to regain his breath, she couldn't quite tell. Then, he continued,

"I'm telling you these things because I know that, whatever it is that's happened to the two leaders of the magical societies of Dufferton, the situation is dangerous enough that they need to band together and protect themselves. If this is the worst case scenario, then both of us are dead or missing, which means that you, my friend, get to take my place as the leader of the Twalnaverra."

The holo-Randy shook his head, sadly, then opened the drawer in his holographic desk and pulled out a tiny book. It looked like the one that Abigail kept her contacts in, and this was confirmed when Randy opened it up and held it out to show her rows and rows of names and physical descriptions.

That's not creepy at all, Randy. Not at all.

"In this book, which you'll find in the second drawer on the top right side of my desk, are the names and physical descriptions of every member of the Twalnaverra, and the Marmara as well. Scry them. Get their help, and explain to them what's happened. You'll need all the help you can get to protect yourself from the ones behind all this. Something bad is brewing in Dufferton."

The hologram pointed to a spot on the ceiling, and then snapped his fingers. A massive, opalescent crystal descended from the spot, both in the recording and in real life.

"I've never shown you this because it was expensive as fuck, and I've been trying to figure out how it works for months now. I finally got it. This marvelous hunk of rock is a scrying crystal, and to use it, you simply touch the tip of the crystal to the palm of your hand and then open the contact book and hold it up. The crystal will simultaneously scry everyone in the book. If you only want to scry one of them, you only say one name. Have you figured out what I want you to do yet?"

Abigail *had* figured out what Randy wanted her to do. He wanted her to scry every Twalnere and Marmaran to come together and join her in helping him.

"I want you to scry every Twalnere and Marmaran, and every rogue too. I want you to get them on your side. I don't care what favors you have to do, I don't want you alone when the shit hits the fan. If I'm gone, and I know I will be if you're watching this, I don't want you in danger. I also don't want any of my other allies and friends to get hurt in whatever hell storm got me. Warn them that something dangerous is going on in Dufferton. Make sure, when you hold your "crystal meeting" that you tell them everything about the night that guy with the ring came to the house. Make sure you tell them of anything suspicious that's happened before or since then. Make absolutely certain no one is left out of the loop in regards to what dangers are mounting. Wherever I am, be it a dungeon, a ditch or the afterlife, I *don't* want to have a meeting of the Twalnaverra where I am. Am I clear?"

Abigail nodded, not realizing that he couldn't see her. Still, he seemed satisfied, and waited a moment before speaking again. This time his voice was back to being quiet and haunting.

"As I've established already, at the time I'm making this record-ing I have absolutely no idea what's happened to me. I do know that it means that I've left you all alone, to take care of my shop and my plants and my damn secret society. For that, I want you to know that I'm sorry. You're one of the few people that I trust more than anything else in the world, and I know that you're strong and capable of leadership. I also know that you may be grieving, because (not to make any assumptions or anything) your friend is gone, seemingly forever. I'm sorry that I left you, Ab. There are so many things that I know I won't get to teach you, because this recording will destroy itself in 30 days, and I could take a lifetime and still owe you more of an explanation."

He ran his hands through his hair, and Abigail felt a pang in her chest.

"I guess this is goodbye, for now. I miss you, Ab. Wherever I am, whatever horrors or death I may or may not be going through right now, I guarantee you that I'm thinking about you. And I'm glad it's me here, and not you."

He put out his arms -seemingly for a hug- and then stopped short, letting them fall back down abruptly. He shook his head, and then the hologram flickered. It wavered dangerously, and he waved a little into the air around him. The light from the dodecahedron slowed down, and became yellow again, and then it stopped spin-ning completely.

Abigail stared at the light for awhile without moving. As the hologram had tried to hug her, her heart had wrenched when she realized she'd put her arms out too. She'd wrapped them around herself and now she still stood, holding herself and closer to tears than she ever wanted to admit.

After a few moments, she numbly took the projector off of the lamp, let it shrink, and then put it away. She looked at the crystal, which was still hanging from the ceiling.

Welp, I guess it's time to open up the world's weirdest conference call.

Several hours later, Abigail stepped out of the office, having recounted her tales and Randy's messages, and convincing the Marmara that he did not, in fact, kill Marlene. She walked out into the tea room and was terrified by the sight of a short, thin man peering into her kitchen cabinets.

"Hey, uh, we're closed."

The man didn't respond at first, then Abigail realized that the reason he seemed so strange was that he was, in fact, not living anymore. He must have been one of several corporeal - leaning ghosts in Dufferton. Why he was in her tea shop, however, was very unclear.

"Oh shit my bad. I uh. Sorry. I was told that I was supposed to replace the big guy?"

Abigail's blood began to boil at the mention of Randy in such a way.

"Who the fuck told you that?"

"My bosses? I mean maybe they're my bosses. I was just hanging out under the highway overpass when two guys came up and asked me if wanted a job. I did, in fact, want a job. They dropped me off in front of here, handed me a vial of purple stuff and a knife and told me to make myself 'useful' or whatever. I was dusting some of your shelves."

Abigail didn't really know what to say, and she didn't really trust the intruder, but he wasn't resisting her attempts to feel his mind and test his intentions. He was obviously sent to attack her (she could tell from a mile away that the vial was full of powdered nightshade) but he genuinely didn't seem to be clued in to that fact. Honestly, he seemed just as confused as she was. She skirted around him, never letting her eyes leave him as she checked with her hand that the deadbolt and lock on the tea room door were fastened. He just watched her curiously.

At least there's no way he heard me while I was in the back office. There's enough charms on that thing to keep out an army of nosy giants.

"Well, thanks I guess. What's your name? And how did you get in here? Keep in mind, I'll *know* if you're lying."

The stranger pushed up the old-fashioned gold spectacles on his face, then held out his hand to shake hers.

"I'm Sidwell Sloan. I'm a ghost."

To emphasize his point, he hopped into the air and then crossed his legs quickly, beginning to float.

"I couldn't get the door open, and I also didn't know where the doorbell was, so I just floated in. I figured you wouldn't mind, since I was helping you out. I thought they would've told you I was coming."

Abigail just looked at him, processing his words and contemplating the implications of his arrival. She tried to think about how best to phrase her next questions, but ultimately just opened her mouth to let them tumble out.

"So you're just a ghost?" He nodded. "And a bunch of random dudes handed you a knife and a vial clearly marked 'nightshade powder' and told you to make yourself useful. And you assumed this had nothing to do with killing me?"

"Why would they want me to kill my coworker?!" He seemed genuinely horrified at the concept.

"I don't work for them! They're almost certainly connected to the people who falsely accused Randy of murder and threw him in jail for life for it! I'd bet my eternal life they'd lock you up for my murder as soon as you committed it! They want every member of the Twalnaverra and Marmara out of the way, dead, or locked up so tight they can't breathe, even if they don't need to."

By the time she was done with her outburst, Abigail was shaking, and her shoulders were tense. Sidwell just looked at her for a minute, then floated backwards slowly. He put his hands where she could see them, and she relaxed a little, blushing in furious embarrassment.

Sidwell, for his part, had absolutely no idea what she was talking about. He was *very* new to the area, and he'd been living in the woods with a friendly herd of deer for a few weeks, but other than them, he really hadn't had any contact with living things since he left the last town he'd been in. The names "Twalnaverra" and "Marmara" were completely meaningless to him, and the angry vampire in front of him was more terrifying than the rabid raccoon that he'd bumped into on his first night under the overpass. He voiced this to Abigail, and then neither party said anything for awhile.

Finally, Abigail mumbled an apology for going off on him, and agreed to let Sidwell work at the Pocket Watch for awhile in exchange for a room to stay in and food, should he get hungry. Sidwell, not wanting to chance meeting with his unfortunate former employers, agreed to the deal. Abigail set him up in one of the mostly-used-for-storage guest rooms on Randy's floor, with strict instructions never to open Randy's door. He thanked her, then floated out the window before she could say anything else to him.

When he came back an hour later, he had an also-semi-corporeal trunk with him which contained clothes that appeared to be peak 1800s wild west fashion, several different Stetsons, a few 1980s wardrobe disasters and a couple of chest binders. She showed him where the laundry room was, and offered to throw anything he needed washed in with her next load.

Abigail went to bed that night uneasy for even more reasons, resolving to immediately start searching for information on who might be targeting the good magic users of Dufferton.

CHAPTER 10: FRIEND OF A FOE

Linda tried really hard to be a good warden.

Less than a week after Randy arrived, a steady flow of inmates began arriving. This caused a huge pile of paperwork to accumulate on her desk, and a huge amount of stress to pile on her shoulders. Several dozen people were sent up the mountain- each told a different thing. Some were told they'd won an all-expense-paid vacation to a ski lodge, some were told they were selected for a special kind of jury duty at a courthouse that was just built on top of the mountain, some were arrested for speeding while their cars were parked, and some were just outright kidnapped. Every time someone arrived, they were given new clothes to change into and everything they had with them was confiscated. She said her stupid little speech and led them to a cell, leaving them in there for an hour or two.

While they got themselves acquainted with their new surroundings or freaked out or whatever, she would go through their things and make sure nothing was bugged by the council before shoving it into a storage closet. Nothing ever was, but Linda was cautious all the same because Roger had made it very clear that he would be watching her very closely, and it seemed like he was keeping his word for the first week or so. Councilmembers would escort inmates in sometimes and listen as she gave her speech, locked away the inmates, and inspected their things. They always had an air of malice around them, as if they were there to threaten *her* into submission far more than the prisoners. There would be at least one of these "surprise inspections" per day, until one day they simply stopped altogether.

When they stopped, Linda was skeptical and cautious. Why weren't they coming up the mountain?

On one hand, Linda was worried that the council was growing suspicious of her and plotting something, but on the other hand...the roads up the mountain were getting worse and worse by the day. To the council, it didn't really matter if a few inmates and a bus driver went off the road one day in an icy death slide as long as no members of the council itself were hurt. This theory was confirmed when one of the last prisoners to arrive showed up without even a guard on the bus.

Linda sat at her desk, re-reading the file in front of her for about the eighth time. *Lilac Fortescue.* The newest inmate was very special- she was Marissa's girlfriend. Marissa was not only the person who'd stood up with her and helped to convince the council that the prisoners should be rehabilitated, but she was also the person who went to the council meetings that were held each month and reported on everything going on at the facility. She'd warned Linda in advance that her partner had been apprehended, and that she would be one of the most powerful inmates to date. Linda appreciated the warning. New inmates always gave her a migraine, but this case was particularly special because with this girl came the need to change a lot of the spells within the prison to accommodate inmate magic use. She'd put Rolf and Ivan in charge of this, as they were her best two guards when it came to the barrier magic.

Man, I'm glad I convinced Felix, Ivan, Rolf and Marissa to join me in this shit.

Linda set aside the file and got ready to meet the new kid. Her abilities were on par with Jefferson, O'Connell, and Von Fer in both their intensity and their volatility. She was able to control electricity, and apparently summon lightning on occasion.

A knock at the front office door pulled her out of her thoughts, and she grunted for whoever was outside to enter. Felix, a young half-elf with sandy gold hair, stepped inside. She waved her hands in a gesture commonly known to mean, "well, out with it. What do you want?" and he nervously cleared his throat again before speaking.

"Good evening, ma'am. I was told to inform you when the new inmate arrived. The dogs spotted the bus driving across the plateau – they'll be here in about 10 minutes." He stared straight ahead of him like he was addressing his superior officer in battle. The thought of someone so young fighting real enemies almost made Linda laugh. He was more than 500 years younger than her. Physically, though, he looked like he was in his 20s, and she could almost picture him in the fatigues of a cadet.

Why the hell is he treating me like I'm a general in the army?

She thanked him for the information and dismissed him, and she heard him snicker a little on his way out.

Ah, so someone dared him to do that. Great, they think I'm funny now.

703 years of life had taught her two things- what it felt like to be exhausted beyond the mortal, physical concept of the word, and that it really didn't matter what people you were in charge of thought, as long as they did as you said.

She made her way out of the office to the front entrance of the prison, her black track pants swishing together with each step. She was using a light glamor at the moment in case there was anyone important along for the ride, so her hoodie looked like a uniform jacket. She pulled her hair back into a high ponytail as she walked, making it to the entryway just as the newbie was pushed inside by the bus driver.

Linda stepped forward and opened her mouth to begin her usual speech, but the girl held up her hand and interrupted.

"I'm sorry, but I can't hear you at all right now. I'm hard of hearing and I use magic to help me hear, so the barrier... thing around this building is making it difficult to understand you." Her voice was apologetic, but Linda still bristled a bit.

She floundered for a moment, unsure of how to proceed. She didn't know any kind of sign language, and she wasn't sure if it was rude to write a note or expect the girl to lip read. She had *very specifically* told Rolf and Ivan to finish fixing those barriers before Lilac's arrival, so that Lilac wouldn't lose her autonomy or ability to communicate. She'd been planning on justifying her actions to the council by telling them that it would be easier to brainwash people when they could hear her, but the council clearly didn't care that much.

In the awkward pause that followed Lilac's words, Linda watched her fidget with one of the snow-white curls on her head. She was taller than Linda by probably 10 inches, and her pale purple eyes were in stark contrast with the melanin of her face. A silver horseshoe peeked out of her nose, and (though it would mean an extra form to fill out) Linda couldn't help but think that it suited her well. Thankfully, as she'd found out when Randy arrived, the "piercings and jewelry" form was very easy to fill out.

Her observations were interrupted when the silence of the entryway was broken by the newbie squealing and bouncing up and down, not unlike a kid being told they had free reign over a candy store. Linda turned around to see Marissa hurrying towards them.

"I apologize for being late, Linda, I was breaking up a fight between Ivan and Rolf. One of them has a couple broken fingers but the infirmary nurse wasn't there-"

"Because I fired her," Linda interrupted. "She kept trying to follow me into my office, and she was generally just...really nosy. The final straw was when she was mean to my dogs, though. Kicked at them for walking near her." Rage visibly burned in Linda's eyes as she recalled the way she sent the council's spying little bitch flying into the snowy parking lot. Sighing, she shook her head to dismiss the emotion and jerked her head towards the new girl and gave Marissa a meaningful look.

"That's your girlfriend, right? The one you *know* isn't gonna to cause trouble with her lightning powers?"

"That's her. Lilac Jane Fortescue, 25 years of age, date of birth December 20th-"

Linda stopped listening to her and checked her watch.

"Right, yes, you told me before. How do I make her hearing spells work? If she places them while she's standing in the office they'll work even when she leaves, right? I don't mean to be rude about the spells or anything, I just have about 90 pages of paperwork to fill out that should've been filed yesterday so the fact that Rolf and Ivan ignored me when I said to set these up before now is really pissing me off."

Marissa nodded. "I understand. I can sign to her for you, and let her know we are going to the office to fix her hearing spells," she said, then added, "and I can do all her paperwork for you if you'd like."

Linda nodded gratefully and Marissa took a moment to explain what Linda was doing as she patted Lilac down and gave her a new set of clothes to change into. Linda thought it would be good, for tradition's sake, to say the welcome speech she'd given to everyone else even though there wasn't much point since the council wasn't listening. She voiced this to Marissa, who agreed, but said she should wait until Lilac could hear. Linda nodded, then began to lead them down the very short front hallway to the office.

Once all three women were inside, the air started crackling with static electricity and Lilac smiled, shaking herself as if banishing stiffness. She started muttering arcane phrases to herself, and a crackling nimbus of electricity manifested around her head. When she seemed finished, Linda cautiously asked, "can you hear me now?"

Lilac nodded, her body sagging back from exhaustion. Linda silently thanked her gods and took Lilac by the arm, starting to talk and pull her out of the office, down the front hall past the lobby and up to the first of two west wing hallways that ran to the back of the giant concrete horseshoe that was The Ark of Light.

"I'm Linda Bernard. I'm the warden here. Yes, my ears are pointed. Yes, I am an elf. While you're here, you answer to me, am I clear? I don't make a point of mistreating prisoners, but this isn't a kiddie fun land, got it?" She noticed Lilac's head lolling to one side, and though she weakly nodded along to show that she was listening, it was clear that she was barely conscious. Linda started talking and walking faster so that she could finish talking and get to her cell before Lilac passed out.

"This facility is called The Ark of Light. You're here to change your path and follow the light of our founders' mission."

Just as Linda finished and opened the door to Lilac's cell, the girl slumped to the side and into the waiting arms of Marissa.

"Oh shit!"

Marissa seemed like she was beginning to panic, so Linda checked Lilac's pulse and listened to her breathing for a minute to make sure that she was still alive. She was, thankfully, so Marissa placed her in her cell on the bed. Linda left Marissa in charge of locking the door whenever she was done tending to her partner, with a reminder to start on the paperwork when she was done. She told Marissa to make a mental note to add "deaf" to Lilac's file, so she could make sure accommodations were always made for her, and Marissa said she'd add it in when she finished with the paperwork about her septum ring.

She made her way down to the end of the hall, past O'Connell and Jeffersons' room, only to find one of the two troublemakers missing in action. She sighed, hoping that he was in the common room at the end of the hall and not off causing a ruckus somewhere. She wasn't disappointed.

She walked to the end of the hall, intending to grab something she was keeping safe in the "Valve" room, and looked through the doors of the hall out into the almost-empty common room. The only two people inside were Jefferson and Von Fer, and they seemed to be talking about something very serious. Linda immediately abandoned the definitely-not-a-bottle of whiskey she most certainly wasn't planning on drinking in the office before resetting the broken fingers of the inmate she'd almost forgotten about, opting instead to sneak up and listen from the shadows of the doorway to their conversation.

"-but anyway, I heard he was her second in command, right? Do you know who was after him on the list of people in charge? I'm willing to bet you money they're the next hit for whatever evil society or whatever the fuck is taking over our town."

Fuck, how much does he know about the council?

Quin said something too quiet for Linda to hear, and Randy nodded.

"Oh I know him. He's a good guy- kind of an ostrich of a person though. He'll want everyone left to flee before more people are dragged up here to Hell. Oh, speaking of which, did you see that fucking creature out the window earlier? Right at dusk, I swear on my mother's grave I saw something with glowing red eyes and pointy ass teeth eat a whole fucking raccoon in one bite. I watched it out the window- I'm not lying! I can see in your eyes you think I'm full of shit, but I'm telling the truth. I almost pissed myself, it was terrifying."

Linda had to stifle a derisive laugh- humans (even magical ones) got scared by the *stupidest* shit.

*I've seen that thing – I guess one of the dumb teen cults that worships the "dark spirit of the mountain" must've summoned it or something back in the day and just... Left it. If it were a little more humanoid I'd call it a soul shifter, but that thing looked **way** too corrupted to have ever been anything that has a human form. Here's hoping that it stays outside the barrier line and doesn't fuck with shit. The elders are going to want **me** to* *deal with it and I have no more patience for monsters of the night than I do for spying nurses.*

She tuned back into the conversation just as Jefferson was covering a yawn with the back of his hand and Von Fer was rubbing her eyes sleepily. As if on cue, a loud electronic bell began ringing insistently over the intercom to signal that lights-out was almost upon them, and both of them jumped. Linda took the opportunity to walk into the room nonchalantly as if she'd been doing a nightly patrol, and she pushed Von Fer towards the main entrance of the common room while pulling Jefferson with her out the side door, down the hallway she'd just come down, and past Fortescue's cell to his own on the opposite side of the hall. He tried to protest, saying that he could walk on his own, but she gave him a look so serious it made him blanch. She seemed to be earning herself a reputation for her "death stare" among everyone at the prison-inmates and guards alike, and she didn't mind in the slightest.

Once Jefferson and O'Connell were safely locked in their cell, she begrudgingly went to the infirmary to deal with whatever cocky idiot had been starting fights earlier that she'd now have to fill out an incident report for- *in triplicate,* because the gods hated her.

"Name?" she asked, not bothering to look at her patient as she washed her hands.

*Medical licenses don't expire, right? Mine should still be valid as long as the paper hasn't turned to dust-and it's **barely** 150 years old. It's still basically brand new.*

"Well, I would hope you know that by now."

Linda spun on her heel and came face to face with Rolf, who was holding his hand gingerly across his chest. His knuckles were torn and bloody, and a few of his fingers seemed to be dislocated.

"Damn, what the hell did you do?" she exclaimed, quickly grabbing some supplies to fix his hand.

He explained that he and Ivan had been figuring out the barrier spells, but they'd realized that they needed Lilac here to fix them properly. They'd then gotten into an argument over who would be the one to tell her, and Ivan had dodged a punch. Rolf was quick to reassure Linda, however, that no drywall had been damaged by his fist, "only a little bit of concrete."

Linda didn't want to hear anymore, so she handed him a towel. "Bite."

"What?" he asked, suddenly seeming worried.

"Bite down on this. I can't find anything to help with your pain, but your fingers are turning blue so I need to fix this now. Bite down and I'll do my best to make this as quick as possible."

True to her word, she reset his fingers and healed his cuts as quickly as she could muster. He writhed in pain, but as soon as it was all over he slumped back in relief. She had him wash his hands and spit out the towel, then explained that Lilac's hearing spells had already been restored.

"Now, I have a new task for you," she said. "Since the council clearly isn't watching us anymore, I'm implementing a new policy. I can see that a lot of inmates seem to know each other from the outside, and they're starting to band together. I've heard some of them start talking, though, and I want to nip something in the bud right now."

She led him out of the infirmary and down the hall to the office.

"Restlessness and organization do not mix. They don't want to be here. They know that we know that they don't belong here. If we have any hope of keeping everyone here safe, and covering our own asses, we need to convince them to stay," she finished.

"We should be running this place like a sleep away camp, then, instead of a prison," Rolf said. When she didn't seem to understand what that meant, he explained that he thought the prisoners should essentially have the freedom to choose their daily schedule, with the exception of mealtimes and lights out. "They'd be locked in their cells at night, and they wouldn't be able to leave, but they could hang out with one another and do things like crafts or yoga or something all day."

Linda looked at him skeptically. On one hand, his proposal was absolutely ridiculous. On the other, though, it was *way* less effort for her. She eventually agreed, on one condition.

"They can like you, but they still need to see me as a horrible evil bitch," she said. She explained that this would keep them in line enough to listen when she gave them orders, which would really only happen if one of her bosses was showing up, and it would give them all someone to scapegoat. Rolf agreed that that was a good idea, and they discussed the logistics of things a bit further. When they finished, she dismissed him to go tell the other guards what they'd discussed.

~~~~~~~~~~~~~~~~~~~~~~~

Several weeks after Lilac's arrival, as everyone seemed to be finally settled in and done causing trouble, she received a letter on a horrifyingly recognizable letterhead.

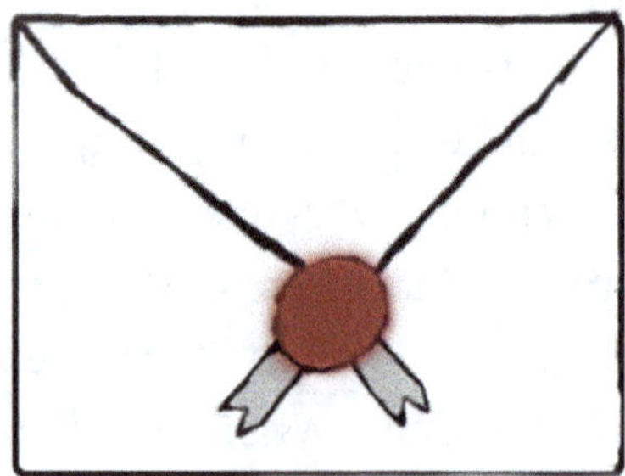
~~~~~~~~~~~~~~~~~~~~~~~

CHAPTER 11: HOWLING AND SCREAMING

Darkness. The musty smell of slick old stone. He can hear his father saying something, screaming something at him. "TURN ON THE FUCKING LIGHT YOU USELESS PIECE OF SHIT!"

He tries to summon the blue-white light that was in the palm of his hand a second ago. He tries to light up the cave. His sister's voice is raised, she's worried. She's afraid of heights- terrified of the dark. She didn't want to go exploring in the caves, but their father refused to take no for an answer.

"Your mom's been gone for two months now. We need to cheer ourselves up. I'm taking you two kids camping- no ifs, ands, or buts. We're going to a lake near my favorite caving site when I was a kid. I used to go there with my scout troop all the time."

The trail was off limits. The caves had "do not enter" signs on them. They went in anyway- without equipment because "no one really needs that shit. Just don't be an idiot."

His father is shaking him angrily while his sister cries, sobs in the dark. She's on a very small ledge. She was trying to get around the side of a ravine. There's water far below her, flowing very, very fast.

His father slaps him and yells for her to shut up. He's breathing hard now, his chest tight and painful. Tears are slipping down his cheeks as he tries to concentrate, tries to reignite the light.

It flickers back into existence. It's very faint, but enough to see, a little. He pushes the light into a ball and sends it floating across the ravine to-wards Lydia. Her tears are still falling as she looks down at her feet. The ledge she's on is so small she has to turn them sideways to fit them on it.

"Look what you did you piece of shit. She was trying to be brave, trying to be a better fucking child than you'll ever be. She tried to keep going in the dark and you fucked her path up. She can't get back from there. She'll have to jump and hope you can fucking catch her."

He tries to cry out, "No! I can't catch her! I'm not strong enough, my arms aren't long enough, dad, no!" but his father isn't listening. He's shouting over his son, pushing him to the edge of the ravine. If they get the angle just right, if she can see him right to aim, she can make it. He concentrates. Their father counts down from five.

She jumps.

The light blinks out again just as her feet leave the stone.

She doesn't know where to put her hands out. He feels her fingertips brush his outstretched hands, but he can't catch her. He hears her scream.

He hears the splash, far, far below them.

He hears himself screaming, his father screaming. Hitting him. Hitting him across the face. Harder and harder and harder and-

"RANDY! I said, wake. Up!!!"

Randy felt a slap across his face and jolted up out of his bed. He could hear shouts coming from other cells, but the voice he was most preoccupied by was that of Mitchell. He was, after all, the one who slapped him awake.

"What the hell do you want?" he replied, his voice unusually thick with emotion and his eyes glistening with tears he was barely holding back. He pushed Mitchell off of him and got out of his bed. His chest was still felt tight from the nightmare, and he was eternally grateful to Linda for leaving low lights on in all the halls at night. They were barely enough to see by, but anything was better than the oppressive darkness of his nightmare.

"You were crying in your sleep about someone named L...iza? Lina? I didn't hear her name but it started with L and I wanted you to shut up. Not that it would do much good, seeing as there's people outside screaming." Mitchell sat back down on his bed.

"Yeah, I can hear that. Why're they yelling, do you know?" Randy went to the door to look out at the hall.

"Oh a giant wolf chased Linda down the hallway a couple minutes ago. I think they ran towards the front office area."

"Wait, What?? Why didn't you tell me that sooner? Get off your bed."

"I didn't think it was anything important enough to mention. Why the heck do you want me to get off my bed?"

"Because I hid a lock pick made out of one of my hairpins in between your mattress and bed frame and I need it? Why do you care? Just move for a second, geez."

"Why did you hide it in my bed!?" Mitchell shouted.

"Because Linda found it last time I hid them in mine? I literally can't survive another trip to solitary."

Without another word, he picked the lock on the door and ran out into the hallway, unbothered by the fact that he was shirtless, barefoot, and running straight into a fight.

I can't let Quin hurt Linda, and I can't let Linda hurt Quin.

He followed the sounds of shouting and howling and the directions of the people in the cells around him, taking a wrong turn at the front office when he heard Linda's dogs barking and mistook them for Quin. Eventually he found the people he was looking for circling each other in the dining hall. Linda's arms were bleeding from several scratches, and Quin had quite a few bleeding cuts on her flanks and back. Linda was holding a bloodied knife in one hand and a stun gun in the other, and as Randy watched, she pulled the trigger and fired the electrodes at Quin's face.

Quin leapt out of the way in time to escape electroshock therapy, and pounced on Linda. Linda's head hit the stone floor with a loud *THUNK* that made Randy's head hurt in sympathy. When she didn't move or fight against Quin, the werewolf howled and sniffed her body, then began tugging at the set of keys that were clasped onto Linda's belt loop with a large blue carabiner.

Randy took his chance, and ran as fast as he could into Quin's side.

Maybe it was the fact that he'd just relived his sister's death at his negligent hands, or maybe it was the fact that he knew the real Quin wasn't here now, and she'd *never* do something like this. Maybe it was just the fact that he didn't want to see Linda's underwear, because Quin would undoubtedly pull her pants off of her body before she could manage to pull the keys off of their carabiner without opposable thumbs. Randy wasn't quite sure, either way, just *why* the fuck he'd decided to throw himself on top of a gigantic, enraged teenage werewolf, or exactly *where* the hell his strength came from, but damn did it come from somewhere. Quin howled again and tried to bite him, then tried to shake him off when she couldn't. He went flying backwards, smashing into the plexiglass top of the servery sneeze guard. Quin bounded after him, and Randy's four functioning brain cells knocked together long enough to give him a brilliant idea.

He rolled backwards and ran at the walk in freezer door, praying that it was big enough for his plan to work. As expected, Quin ran after him, and before she could stop herself, she barreled past him into the freezer. He slammed the door shut, ignoring her as she howled and clawed at the metal, and turned back towards Linda.

Several guards (who looked like they'd just woken up from a nice werewolf-induced power nap) were around her, trying to make sure nothing was broken. He came over to them and told them what little of the situation he knew. Linda started to stir, and he murmured as many healing spells as he dared try within the barriers of the Ark.

After several *more* minutes of explaining everything to Linda, he was escorted back to his cell (instead of solitary) with the promise that, as a thank you for probably saving her life and *definitely* saving her dignity, he would get a nightlight by the end of the week.

He told Mitchell not to ask about what had happened, as he was too exhausted to breathe properly, let alone explain himself for a third time.

Thankfully, his next sleep was dreamless, which meant that it was longer, calmer, and more fitful than his last.

CHAPTER 12: DO NOT ENTER

"Are you gonna tell me what happened last night?" Mitchell asked the next morning, conscious of the distinct lack of both Quin and Linda from the breakfast line.

Linda was fighting a giant wolf last night-wait. What if the wolf was Quin?! She's a werewolf? Oh, wait, I remember Aunt Edith talking to someone on the phone once about meeting at "the werewolves' ranch". Is Quin one of those werewolves? Oh my gosh, is Quin okay?

The voices that had chased him away from his house (and into the waiting arms of the cops who framed him for arson) had disappeared almost as suddenly as they'd appeared- they were gone before he even set foot in the Ark. Still, he was left with more questions about magic than he would ever have an answer for, and even if it wasn't full of whispering monsters, his head was still full of heavy thoughts.

Aunt Edith never taught him about magic, other than that he should try never to use it. Here, he saw people using small amounts of magic, or talking about their powers, or just...existing? without the shame he'd been conditioned to associate with the open use of his powers. He found himself asking Randy a *lot* of questions about having powers, and what it was supposed to feel like when he had magic.

There's so much Aunt Edith didn't teach me.

He was pulled out of his thoughts by Randy shaking him lightly and saying, "Hey, are you even listening? I *said* "do you really want to know" and you just ignored me. I'm still exhausted, man. If you really want to hear about what happened last night I can tell you, but if you're just gonna zone out the whole time I'm going back to the cell to take a nap." Mitchell shook his head and focused on Randy, then asked him to continue.

"So, you got a look on your face a couple of minutes ago like you realized something. What do you think you know?" Randy took a long sip out of a steaming mug of hot chocolate as he looked over the blue and green edge of his glasses at Mitchell.

"Uh, I think Quin was the wolf? Since she's not here and Linda's also not here, and Linda was fighting a wolf. And I heard my Aunt Edith talking about going to a meeting at a ranch on Mt. Wapetona owned by werewolves- didn't Quin live on a Ranch on Mt. Wapetona before she came here?" He was unsure of himself, and it showed in the slow, drawn out way he shared his hypothesis with Randy.

His cellmate nodded at him, holding in a yawn and making his jaw shake like there was a jackhammer hitting it in the process.

"Yeah, she does. Good job, gold star. You know where your crush lives, and not even in a creepy way!" Randy playfully punched him in the arm, which made him blush a little. Randy noticed and cleared his throat awkwardly, taking another sip of his hot chocolate. "But no, in all seriousness, yeah. Quin was the wolf fighting Linda last night. They're both resting up in the infirmary at the moment."

Mitchell's eyebrows raised in alarm, and he opened his mouth to speak, but Randy put his hand up.

"Before you freak out, they're both fine. Quin has some shallow scratches on her legs from Linda slashing at her with a pocket knife, and (even though it took them almost three hours to get her to consent to medical care that wasn't her operating on herself) Linda was checked out by a doctor and she doesn't even have a concussion, just a hell of a bruise on her head and a lot of scratches...and some bites. Your girl gave her a run for her money, that's for sure."

Why would Quin try to break out? She said she was afraid of what might happen to her family if she went home! And Linda might be mean to people who annoy her, but she's not evil! She's holding us here, sure, but she's only doing her job! Quin likes her, even.

"Woah, hey, what's the look of abject horror for? Talk to me, flames, you look like someone just told you Quin was getting executed for her crimes."

Wait oh gosh oh wait oh no she's gonna be in so much trouble! What if they really do take her and-

"Mitchell, I'm counting down from ten and by the time I get to one I expect you to be actually breathing again and telling me what you're freaking out about."

Randy sounded serious, so Mitchell closed his eyes and took several deep, measured breaths to calm himself down. By the time Randy had reached five, he was fine enough to explain himself.

"Randy," he started, tearing up a little just at the thought of something happening to Quin. "Randy, she likes Linda. She said she was afraid of people coming after her family if she tried to escape or leave the Ark in any way. Why would she break out of her cell in the middle of the night and attack Linda? What are they gonna do to punish her?"

"Because it was the full moon," Randy replied nonchalantly, finishing the last dregs of his hot chocolate. "She doesn't have a window in her cell, but it's been getting darker earlier and earlier, and the moon was out well before lights-out. She was in the common room earlier in the evening and left really quickly after looking out the window. I meant to ask her about it or tell Linda, but I forgot. She was probably fighting off a transformation for a couple of hours before finally giving in. I thought the barriers around the Ark were keeping her from transforming, but I guess the super moon last night was too powerful for either Quin or the barriers to handle. I already asked Linda what was gonna happen with Quin now, and she said they were just gonna move her into a more heavily enchanted cell and keep closer track of the lunar cycles. She's not in trouble. They don't blame her."

Relief flooded Mitchell, and he slumped forward to lean on the table.

"Oh thank goodness. I was so worried."

He looked down at the table in front of him and was surprised to find a plate of uneaten breakfast food in front of himself. It wasn't warm anymore, so, feeling slightly brave, he put his hands out over the plate of bland scrambled eggs and under cooked, thinly sliced bacon and whispered, "ignis."

Both of his hands burst into flames, startling Randy and a few other inmates who were sitting nearby. Randy cursed (which Mitchell hated to hear) and pulled his long, curly hair as far away as he could from Mitchell so that he didn't light it on fire. After a few seconds of holding the flames just enough above the plate that they didn't light his food on fire, he let the flames die out, and took a bite of his (now) over-cooked eggs.

A few bites in, he realized that something felt wrong. He felt sluggish, and his arms didn't want to move as fast as he was trying to move them. The same feeling of concrete being poured over his body that he had felt when he'd first entered the barrier around the Ark was hitting him again, only this time stronger by a factor of twelve.

"R-randy?" he asked shakily, his voice quiet and a little breathy.

"Hm? Wait are you okay? Ohhhhhhh gods you used too much energy lighting that little bonfire in your hands, didn't you?" He looked alarmed, but Mitchell was too tired to fully understand why. He could feel himself slipping slowly out of consciousness now, and he vaguely worried that if he passed out he'd land in his breakfast and ruin the extra-crispy bacon he'd just made.

He closed his eyes for a second, then felt someone shaking his shoulders and yelling something garbled into his ear. Everything sounded like he was under water, and he scrunched up his face at the unpleasant sound as he leaned into the person holding onto him. Blackness started to close in on him, and he gratefully accepted it, letting himself drift off to sleep.

When he woke up, he was in the infirmary. He checked the combination clock, calendar, and thermostat that was hanging on the wall above his bed, and to his alarm he realized that it was 8 am on December 20th, meaning he'd slept for an entire day, and was now late for breakfast.

He sat up quickly, instantly regretting it as the movement made his head ache. He swung his legs over the side of the bed slowly, then stood and felt something tug painfully at his hand. He looked down to see an IV of fluid stuck in his hand.

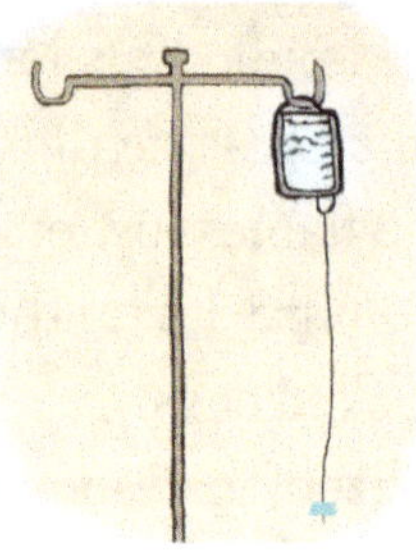

He gulped back the bile that rose in his throat at the sight of the needle and quickly pulled it out, inwardly hating the few tears that slipped down his cheeks as he looked away and rubbed his hand. He quickly made his way out of the infirmary and down the short front hallway to the dining hall, where he was happy to see Quin sitting in her usual spot at the breakfast table, across from Randy.

He went through the line and saw, to his delight, that there were doughnuts laid out for everyone to enjoy. He grabbed one and went to join his friends.

"Hey sleeping beauty, how do you feel? You were worse off than I was when they brought you in. I was about to leave, but Linda let me sit with you for awhile because she didn't want to sacrifice any guards to actually watch you, and she fired the nurse because she was a drug addict. You barely had a pulse, man." Quin gave him a one-armed hug, seeming happy to have him back.

"Yeah, man. They must've given you some *strooooong* stuff in that IV," Randy chimed in, ruffling his hair from across the table.

Mitchell didn't answer, just went to take a bite of his doughnut. Before he could, though, someone started singing "Happy Birthday," and soon everyone in the dining hall joined in to wish someone (Lilac, as they found out) a happy birthday. He clapped politely as she stood up and took a bite of her doughnut, then sank his teeth into his.

He engaged in polite conversation with his friends for several minutes until the boisterous atmosphere of the dining hall was interrupted *again*, this time by Linda standing up at the front of the dining hall and shouting for everyone's attention.

"Alright, listen up! I have an announcement to make. There are some changes that will be happening around here. First and foremost," she said, pacing back and forth and looking some people in the eye as she spoke, "We're gonna lighten up a little bit. Now, you will begin to have free reign of this facility in *most* aspects- daily activities, when you get up, whether or not you eat, what you do with your time. But when I say it's lights out, you damn well better listen to me. I am giving you all one chance to have a little freedom in this place, extending an olive branch, if you will. By doing this, I'm expecting that all of you will listen when I *do* tell you to do things, because you know that if I'm giving instructions they're to save my ass and yours. Remember, this place is to turn you into your best self, and we're going to do that by giving you the freedom you need to grow."

The room went completely silent, unsure of what to make of Linda's announcement. She seemed genuine enough, and Mitchell was excited to have a little more freedom, but the others around him seemed very skeptical that what she was saying was true.

"In giving you this freedom, we hope to make it a little more bearable to be here. No one can say how long your stay at the Ark of Light will be, but I know that the more you hate it here the more likely you are to try and start something you won't be able to finish.

We'll be filling your time with fun distractions so that that doesn't happen. I don't feel like talking to you all anymore," she said, the slightly caring tone dropping once more from her voice, "so I'll let Rolf take it from here."

Just like that, she pointed to one of the guards standing nearby and walked out of the dining hall. He fumbled for a minute to pull out a crumpled sheet of paper from his pocket, then stepped forward and said,

"I'm supposed to say that I'm *"excited"* to announce that we will be having a talent show next Friday! Use of powers and magic is prohibited without prior authorization, and I can tell you right now that Linda's almost certainly not going to authorize anything because, and I quote, 'I'm not doing all of that damn paperwork for everyone.' So, no magic. If you use magic we're throwing you in solitary for a month. Other than that, we don't care what you do. If anyone has props or instruments that they want to use, please come talk to a guard and we will make an appointment for you to talk to Linda in the front office. If you do so before Monday, she says she will try her best to get them for you from somewhere." He put away the paper and looked nervously around at everyone who was staring at him.

"Okay well, that was all. Go back to your doughnuts, and start thinking about what you want to do for the talent show. Remember, no magic or we lock you in solitary for a month!!"

With that, everyone turned back to the people around them to discuss what had just happened.

The table's conversation buzzed anew, and Mitchell found himself caught in a heated discussion of possible performances that their little friend group could do. Before breakfast was over, he'd found himself roped into a drum and electric guitar duet with Quin.

He was sitting in the common room a few hours later, still nursing the last traces of his headache, when Linda came back in with a scowl on her face and a stack of papers in her hands.

"That's enough! Quiet!" she yelled, startling everyone in the room and sending a shock of pain through Mitchell's head.

"It took almost an hour because our stupid copier is cheap garbage, but I printed some posters for the talent show. O'Connell, Reeves, Martinez, and, uh, you-" she pointed to each person as she said their name, and then pointed to the stack of paper in her hands- "you're gonna decorate and hang these around. I was told I had to make posters and decorate for the talent show. I made the posters in like two minutes on the computer- you guys get to hang them because I said so. If you wanna decorate them you can, I guess, but if I see any of them hanging around with dicks drawn on them, I will find who did it, and I'll tattoo an anatomically correct diagram of a penis on your forehead. You've been warned." She thrust the posters into Mitchell's hands before he could say anything, then turned around and walked back out of the room.

Well, I guess I know what I'm doing for the rest of the day then....

Mitchell looked around at the others she'd named, and none of them looked even *remotely* interested in helping him, so he sighed and took a few of the markers from the table in the common room.

This place is like a daycare facility for parents that don't want their kids anymore. I mean, come on. Quin's the youngest person here. None of us are the kids these coloring books were made for.

He scoffed and pushed aside the fairy-princess-unicorn themed book on the table in front of him and sat on a small, brightly-colored chair to start his design process. He drew a stage on one poster, a pair of red and blue spotlights on another, and an electric guitar on a third. At some point, Quin found him and helped him draw some retro rock star-themed designs on the remaining sheets of paper, and then the two enlisted Randy to help them hang post-ers everywhere.

They split up, each taking one section of the building. Randy took the east wing and started with the small "multipurpose room" at the back of the building that was full of gym equipment (that had clearly been salvaged or stolen from a middle school PE supply closet) and incomplete sets of weights. Quin took the front hall and dining room, and was subsequently pulled into the kitchen to help the group of inmates doing dishes there. Mitchell started in the common room and moved down the far west hall, leaving a couple of posters behind him as he turned the corner of the first west wing hallway and headed back up the second. He left the poster he was most proud of- one which had a detailed drawing of a dragon juggling fireballs and a person- on the wall next to his cell door, so that everyone who walked past would know that he was the one who did it.

He had one poster left in his hands, and he was getting ready to put it on the wall at the end of the hallway and enter the common room through its side door when he brushed against the door to a room labeled "valve room". It was the last room at the end of the hallway, and the instant his skin came into contact with the cold, rough wood of the door, every hair on his body stood on end and the shiver that ran down his spine was so powerful, he physically convulsed a little. He recoiled from the door, and something deep inside of him told him not to touch it again. The voice of reason was, however, not very strong compared to the rest of his brain, which was burning with red-hot curiosity and screaming to open the door. He put his hand on the doorknob out of curiosity and bit back a startled yelp- when he pulled his hand away it was singed as though he'd touched a hot iron.

*Ow, geez. That's one of the only burns I've ever gotten, and it's not even from doing something stupid this time! Well, Maybe it's from doing something a **little** stupid.*

He looked more carefully at the door knob, and noticed two things. The first was the fact that it had a deadbolt above it, unlike any of the other doors at the Ark. The second thing that he noticed, which piqued his curiosity even further and made him *really* wonder what was in the room that definitely *wasn't* a valve room, was the fact that the keyholes in both the deadbolt and the doorknob were glowing a little.

Mitchell stepped back from the door quickly, not wanting to mess with whatever was inside, and hung his last poster at the end of the hallway. He slipped back into the common room just as Randy and Quin were arriving, and motioned for them to come over and sit with him in the corner of the room farthest away from "the valve room".

"What's up man? You look like you've seen a ghost or something," Randy said as soon as he got to the couch Mitchell was curled up on. Quin perched on the armrest next to him, resting her arm on his shoulder.

"Hey, uh...do you guys ever feel weird when you're in the presence of large amounts of magic? Like, your-"

"Hackles rise?" Quin asked.

"Your heart pounds?" Randy continued.

"Like something's crawling up your spine?" Quin finished, and they both looked eagerly at him for an answer.

Mitchell gulped, then nodded, launching into the story of what had just happened to him, while the others listened with bated breath. By the time he was finished, Quin looked worried, and something dark and curious glowed behind Randy's eyes.

"We have to find out what's in there. I'll create a diversion-you've seen me use my powers before, right?" Mitchell and Quin stared at him blankly. He rolled his eyes and blew his hair out of his face, then pulled them both over to the window, instructing them to watch carefully. He channeled as much of his strength as he could into controlling the dying ivy vines that were growing along the side of the building.

As Mitchell watched, the vines twisted and grew two feet higher than they'd been before. Randy was breathing hard, and his face was growing red with the effort of the magic, but he whispered a barely-audible, "and now I'll show you my real powers" and suddenly, a ball of blue-white light flared in the air just outside the window, morphing into a butterfly the size of Mitchell's hand. It lasted only a moment before flickering and going out, and then Randy collapsed backwards into Quin's arms, almost knocking her over. Thankfully, Mitchell saw the slow, old, rotating security camera on the corner of the roof swivel back to a position it could've seen the light show from *after* Randy had already finished, and thankfully the common room had been empty for a while now.

Quin helped Mitchell carry Randy back to their cell, and they discussed the talent show for a few minutes. It was decided that Randy and the twin sirens that lived next to Quin would hypnotize the audience long enough for Randy to break into the enchanted room. Quin said goodnight to them and headed down the hall to her own cell just as the bell for lights out rang through the hallways.

Mitchell woke up very, very early the next day to the sounds of thrashing and muffled sobbing coming from the bed across the room. He turned over on his side and whispered, "hey, Randy, y'okay buddy?" into the darkness, hoping his friend could hear him.

The crying got a little louder, and Mitchell sighed softly.

This is the second week in a row that he's had nightmares every night. I'm willing to bet money that they were this bad when I was in the infirmary, too. Man, what happened to him?

He got up and wrapped his cover around his shoulders, then sat down gently at the edge of the other bed. Randy was still thrashing, and as Mitchell listened, he could make out some of what he was sobbing into the void of his dreams.

"Please! Dad, please! I'll be good! I'll kill all the plants, see? They're dead now! I'm not gonna grow any more of them! Please, leave the light on. Dad, please, it's so dark!"

Randy's body jerked like he'd been struck across the face, and he cried out in pain, his face crumpling.

"Please! Dad, please!" He beat his fists against the air as though he were beating against a door. Mitchell had to dodge his cellmate's fists several times before he finally let his arms droop down in front of him, sobs racking his body. Mitchell found his own cheeks a little damp from the scene, too.

"Hey, Randy? Can you hear me, Randy? It's me, Mitchell. You're safe. I'm here. Come on, man, it's a dream."

Randy didn't seem to comprehend him, but he looked up at the ceiling with unseeing brown eyes, and his breath hitched as if he'd heard the voice, if not the intention behind it.

"Lydia? Lydia are you there? I'm so sorry, Lydia. I'm so sorry. I deserve to be in this hell hole. Dad was right to lock me away in the dark- I couldn't keep my light on for you, why should I deserve to see the light again for myself?" His voice was steady at first, but then it broke, and he shook again with now-silent tears.

WAIT! This all started after Linda put him in solitary for two days! Those cells are pitch black, no windows at all! Ugh, come on Linda! I'm telling her about this tomorrow morning, and I'm making her apologize. Yeah. Wait, but how do I get Randy to stop screaming in his sleep.

Suddenly, Mitchell had an idea. He leaned down, close to Randy's ear, and tried to do his best little-sister impression as he whispered, *"shhh, Randy, I forgive you. It's not your fault. It was never your fault. Stop blaming yourself. Let yourself heal. Let yourself move on. Know that I forgive you, and I love you. This. isn't. your. Fault."*

Randy relaxed as Mitchell said the words, and by the time Mitchell had drawn back, Randy was still sniffling, but no longer crying as hard as before.

The next morning, Mitchell skipped breakfast in favor of marching to the front office and giving Linda a *very* stern talking to, one that even she was a little wary of. He stayed in the room as she made some calls, and after finally getting into contact with Randy's old business partner, he listened in as she arranged to have the enchanted blanket, that kept Randy's nightmares away during hard times, sent to the Ark on the next bus up. He didn't expect the bone-crushing thank you hug that Randy gave him when the blanket arrived a few days later, but he returned it willingly all the same.

Mitchell wasn't awoken by another nightmare again in his time as Randy's cellmate.

CHAPTER 13: BONNE NUIT

"Abigail? The lady on the phone says she *specifically* wants to talk to you. She says she's the warden of-"

Without a word, Abigail took the cordless phone out of Sidwell's hands and took the caller off hold, sprinting out of the room faster than the human eye could track.

"Hello?" she asked as she locked herself in the back office, voice steady and wary.

"Hello, Ms. Stern. Please pardon me for interrupting your daily life, but you were listed as the next of kin for Randolph A. Jefferson?" the caller asked, her voice bored and the question obviously-rehearsed.

If Abigail's heart had been beating, it would've stopped when she heard the question. As it was, a dreadful, chilling knot of feeling tied itself around her stomach.

Oh my god, what did they do to him? Please, please don't let him be dead!

She wasn't quite sure where the emotion came from, because it wasn't like she'd *missed* Randy in the month he'd been gone. She *certainly* hadn't kept herself awake for multiple nights in a row, digging for information on the people and organization that had taken him because it was easier than trying to fall asleep without the comforting sound of his snoring a floor below her.

"Wh...what, ahem, what's wrong?" she asked into the receiver, clearing her throat to try and sound natural.

Shockingly, the woman's voice was...reassuring?

"Oh, no, nothing's wrong Ms. Stern. This facility's policies are changing- we are focusing on rehabilitation and research shows that having familiar or favorite items could help that process." The woman still seemed bored, like she'd repeated this half a hundred times, but it was clear she was trying not to alarm Abigail.

"Rehabilitation? Rehabilitating what, exactly? Didn't they try to claim that Randy would never be able to redeem himself? This isn't adding up," Abigail said. The person on the other end of the line dropped all pretense of formality and responded,

"I'm gonna level with you. Randy's been very freaked out every night at lights out, even though we don't even really *do* the lights out protocol anymore. Something in the last week messed with him to the point where he asked his cellmate to light a fire in the corner of their room for light."

"Did you lock him in a solitary confinement cell in the dark?" Abigail asked, relieved that he wasn't dead, and now *much* more angry than she probably should have been, as someone who was "just a friend". The warden answered in the affirmative, with only the defense that she had nothing in his file to tell her *not* to lock him in a tiny dark room for hours or days on end. *That* made Abigail's cold, undead blood *boil*.

"You fucked him up and now you want me to fix it?" Abigail bit back icily, her irises shifting to a dangerous shade of red that the woman unfortunately couldn't see.

The warden (who was obviously an elf- Abigail could taste the self-righteous pretentiousness coming off of her from the Pocket Watch) defended herself angrily with an argument Abigail was too pissed off to listen to properly.

"Look, just shut up, okay? I'll send you the enchanted blanket he uses to block out things he doesn't wanna remember, but don't *ever* lock him up like that again, you hear me?" Abigail was struggling to keep her cool.

The warden agreed quickly, clearly unsettled by the dangerous edge in Abigail's tone. She also asked, quietly, if Abigail could send over whatever nightlight Randy used when he didn't have enough energy for magic, because she'd promised him one in exchange for apparently saving her life or something. Abigail smirked at the thought of this probably-pantsuit-clad bitch stuck helpless with only Randy's merciful, way-too-kind heart to save her. She agreed to send the nightlight too.

"Thank you," the warden said, sounding relieved. "I know you probably think I'm an awful person-"

"I do. Very much so," Abigail shot back.

"Right, yeah, that's fair. But please understand something. I am doing my best to ensure the safety of everyone here. I *know* it's not fair that some of the people I'm in charge of are here. I know that. But truly, there's nothing I can do but make them more comfortable while I keep them here."

Abigail's contempt of the woman on the other end of the line ebbed, replaced by the trickle of fear that ran down her spine. Carefully, she asked, "What are you talking about?"

"I can't tell you that. Really, I very much shouldn't have said this much but it's too late to really do anything about that now. All I can say now is that if you want to do what you can to help your friend, send me the things I've asked for and whatever toiletries and clothes you think he'd need. Other inmates are being given their own clothes and things back, and anyone who didn't bring those and have them confiscated is getting a call home for a care package. If you want to help, make Randy one of those."

Abigail's mind started to race, and she immediately thought of a thousand different things she could put in the care package to help Randy escape. Unfortunately, the elf was one step ahead of her.

"Oh, and we'll be checking through everything you send of course, so don't even try sending things to escape with. They'll just get thrown outside in the snow, or added to my cool weapon collection."

The conversation ended soon after that, and Abigail was left with a mind swirling with questions. If what the warden seemed to be hinting at was true, then there was something deep rooted and dark lurking beneath the surface in Kacapa County. A knot of unease settled in her stomach and she tried to take deep breaths. She had to keep working to free Randy.

Mechanically, she began to gather the things for him, looking through his library at the same time to try and find a book she hadn't gone through yet. He had hundreds, so soon enough she found one. She took the care package for Randy, set it out to send up the mountain, and went up to the attic, a book of arcane occult forces in one hand and a pot of strong tea in the other.

For the next several days, the Pocket Watch was busy- though not unusually busy, considering the various winter holidays celebrated by the people of Dufferton and the fact that it was much cheaper for young, broke people to trade something like a jar of snow taken from under the full moon and get a nice, lightly enchanted Christmas present for their grandma as opposed to trekking over to the local Bullseye Outlet to spend half their savings on something mediocre.

Abigail spent her time evenly divided between teaching Sidwell how the curiosity shop's trading system worked, teaching him how to make Pinecone Spice Tea lattes (why those were even a thing she didn't really want to know) and other winter-specialties, going behind him to make sure he carded everyone who ordered mulled cider or Smoking Bishop, and throwing herself down various rabbit holes to try and find out who was picking off members of the Twalnaverra and Marmara.

She was beginning to lose hope in her weeks-long search for answers when she stumbled upon a name in an old phone book that had an "M" next to it. Well, to be more exact, it had a crossed-out "M" next to it. She committed the name to memory and went back to helping customers until noon, when she sent a quick prayer to the major gods of a few local religions in the hope that at least *one* of them would keep things under control while she sequestered herself in the back office to scry the name from the phone book.

~~~~~~~~~~~~~~~~

"Hello? Betty Winters? Is anyone there?" she didn't fully expect an answer- what with it being noon on Christmas Eve and all, but she was still hoping for *something.* Even a "I'm with family leave me alone until new year" would be better than no response at all. She was pleasantly surprised when someone's face appeared in Randy's scrying crystal- an old woman with piercing green eyes and a thin, wrinkled face glared at Abigail, her curly white hair pulled back away from her face and her hands out of frame, but obviously preoccupied with something.

"What the hell do you want? Who gave you my name? Why are you scrying me when I'm in the middle of cooking Christmas dinner for my family?" the old woman asked angrily, looking past whatever mirrored surface she was using to perpetuate the contact with Abigail like she was reading the timer on an oven.

"I'm sorry to bother you, ma'am, but I found your name in Randy Jefferson's contact book and I thought-"

"You thought that because I left the Marmara I have something to do with his conviction? No. Why I left the Marmara after my husband died is my business, but it has nothing to do with any of you," the woman interrupted, angrily brushing a strand of her hair out of her face and reaching out of frame to pick up a jar of nutmeg.

"Of course not, ma'am, I was just asking everyone from both sides if they had any ideas as to what's going on. It's not just Randy- magic users all over the county are going missing or being convicted of crimes they didn't commit. Everyone's being sent to a facility up on Two Peaks mountain. I know it's not my business what your powers are, but I'd think you'd want to help me protect your family from whoever's behind this."

Mrs. Winters was now completely focused on Abigail, her face unreadable. Abigail swallowed and continued:

"I know that I'm not doing a very good job of convincing you to help me- you're probably asking "what's in it for me?". I'm a vampire, but I've spent the last hundred or so years regularly
~~~~~~~~~~~~~~~~

communicating with spirits and ghosts. If you can help me find out something, *anything*, about the people behind all of this, I'll use every occult practice at my disposal to help you speak with your husband again." Abigail was counting on the fact that Mr. Winters wasn't a terrible husband and Mrs. Winters would want to talk to him again. By the damp shine in Mrs. Winters' eyes and the silent contemplation on her face, Abigail could tell that she'd picked the right offer to make.

"Fine. I'll help you," she finally replied quietly. Abigail pretended not to see her wipe a stray tear from her cheek, and thanked her for her willingness to help.

"I have a few theories. The most plausible one, I suppose, is that maybe some quotidians found out about the magic around here and decided that they don't want anyone who's not like them around? I'm still not sure how they would've gotten all of our names or anything but-" Mrs. Winters laughed, interrupting Abigail.

"Quotidians? Hah, no. They're all either completely oblivious or they like what magic gets them. Even if there are some like what you said, none of them would have the power or influence around here to do anything. No, I know who's behind this. It's- oh hang on, I have to pull my gingerbread men out of the oven." A timer went off and she stepped away for a moment, and Abigail anxiously stared out the kitchen window in the corner of her view. There seemed to be nothing around the house except deep, dense forests. Abigail could see a shimmering aura of thick, protective magic around the house- she guessed that there were at least ten shielding spells around the property. When Mrs. Winters came back, Abigail asked about the barriers.

"The Council of Blight are the ones behind your disappearances. They tried to recruit me, right after Edwin died. Said some things about "getting back at the quotidian bastards who had no idea how to heal him" and "taking back this realm from the non-magic users and putting people with real power in control." The two people who came to my door went on their long rant about how the Council of

Blight was going to bring the quotidians to their knees- I genuinely thought they were off their rockers. They asked me if I wanted to join them and I said I'd consider it, then two days later I moved into the middle of the woods and hid my house with a bunch of magic because I didn't want to deal with them coming back for an answer."

The old woman mentioned the council as if Abigail should've already heard about it, and when Abigail asked her to explain their ideology, if she could remember it, she actually scoffed.

"What, are they not trying to recruit everyone? Well then I guess I'm a little offended. They believe that, for one thing, all quotidians should bow before us magic users. They literally want to enslave them, or kill them if they refuse to answer to the council. They also want to enslave any magic users who don't also bow before the council in exchange for minuscule amounts of power over the "weak useless filth" that is the Quotidian race. They want their Council of Blight Elders to be in charge of the whole world, and they're starting with Kacapa county. I'd bet my life they're the ones rounding up the "dissenters" around here- anyone who might be sympathetic to the Quotidians. And before you ask, I only said I'd consider it so they'd get off my property without me having to directly make them my enemies by calling the cops. The only reason I can think of that they would've come to me, other than to flat-out brainwash me, is the fact that I'm just a widowed old lady who stays on the sidelines of things around here, and I'm known for keeping my eyes open around town. No one would suspect a thing if I just *happened* to be a witness corroborating something that they claim happened."

Abigail was left speechless when Mrs. Winters finished, fear rising in her chest at the depth of this council's power and the vileness of their plans.

Is this what the warden was talking about?

Mrs. Winters actually had to ask her if she was alright, and didn't fully seem convinced at her reply that yes, she was. Abigail thanked her for the information and they spoke for a few minutes about when and where they would meet for Abigail to hold up her end of their bargain, and then they wished each other happy holidays.

When Mrs. Winters' face faded from her view, Abigail immediately grabbed Randy's contact book and, like before, scryed everyone she could. She told them everything she'd learned from Mrs. Winters, but kept the warden's words to herself, for now. As expected, everyone immediately went into an uproar when they found out about the Council of Blight. By the time everything was sorted out, it was almost time for the evening "happy hour" tea service, and Abigail's attention flicked between checking her watch and moderating the discussion.

On the one hand, most of the Marmarans wanted everyone to go into hiding from the Council of Blight, saying that anyone taken by the council was probably a goner at this point anyway, so they needed to focus on protecting everyone who was left. On the other hand, a very vocal group of Twalneres began to call the Marmarans cowards, arguing that everyone should focus on trying to rescue the others and destroy the council in an epic magical battle for all to see. After an hour of back and forth and several times where Abigail had to tell grown adults to stop calling each other names like children, she finally managed to get everyone to compromise.

She called the Marmarans out for their refusal to even *try* to rescue their friends and family from the council, and tried her best not to sound like an irritated schoolteacher as she explained to the Twalneres why "an epic battle for all the quotidians to watch" was probably a bad idea, since they were trying *not* to make the Quotidians associate magic with violence. In the end, everyone agreed to rescue the others and stop the council, but try not to bring too much public attention to the magical community. The scry ended shortly after that, and Abigail left the office.

She staggered into the packed tea room, barely conscious from the amount of energy she'd just used, and managed to keep herself on her feet until closing, when her knees went out from under her. Without a word, Sidwell slung her arm over his shoulder and helped her up the stairs, laying her down on Randy's bed so she didn't have to walk as far. She was out cold before her head touched his pillow.

As the new year came, Abigail told Sidwell everything she'd learned, and he was (justifiably) angry that the council had also tried to recruit him. When he heard about the Twalnaverra and Marmara, he agreed to join the Twalnaverra, at least while he was in the area, to help build up their ranks. To placate the anxious Marmarans under her supervision, Abigail had promised to try and find some spells to protect people, and she started gathering as many healing herbs, protection talismans, and enchanted weapons and armor pieces as she can get her hands on. She mostly left the tea room and shop under Sidwell's care as she built up her arsenal and buried everything she found in the greenhouse to keep it safe in case of emergencies.

Two weeks into the new year, on January 12th, a large group of police officers showed up at the Pocket Watch. They had warrants for both Abigail's and Sidwell's arrests for "suspicious activity possibly connected to the actions of Randolph A. Jefferson." Abigail didn't bother to call out their bullshit as she was pulled out of the tea room, and stifled her laughter as they tried (and failed) to break into the greenhouse.

"No one but Randy can open it, sorry. He protected it with more wards than anyone's ever used on anything, because those plants are like his children. Not even I can get in there," she said. The policemen around her angrily pulled her back inside, then led her out front to a waiting squad car.

On her way into the police station, Abigail found out the hard way that she wasn't wearing her sun protection talisman. As she was pulled out of the squad car and into the sunny Sheriff's office parking lot, her skin began to burn painfully, and she tried to thrash away from her captors to get to the safety of the shade. She was unsuccessful, and was additionally charged with resisting arrest. She was locked in a holding cell with Sidwell, where they both waited to be sent up Two Peak mountain to the Devil's Bed Plateau and the Ark of Light.

CHAPTER 14: FAIR WARNING

~From the desk of Roger Callsworth~

Ms. Bernard,

The council will be coming to inspect the facility on December 28th of this year. You are to have a concrete plan in place and already beginning to be implemented that will guarantee that everyone at The Ark of Light will begin to see things our way before spring. If you do not, there will be very unpleasant consequences for you.

Do not disappoint us.

R. J. Callsworth.

~~~~~

Oh god. Oh god oh fuck.

Linda clutched the paper in her hands, pacing quickly back and forth across her study floor. She carefully avoided stepping on loose papers, but in her focus on those she ended up barking her shins on the weapons chest by her chair. She swore, moving to sit in the chair and mutter healing spells over her freshly bruised leg. Roger had given her warning that he and/or one of his favorite cronies would be paying her a visit, but that hadn't truly prepared her for the sight of Roger's black sedan slinking up the mountain through the high snowdrifts. He had given her a warning just before Quin had lost control of her powers, and though Linda had tried her best to get everyone to understand that they needed to fear her, she worried her plan to keep them contained while Roger was here would fail.
~~~~~

As soon as Roger's car was visible, she rushed to her study to change out of her usual half-assed "uniform" and into her cleanest set of professional clothes. She'd warned the other guards that he was coming as soon as she'd seen the car, and now she knew they'd be yelling sobering spells at each other and trying to get rid of the "special brownies" that Marissa had brought in. She brought her dogs with her to the study, and left them there with food and water.

She glanced at the monitor on her messy desk and saw in the security feed that she'd set up. he was thankfully far enough away for her to go through with the emergency protocol she'd just thought of.

She pulled her hair down from its usual ponytail, then twisted it up into a bun as she made her way out of her study and locked the door behind her. Someone was in the hallway near enough to see her, so without bothering to see who it was, she knocked them unconscious with a the word, ignoring the drop in her energy and taking a moment to locate the unlucky inmate's cell to throw him inside. She kept walking down the hall, stopping every inmate she saw to tell them to go back in their cell or face solitary for the next year. She found Von Fer and grabbed her wrist, refusing to answer the girl's frantic questions as she dragged her to the door of the guard room.

"Felix, put her in solitary. If Roger asks, she's been in there since she tried to escape." She handed Von Fer off before anyone had time to ask for an explanation, making her way towards Jefferson and O'Connell's cell.

"Jefferson, I'm giving you one warning and *only* one warning," she said as she burst into the cell. Jefferson was sitting on his bed braiding his hair, and he jumped when the warden flung the door open. He opened his mouth to say something (probably stupid) at her unexpected entrance, but she held a hand up and shot him a look so full of vitriol that he went pale and stayed silent.

"My bosses *want* me to give them a reason to kill everyone here. Keeping all of you alive and rehabilitating you is a huge hassle, and the only reason they're bothering to help you see the light is because I stood up and asked them to try. Your crimes were supposed to be punished with the death penalty, but I asked them to give everyone here a chance to change. If you're not on your goddamn best behavior when my boss gets here for the surprise inspection he decided he's pulling today, I won't say a word in protest when he puts your ass in the electric chair.I know you can speak with your mind, so go ahead and tell your band of mischief making friends – if any of you try to pull shit, you'll be fucking yourselves over."

She was gone before he had a chance to process everything she had said, locking the door of the cell behind her. She could tell he didn't believe every word she'd said, but she didn't have time to think about telling the truth.

Linda found O'Connell in the hallway, heading towards his cell, and had a guard escort him back to it. She glanced out of one of the hallway windows at the rapidly falling snow and quickened her step.

She came to the guard room just as her on-shift guards were arriving back from throwing all of the inmates into their cells.

"Did you put them in trances?" She asked, glowering at Felix as he joined the group late. They all responded that they had, and she nodded.

"Get to your posts and look angry. He'll be here in-" she checked her watch and looked at the screen of the grainy "official" security feed. "-five minutes. Tops. He's pulling up to the parking lot now. Sing my praises and I'll bring you each a bottle of the elf booze from my stash. Hit an inmate for being "uncooperative" while he's watching and I'll get Jefferson to grow you a bag of the really good shit."

The guards disbursed, and Linda straightened her blouse and squared her shoulders, marching to the lobby. She was standing at attention as Roger opened the snow-covered door and stepped inside the Ark of Light.

~~~~~~~~~~~~~~~~~~~~~~~
~~~~~~~~~~~~~~~~~~~~~~~

Roger's heels clicked behind her as she made her way through the halls of the Ark. He had ordered her to take him on a tour of the prison and to show him what she was doing to control the inmates.

First, she took him to the dining hall, where a handful of miserable, silent inmates stared straight ahead of themselves as they robotically did the dishes. He watched them for a few minutes before grunting noncommittally, a signal for the tour to continue.

She led him past several cells, including Jefferson and O'Connell's, and stood nervously behind him as he stopped at each one. Jefferson stayed true to his word silently sitting on his bed and ignoring his cellmate as Linda and Roger came to the door. Roger asked him a few questions (mostly about whether or not he regretted what he had done) and Jefferson did a perfect impression of someone who actually gave a fuck about getting out of jail on good behavior and changing his ways. Linda made a mental note to give him extra free time once a Roger was gone. O'Connell just seemed... catatonic. Roger really seemed to like that, and as he saw more inmates who looked the same, Linda allowed herself to feel a little less scared that he was going to kill them all.

When the tour was over, he walked back with her to the front office where he closed and locked the door behind him.

"Your work impresses me, Ms. Bernard. I know, however, that these changes are far too recent to be a true reflection of the conditions which led up to the attempted escape of Ms. Von Fer, even if, as you say, she was wholly under the influence of the lunar cycle and is an otherwise exemplary inmate who displays a sympathy to our teachings. *I do not like liars Ms. Bernard.*"

As he spoke, he advanced towards her, backing her up against the main office desk. He lowered his voice to a furious growl for the last line, and he grabbed her right hand when he was finished speaking.

Sheer terror was coursing through her veins, because Linda could plainly see the hatred in his eyes that mirrored the manic anger he'd shown as he spoke about the list of traitors during the first meeting about the Ark of Light.

So, this is how I'm going to die, huh?

That was the only thing Linda had time to think before Roger barked,

"Allow me to show you how I deal with liars, Ms. Bernard!"

He took her hand and sunk his fingernails into its palm, making her cry out in pain. He seemed sadistically joyful at the sound, and he dug his nails in harder as he began speaking in a tongue too foul to be comprehended by mortal minds. He let go after a few seconds, leaving bloody crescent moons in her palm, from which swirling trails of black magic emanated. When he let go of her completely, Linda's knees buckled and she dropped to the floor, clutching her hand close to her body and swearing in German. He smiled down at her, then merely said,

"I'll see myself out, Ms. Bernard. Do not make a mistake like this again."

Linda wasn't quite sure how long she laid on the floor of the front office, but it couldn't have been long, because none of the guards came to look for her before she regained herself enough to stand and stagger out of the room. She stopped Ivan, the first guard she passed, to let him know that Roger had left, then ordered him to tell the others that the coast was clear. Before he even had a chance to ask if she was all right, she headed down the hallway towards her study. He knew better than to follow her there.

As soon as she got to her study, Linda let herself collapse again – this time into the leather armchair in the middle of the room. She looked down at her hand and was alarmed to see that not only had it not stopped bleeding, but that her blood was actually starting to turn black. She couldn't really think straight, but some part of her vaguely wondered if Cindy had ever been poisoned like this before. She found herself quietly wishing her mother were there, yet at the same time, glad that she would, at least, be spared the pain of watching the child she just got back die. She drifted farther and farther from herself with each second that passed, and she even began to forget the searing pain in her arm and hand. She didn't care about the inmates or the other guards anymore. All she knew now was that she definitely wasn't getting paid for Roger's death if she was dead.

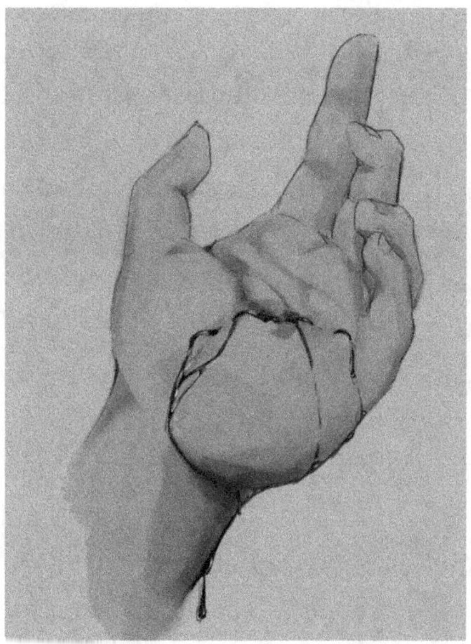

Perhaps it was her stubbornness, or perhaps it was her desire to see the shadow–souled bastard dead that kept Linda alive. Maybe the thoughts she'd had of her mother had called Cindy to her. Either way, some things seemed to intercede on her behalf, because while she was unconscious and rapidly bleeding onto the floor, her mother managed to get out of the house for the evening.

Cindy'd convinced Roger to let her go up the mountain to get something he'd forgotten there- some set of somehow important papers. When she arrived at the Ark, she immediately knew something was deeply wrong. Linda was nowhere to be found or felt, and all of her guards had simply said she'd been spending all of her time since Roger left in her study. They hadn't seen her for hours.

Cindy had her own "study", so she knew what to look for. She wandered the halls of the Ark, ignoring curious inmates and searching for the tell-tale signs of a pocket dimension. When she found a door with a glowing lock at the very back of the building, she immediately knew that her daughter would be inside. She raised a hand and said a word and the door swung lightly open, and Cindy cautiously stepped inside.

"Linda? Linda, are you in here?" She called softly, not bothering to close the door. Everyone else in the prison was either in a cell or in the guard room smoking pipes that smelled like skunks. Linda's dogs cowered in the corner. When she walked up to the chair in the center of the room, she gasped as she saw why: She had found Linda.

Linda's veins, where visible, were all surrounded by purple-black bruises that looked like trails of smoke. Her veins themselves looked as though they were filled with ink, and black-red blood was dripping between her fingers from five crescent-shaped gashes. Cindy's own blood began to boil at the realization that those were *claw marks. The kind that Roger left on people who opposed him.*

She ran a feather-light touch against Linda's neck to check her pulse, then repeated the action against her wrist. Luckily, she could feel blood pumping beneath her fingertips, which meant she wasn't too late.

By some miracle, Cindy managed to find almost everything she would need to heal Linda's wounds in the (oddly hidden) cabinets of her study. Cindy knew how to heal the kind of wounds that Roger left on people from unfortunate personal experience, so she was confident that Linda would live. The hard part was trying to find the right amount (or *any* amount) of the flowers she would need to properly poultice her hand. Linda's supply of medical herbs was... limited. *Ridiculously limited.*

While she stood searching through Linda's cabinets for Dros petals and Goldenroot leaves, Linda began to stir. She coughed thickly and tried to sit up, scaring the life out of Cindy.

"Oh, thank my father, you're awake. Where do you keep your Dros petals? I can't make a poultice to heal you with nothing but rubbing alcohol, tourniquets, and 9 different kinds of gauze."

She kept her tone even to keep Linda calm, but on the inside, Cindy was crying with relief.

Linda groggily said...something that Cindy didn't catch. When asked to repeat herself, Linda just groaned and reached her mind weakly out to Cindy, too tired to part her lips again.

"I don't have any, Cin. N-never needed any." Her mind was barely a touch across Cindy's, and the demigoddess frowned. Before she could ask anything else or try to see if Linda was okay, the weakened elf continued,

"Jefferson can probably grow you some. He's usually a fuckin' insuf'rable twat who gets in my way and gives me headaches, but he can grow plants pretty well with his... mind or something. Saved my life once, too, so I think he might be willing to do it? Maybe..." Even through telepathic communication, Linda was managing to slur her words and her mind had grown so weak Cindy could barely feel it. She was slipping out of consciousness again.

Cindy made a quick decision- she bundled the supplies she'd collected under one arm and carefully slipped the other under Linda's shoulders, hauling her up out of the armchair. Linda whimpered in protest and tried to fight Cindy off, but she ultimately gave in and let herself be hoisted up. The two took small steps down the hallway with Linda wrapped in Cindy's tight embrace (which was really the only way she could stay upright), stopping on the way to the front office to call Jefferson out of his cell.

The curly-haired man was very confused, but Cindy refused to explain the situation until the three were all standing in the office with the door closed. When Randy was told what happened, he immediately agreed to grow the plants that Cindy needed, remembering what Linda had said about being the reason that the inmates were being kept alive. The least he could do, he said, was return the favor.

"Can you hold her arm down, dear?" Cindy asked Randy as soon as she made the poultice.

The room smelled of sweet flowers and blood, and Linda tensed up at the realization that they were going to dress her wound. Cindy could see a cloud of memory behind her eyes that made her heart ache for her daughter. She didn't have time to ask what memories Linda was plagued with, though, because as soon as she placed the herbs in Linda's hand and began wrapping the bandages around it, Linda stifled an agonized to scream and clutched her arm, her legs buckling beneath her. Randy cried out a little and caught her just before she fell. He set her down and she immediately curled up on the floor in pain.

Randy looked *terrified* at the concept that his warden, the woman who had undoubtedly displayed herself as the pinnacle of strength and emotionlessness, could be brought to such a state. Cindy made a mental note to erase the memories of everyone in the prison so that no one would remember the past day – Linda didn't need people thinking she was weak, or cruel. If she was going to manage to keep everyone in line and alive long enough for their allies on the outside to save them, she would need to keep up her strong appearance.

As the herbs worked, Cindy sat back on her heels on the floor and stroked Linda's hair gently, wishing that there was more she could do to end her daughter's pain. After a few minutes, Linda seemed to shift into unconsciousness as what little strength she had left ebbed so that her body could heal itself.

~~~~~~~~~~~~~~~~~~~~~~~~~~~

When Linda was next coherent, it was nearly midnight. Cindy was on the prison's landline phone and Jefferson was sitting under the desk in the guard office, doodling on a piece of paper with one of the crayons from the common room. He looked up at her as she
~~~~~~~~~~~~~~~~~~~~~~~~~~~

shifted and put his finger to his lips, pointing at Cindy so that she would know not to talk. Linda began to listen in on the conversation and she realized that Cindy must be talking to Roger.

"I know dear, it's absolutely hideous. The snow up here is in drifts almost four feet high in some places. I tried to leave earlier as soon as I picked up your paperwork, but the car wouldn't even start because it was too cold."

Linda hoped, for Cindy's sake, that Roger would believe her. While it *was* snowy out, it hadn't been cold enough to stop a car from working. At least, it hadn't been before she passed out...

She noticed that Cindy was clutching a glowing pen, and when she threw a quizzical glance at Jefferson, he mouthed "L U C K C H A R M" at her in explanation. She nodded slightly and suppressed a cough. While Cindy finished up her phone call and managed to convince Roger to stay at home and let her stay the night at the Ark for her own safety, Linda looked down at her arms and hands. The veins in her arms were normal again, and her hand was fully healed, no longer bandaged. She looked up when Cindy hung up the phone and walked over to help her up off of the floor.

"He thinks I'm staying in the guard room, and that you healed yourself before I got here. He genuinely didn't think he did that much damage to you- kept talking about how, once you "caught your breath," you wouldn't make another mistake or something like that. I think he thought his poison would brainwash you or something. It was awful having to act like I thought he did the right thing."

She pulled Linda into a tight hug, and Linda had to suppress the urge to melt into her and return the embrace. She had to preserve what little dignity she had left- especially in front of her least favorite inmate. Eventually, Cindy let go and Linda just stood awkwardly next to her, hoping her mother could sense how grateful she was for the comfort.

Cindy herself seemed angry when she pulled away, and the longer the trio stood in the silence of the front office, the angrier she seemed to get. She glared down at Linda's hand, a dark cloud seeming to form behind her eyes that Linda had never seen before. She quietly ordered Jefferson to leave, mustering the strength to close the door behind him when he complied.

Cindy watched him leave, then closed her eyes and muttered something for a moment, and then Linda saw a shimmering nimbus leave the vicinity of her body and travel towards the nearest air vent, off to spread through the prison.

"I made it so that everyone will forget the events of today and tonight," she said in answer to her daughter's unspoken question. "Randy will be no different- by the time he gets back to his cell, he'll have forgotten why he was ever outside of it. Your study is locked up already. Linda, I- words cannot express how furious I am right now."

Linda's stomach dropped, immediately assuming the worst. She'd pissed off enough superior officers and bosses and kings to fear retaliation.

Fuck, does she blame me for this? Does she think I was stupid enough to attack Roger, or that I made a mistake by letting Quin almost escape? Shit, is she really mad at me?

She opened her mouth to apologize and realized that Cindy was actually crying. Tears were streaming down her cheeks, and when she wrapped her arms around Linda this time, the elf didn't flinch away. She returned the hug gently, if awkwardly, and waited for Cindy to explain herself.

"HE COULD HAVE KILLED YOU, AEMENORA! When I got here, you were barely breathing. That sick son of a bitch will pay for hurting you. I swear it on my father the moon and his brother, the sun, and all the armies of stars in the sky."

Cindy was shaking with anger, but after her outburst she seemed to calm down a little. Linda tried to think of a way to lighten the mood, because she didn't have the energy to babysit an upset demigoddess- especially the one who'd sung her into existence.

"Hey, uh, speaking of your dad," she started, snapping Cindy out of her furious mood and drawing a snort of amusement out of her, "I didn't forget your birthday. I know we always used to make offerings to the Moon King together, back before- well, it doesn't matter." She took a breath for a moment, reaching out to lace her fingers with Cindy's and look down at their intertwined hands. "I just thought you should know, I never stopped. They got less fancy once I was stuck on my own, but I'd always pour him a glass of beer or rum or whatever on the winter solstice. I was gonna ask you to come up here this year, since you were actually *alive* and all, but I didn't know if Roger would.... Anyway," she rambled awkwardly, her words halting every once in a while. "I'm glad I got to see you, even if it was for a shitty reason. Happy belated birthday, Caeda."

This time, Linda was the one who initiated the hug. She wrapped her arms around her mother's neck and rocked back and forth for a minute, at first silently berating herself for not getting her any real gifts. By the way Caeda held her, however, she soon realized that perhaps this time together was enough of a gift for her.

Linda would've happily spent the rest of the night talking with her mother and plotting against Roger, but both of them were exhausted. So, she let "Cindy" take her place on the armchair in her study (after they covered the dried bloodstains with an old quilt) while she slept (for the first time) in the guard room on one of the empty bunks. By the time she woke up the next morning, Cindy had already left, and Linda found a note from her on her study desk.

Sorry to leave in such a hurry, darling, but I have to get back to the monster. He'll be in a good mood for awhile- he always is after he gets to beat someone up. It's sickening, really, but it's better than him being furious at me and still wanting to kill you.

Thank you for the birthday wish, by the way. It warms my heart to know that you never forgot me. If you want to give me a gift- do me a kindness and give our friend Randy extra free time or something, courtesy of me. If it weren't for him, you would be dead.

Anyway, I just wanted to leave you with something to remind you that I love you. Please stay safe, Aemenora. The stars will shine for you always.

Love,

Your mother, Caeda

CHAPTER 15: SHOWSTOPPER

Randy couldn't quite remember why he'd been let out of his cell, but he wasn't particularly upset about the opportunity to cement his plans for the talent show. He was halfway down the front hallway, standing in front of the only cell next to the infirmary, when he decided that now was as good a time as any to make sure that the siren he'd been talking to for most of...yesterday, since it was after midnight, was still willing to perform with him during the talent show. She'd been brought to the Ark with her sister because they were both members of the Marmara, so Randy wasn't entirely sure that she would agree to work with him. So far, most of the Marmarans he'd talked to seemed to have accepted their fate and resigned themselves to be prisoners in the magical baby jail they all would call home for the rest of their lives.

He kept looking behind himself as he carefully made his way back across the building, past the front office where Linda and some woman he'd never seen before were talking and...crying? He didn't really have time to eavesdrop as much as he would've liked.

When he got to the far east hall of the prison, he walked up to the siren siblings' cell and knocked twice, hard enough to be heard by the women inside but not loud enough to wake anyone else up. There was a pleasant lack of guards walking around, which made what he was doing easier, but he still didn't want to cause a ruckus.

He wasn't quite sure why anymore, because he couldn't recall anything from earlier that day, but he felt very deeply unsettled and something deep inside told him that it would be very dangerous to upset Linda- that she had power over everyone in the prison unlike anything anyone would imagine. He just...couldn't remember what it was.

Randy was snapped back to the present by the sound of someone shifting behind the heavy metal door of the cell.

"Theresa? Can I talk to you?" he called softly. Someone shifted on the other side of the heavy metallic door, clearly trying to fumble across the room in the dark with only the sliver of light of the door to guide her.

"What do you want, Randy? What time is it, anyway?" an ethereal voice called back. Before he could respond, she continued,

"Hey, wait. How the hell did you get over here? Your cell's on the "frequently checked" side of this place, plus you'd have to get past *both* guard rooms *and* the front guard office where Linda stays all night...seriously, *what are you doing here?*"

Randy took a moment to think.

*How **did** I get here?*

He tried to remember *anything* from earlier that day, but drew a complete blank. He could hazily remember going to bed last night, and then talking to...someone. About something upsetting. Then...nothing.

There were several beats of silence as he wracked his brain, but ultimately, all he came up with was a halfhearted, "I...don't actually know. I don't remember today. I just kinda...got here."

Theresa stayed silent, as if expecting the answer to a second question. After a moment, Randy remembered the other thing she'd asked him.

"Oh, yeah. I'm here because I don't remember- did you tell me that you would perform with me? You mentioned yesterday that you'd think about it and get back to me today- do you remember what you told me? And when?"

Theresa didn't say anything for awhile, and Randy almost wondered if he should ask again, when she quietly muttered,

"I don't remember today, either. I...I'll sing with you. But I'll warn you, I can't sustain my powers for very long here. I can't even hum without feeling the drain on my energy. At most, I can sing for, like, five minutes. If that. Your violin can take up most of the song; as long as it begins and ends with my voice, the trance spell will work. What exactly are you trying to do, anyway, break out? The barriers will be too strong, even if you manage to get Linda's keys or whatever. Besides, it's so cold out, and the snow's so high- no one could make it back to town in that. You'll freeze to death."

Randy hadn't told her what he was going to do? No, he hadn't, that was right. He shook his head, forgetting that she probably couldn't see him.

"No. I...It isn't like that. I'm trying to learn more about Linda, to see if there's any way out she knows about, or any paperwork I can forge to get us all released or something." He hoped Theresa wouldn't think he sounded cagey enough to question.

I want to know who she's working for.

Theresa seemed to accept that answer, and Randy heard her muffle a yawn. God, what time was it? He had no way of knowing, as Linda hadn't hung any clocks in the hallways, and he hadn't been allowed to bring his pocket watch with him to the Ark.

As he bid Theresa goodnight and began to make his way back to his cell (past the office with Linda and the lady he didn't recognize), he found himself wishing he could hear the reassuring tick of his watch. It had been a gift from Marlene on his last birthday, a beautiful silver and glass masterpiece that he could watch whenever he needed to take his mind off of something or he needed to concentrate on something important. She'd etched tiny flowers into the silver of the face, and even the hands were shaped like leaves. She'd tried to make the gears into flower shapes, but had only half succeeded. He stored energy in it like it was a rechargeable battery, and he couldn't help but think that if he had it with him it would help him find a way out.

Thinking about the watch, about Marlene...He had to find out who was behind this. Who had...he couldn't let himself believe they'd really killed her.

When he got back to his cell, he found that the door was already unlocked (saving him the energetic drain of opening it with magic) and Mitchell was sound asleep. He got inside and laid down, suddenly realizing how utterly exhausted he was. It was as though he'd used a lot of magic- enough to grow a patch of magical wildflowers.

That night, he dreamed of his shop, and of Abigail, and lilting strains of violin music wound their way through his mind as he slept. In the morning, he committed the song to memory and decided that *that* was what he would perform during the talent show.

~~~~~~~~~~~~~~~~~~~~~~~~

Randy took a breath in, then stepped up onto the stage set up in the dining hall, crossing the cold wooden planks that no one really knew the origins of, and came to a halt in front of the chair and half-broken microphone stand that someone had been kind enough to set up for him. Linda had placed a rented violin on the chair, and he picked it up and examined it to make sure it was tuned properly.

He felt Theresa's weight add itself to the stage, and in the dim light beyond the poorly engineered stage "spotlights", he could make out the bored faces of the hundred or so inmates that were being forced to watch the talent show.

He fought the rising dread in his chest at the reality of everyone *actually* watching him play when it was the first time he'd done so in several months, nodded once to Theresa, and put the bow to the strings.

Theresa's voice rang out before he played the first note, a high and clear beginning that sent a slight chill down his spine. She wasn't singing *words,* per se, but there was a clear *emotion* in the sounds that came out of her throat. She was singing of freedom, and of lost souls. If he hadn't been protected from her spell with a quick hearing ward before they got on stage, Randy was sure he would've fallen in her thrall.

He played slowly at first, a sad, haunting melody, but gradually he sped up in tempo, playing quickly in an upbeat frenzy. His eyes darted out into the audience, trying to gauge the reactions of his
~~~~~~~~~~~~~~~~~~~~~~~~

listeners, and he smiled as he saw the glazed-over look of wonder in their eyes. No one seemed to notice when Theresa ended on a high note by looking over at him and didn't pick the vocals back up again.

Someone near the back started to tap a primitive drumbeat onto their legs, and several people joined in. Looking out the window, Randy was pleased to see plants stirring outside and ivy beginning to crawl in long tendrils under the window, sliding it up as the plants began to invade the room and sway to the music.

To the phyllokinetic's utter delight, everyone else was ignoring the dancing plants in favor of the bewitching melody of the bow sliding over the instrument's strings that swirled from his fingertips as he played on.

Randy's smile grew even wider as he saw that now, every guard was tapping their feet to the rhythm of the song. The entire audience, even those keeping time with his violin, seemed to be in a dreamy haze. No one seemed fully awake and even as the tempo increased, it was as if the song was the most soothing lullaby in the world. Randy watched as the eyes of everyone in the room slowly closed. The percussion slowly became quieter as people started falling asleep in their chairs.

Randy kept playing, even as several people started snoring, and Linda slumped forward in her chair in the front row. He kept playing as someone yawned loudly, and as the guards that stood at the doors slumped down the walls. Even when he knew everyone was asleep, Randy kept playing until the vines had crept into the room, covering the floor in damp, green leaves and yellow and white honey scented flowers. He kept playing, even as the vines took over the percussion and restarted the drumbeat. He kept playing until they snaked across the floor to his feet, wrapping around themselves and building themselves up into a body that mimicked his own.

When the vine-person's hands reached toward him, begging for the violin, Randy didn't want to hand it over at first. He loved the feel of sliding a bow across a set of strings. However, he knew that he had to hand it over, so he could do what he needed to do. He let the vines wrap around the bow and strings carefully, and when the drums had momentarily drowned out the violin, he handed his instrument over. He waited a moment, listening to the vine-covered violin play itself.

When he was certain that no one had woken up or been disturbed by the change of violinists, Randy stepped carefully backwards, navigating over roots. Theresa stared at him, mouth agape, and he pressed his fingers to his lips and made a chair for her out of roots before turning around to leave. His feet were sinking into a deep moss blanket that had covered the ground. He snuck towards the door, painfully aware of his own movements. When he was nearly at the door, Randy heard stirring that made his heart seem to stop, and his head whipped around to look at the source of the noise.

Mitchell was shifting quietly in his sleep. The music didn't stop, and Randy let out a sigh of relief when he saw his roommate shift to a better sleeping position without opening his eyes. Randy sighed with relief and returned to picking his way over moss and roots until he finally made it out of the room.

~~~~~

He traveled quickly down the hall in the direction that Mitchell had said to go. Randy was looking for a door, one that was nondescript. Commonplace. A door which had set off every alarm and call for caution within Randy's roommate. He searched for what seemed like hours before finally finding it.

The last door in this hallway, in the recess outside of the common room. Labeled "valve room".

Randy remembered Mitchell's words as he muttered protective spells on his hands. He tried just turning the knob, and when that didn't work, he resorted to wasting a little bit of energy to pick the lock with magic. It swung open in a few seconds, spilling light into the dim corridor. What he found inside was completely unexpected.
~~~~~

Randy had thought it might have been a torture chamber, or a meth lab, or some other scary room that he could totally believe Linda would have. On the contrary, what he found was a cozy study. Its walls were lined with bookshelves and half-hidden cabinets.The wall right across from the door, however, was what truly caught Randy's attention. It was a wall of screens, each showing a different camera feed. A desk sat in front of the screens, covered in papers and books and old snack wrappers.

The quality of the video was much, *much* better than the quality of the "official" security cameras in the guard room, and they seemed to be focused very precisely on things that weren't the inmates. One camera showed a view of Lake Tamory, the body of water between Two Peak and Mt. Wapetona. Another showed a live feed of the Devil's Bed Plateau. It was zoomed in on the mouth of the road that led up the mountain, and Randy couldn't help but wonder who Linda was watching out for.

Below the camera screens was an old desk, made of dark mahogany wood. It had several drawers, a few of which were open. One drawer seemed to have dirty laundry in it, while the corner of a blanket poked out of another. On top of the desk, several files and piles of paper were strewn across its surface. Randy quickly made his way over (aware of how little time he had and how much energy his spells were consuming) and picked up one of the loose papers.

He found a note on the desk from someone named "Cindy", and in it he found very interesting information. All the missing memories flooded him from the last 24 hours, and he realized that Linda was doing much more for them than anyone knew. A second note, this one "From the desk of Roger Callsworth," confirmed this. Details of the ways she was to break their minds and torture everyone, should they seem to be refusing "conversion to the council" were laid out in the note, but elven runes scribbled in the margins said things like "fuck off you dickhead" and "that's so asinine why the fuck" reassured him that she wasn't planning on following orders anytime soon.

Randy tore his gaze away from the papers and placed them back exactly where he'd found them. There was a horrifyingly unkempt pile of books beside the desk, and one of them near his foot caught his eye. It seemed to be one she'd read a few times, as its spine was worn, but he could tell by the thick layer of dust on top of it that she hadn't picked it up in a while. He gently took it and read the cover, surprised to see that it was some kind of "guide to defeating umbrakinetics". The fact that she needed to know that information *deeply* worried him, and he thought back to what she'd said before about her bosses -the council, he now realized- and how badly they wanted him and everyone like him dead. Was this "Roger" that Linda's friend Cindy had mentioned her boss? He decided to take the book with him, as well as another few defense-related magic books from near the bottom of the pile, and hide them in his room.

He turned around, allowing his attention to fall on a large wooden chest which sat next to a brown armchair which bore the marks of years of love and use. Going to it, he was quite surprised to find no complicated combination lock or steel deadbolt keeping it shut. Instead, the chest had a simple lock mechanism set into the beautifully carved wood. More runes ordained this box, and Randy could make out the words "keep my...safe", as well as what he guessed to be a personal sigil engraved above the lock mechanism.

Fingers nimble, Randy picked the lock to the chest and carefully opened the lid, standing behind it so as not to fall victim to a booby trap or other attack. When he was convinced that he wouldn't be killed by anything in the chest, Randy stepped back in front of it and looked inside.

The chest was full of various weapons, ranging in age from the 17th century to the twentieth. The chest was not well-organized at all, with guns and weapons and even a small crossbow stacked on top of each other haphazardly. The only things that were well-organized were the knives, which were held securely to the lid of the chest. Several hunting knives and what looked like a dagger or two were strapped there, but what caught Randy's eye the most was the gorgeous set of shiny, steel throwing knives. Though 8 inches in length, the weapons had no handle except for a set of runes set into the lower half of each knife. They seemed the perfect weapons for someone like Linda.

Wordlessly, Randy ran a finger across the flat of the blade of one of the hunting knives.

She won't miss it, and even if she does, there's no way she'd know who took it.

He slipped the knife out of its casing, sorely tempted to take it with him. It could be useful to have a weapon, but Linda would *definitely* find out, and he'd really rather not find out if her guns still worked.

He quickly replaced it and resealed the chest, stepping away and deciding to try one of the bottom wall cabinets. When he got to it, however, he was disappointed to find that every cabinet door within the room's wall seemed to be sealed with a barrier that he couldn't pierce with his power. He decided to leave them be.

I wonder what Linda's hiding in there? Randy thought to himself, attempting to stand up. As he did, he felt a wave of dizziness wash over him and he felt lightheaded. Alarmed, Randy realized that he'd been in Linda's office for nearly ten minutes, and the energy his spells were taking from him was becoming dangerously too much to bear. He made his way as quickly as possible from the study, making sure to leave everything (except what he stole) as he found it and locking the door securely behind him. He stopped by his room on his way back to the stage, painfully aware of how labored each of his heartbeats had become, and buried the contraband books beneath his mattress, under his dresser, and inside one of the tiles of the ceiling.

Suddenly he felt a horrible pang in his chest that signaled that the magic was dangerously overworking him, but as he turned to rush back to the stage, and an idea struck him. He tore down the poster Mitchell had hung by their door about the talent show, then ran to the secret room. He borrowed a green permanent marker he found on the floor and scribbled the symbols of the Twalnaverra and Marmara, along with a message, on the back of the poster. He searched for a good place to leave the note, then noticed the edge of a dartboard poking out from behind some coats on the back of the door. Dimly, he reasoned that the dartboard might be a nice ominous place, so he decided to hang it on there, making sure to leave the coat slightly askew so she might find the note. Then he rushed out of the study and back to the dining hall.

When he finally got back to the stage, Theresa gave him a very concerned look. He felt weak, and he was shaking hard enough that he felt like he might fall over, but said nothing to her. He told the vegetation in the room to go back outside, and watched as it slowly did. During a lull in the violin's part, he took his opportunity and took the instrument from the vines that had been playing it, which lost their shape and crept back outside. He played again, slowing the song down from its fevered tempo and beginning to end the song while Theresa picked up the vocals again. People began to stir as the sound of the violin became slower and louder, and the siren sang them back out of their stupor.

When the last traces of vegetation were out of the room, Randy began to bring the song to a close. He ended the violin part on a dark vibrato, then stood onstage, quietly panting as his audience came back to themselves. Theresa's voice echoed throughout the room on the last beat of the song, and everyone fully shook off the last of the effects of the magic.

Randy looked back out into the crowd as the last note faded and Theresa closed her mouth. One by one, people began to applaud the song, and Randy set the violin back in its case, shaky hands fumbling with the strap made to hold down the bow. He took a deep breath and stepped sideways to take Theresa's hand for their final bow, acutely aware of the darkening edges of his vision. He could see, even in the dim "stage lights" that she was pale and drenched in sweat. He bent forward at the waist mechanically and his vision went nearly black. He struggled for breath, straightening back up and stumbling down the side of the stage. He went to the back of the seating area, trying to avoid the worried expressions of his friends as he sat down. He looked back towards the stage, where Teresa's twin, Helen, was walking her off to the side.

He fought to stay conscious and coherent through the last two performances of the night- a one-act play and a juggling demonstration. His eyelids felt like they were made of lead, and every breath felt like he was filling his lungs with water instead of air. He could feel his forehead burning but his whole body felt strangely cold.

By the time the last act was done, everything sounded tinny and hollow, and he stayed seated when everyone else began to file back to their cells.

He felt a hand on his back and he lifted his head a little. Quin was standing in front of him, and she looked concerned. He tiredly furrowed his brows, and Quin said something he was too exhausted to catch. She said it again, but all he heard was a metallic echo. She brought her hand up to her nose and then down to touch him, brushing across his upper lip with her middle and ring fingers. She drew them away to show him that they were covered in blood.

He didn't really feel his lips move, but he heard an airy whisper come out of the back of his throat.

"Aw, hell."

He coughed suddenly, hard, and Quin had to catch him as he listed forward. He caught his breath after a few seconds, but his throat felt as though it was on fire. His nose was still bleeding as if someone had broken it, and he knew that if he tried to stand, he would faint. All he could do was look at Quin with watery eyes and listen to the chiming of the lights out warning bell ringing through the halls.

At some point, he closed his eyes and didn't hear Quin walk away. He felt a warm hand wrapped around his wrist and he opened his eyes to see Linda looking at him with a rare measure of concern. She seemed to recognize his symptoms for what they were–

magical exhaustion. He desperately hoped she wouldn't put two and two together.

She was speaking loudly at him, her voice muffled like he was hearing it through several bolts of fabric. A low whine escaped his throat at all the noise, and it was apparently shocking enough for Linda to draw her lips into a serious (and thankfully silent) line. She placed her inner wrist against his forehead, as if to confirm a suspicion, and then brought something in her other hand up to his face. He struggled against her for a second as she held a strange-smelling cloth over his mouth and nose, but ultimately, he gave in and went limp in his seat.

He woke up over a week later in the infirmary, no longer drained of energy and, *very* surprisingly, not in trouble for breaking into Linda's study. The memories he'd regained when he'd stepped inside ran through his head, and he realized that she'd probably assumed he'd used too much of his energy *helping her* the night before the performance, and then she'd figured he'd used some magical auto tune or something that completely sent him over the edge. She'd probably let his comatose state be punishment enough for breaking her rule.

His voice scratchy and weak from disuse, he called to the definitely-stoned guard who was dozing in the doorway, and after awhile a vaguely terrifying man in a doctors' coat (who Linda had probably kidnapped to keep at the Ark) came in at the guard's request and ran a few tests on him. By the end of the testing, Randy had found out that 1) it was past dinnertime, and 2) that it was now January 14th. He was a little sad that he'd missed New Years' with Abigail, but more sad that he wasn't going to get to eat dinner.

Finally, the doctor turned away and told him that he was free to go, as long as he could walk, and that he should be fine to return to his normal activities as long as he was careful to rest when he felt drained. Randy looked away briefly when the IV was removed from his hand, then got up and shakily made his way out of the infirmary and down the hall to his cell.

On his way to his cell, he heard someone being yelled at by Linda, and the sounds of a scuffle down one of the halls. Part of him was worried about Quin, because her cell was in the direction of the shouting, but in truth, he didn't really care that much. He just wanted to go ask Mitchell to tell him what he'd missed.

"Hey Randy! Welcome back to the land of the living! How was your, uh, 8-day nap?" Randy snorted at Mitchell's question.

"Honestly, it was very boring. I didn't dream or anything, which is both relieving and a little disappointing. I was hoping I'd get to have one of *those* dreams, if you catch my drift. What'd I miss while I was out?" He sat down against the head of his bed, fishing one of the stolen books out from behind him.

"Oh, nothing much. Linda's been super busy (like, I heard the guards say she's been found passed out in the front office every night all month, but it's even worse now) because we started getting a bunch of new people the day after you passed out. Two of them arrived today, actually! One's a really cool ghost cowboy, and I heard Linda had to make his cell into some weird enchanted chamber so he couldn't float through it."

Mitchell seemed content to let the story stagnate as he settled down into bed for the night, then he peered over at the book that Randy had just cracked open. He looked like he was thinking for a moment, and then said,

"Oh, hey! You never said- what'd you see when you went in the weird magic room? Obviously you found some books you wanted to borrow."

Randy sighed and took his glasses off, setting them inside the book as he paused to rub his eyes. Even though he'd slept for so long, he was still quite tired. Mitchell seemed to understand that this meant, "I'll tell you tomorrow," because he mumbled, "never mind. You can tell me later" into his pillow and turned over in bed.

Randy settled down as well, closing his eyes and trying to fall asleep. He was just starting to drift off when a thought occurred to him that sent ice running through his veins. He pushed his mind out through the dark halls, carefully avoiding actually contacting any of his fellow inmates as he searched the new minds for the familiar feeling of the one person he hoped to *never* see again, if he was to live out his days in the Ark of Light.

Just as he began to give up, he found her, and she found him. His mind, filled with horror, immediately mingled with hers, which was flooded with relief and something that another person would have taken as love. Their connection was tenuous, as she could sense him fading with panic and tiredness, and she bid him a hasty goodnight as his mind came fully back to him alone. Silent tears sprung to his eyes and trickled down his cheeks when he realized what this meant.

Abigail was in the Ark. The council had captured her and a bunch of her Twalnaverran friends, too. More than half of the resisting force was now captured.

The Council of Blight was winning.

CHAPTER 16: WHO ARE YOU?

Gods, I want a drink.

Linda rubbed her temples and leafed through the last of the gigantic piles of paperwork on her desk. Ever since her...*meeting* with Roger, new inmates were arriving daily. First, Jefferson had used some kind of spell at the talent show (probably a little auto tune) and nearly killed himself from the strain of using magic when he was already exhausted after helping her the night before. It couldn't have been something too intensive, could it? She didn't think he would've had much energy left for mischief making. Besides, she'd gone over the Ark with a fine-toothed comb for days, but she hadn't found anything out of place, and she could always interrogate him later if he started acting suspicious.

Not to mention, just when she'd finished making sure he wasn't gonna kick the bucket and new inmates started pouring in, she'd had to send her dogs down the mountain to stay at a kennel indefinitely, out of fear that the next time Roger came up the mountain, he would find and hurt them. 42 new inmates in just over a week was...overwhelming. She had barely left the front office since the talent show, and she'd been craving her favorite vice for days now. She signed her name and dated the last entrance acceptance report, then sat back to take stock of what was left for her to do.

"Oh damn, I think that was actually the last form," she muttered under her breath, then quickly knocked three times on the faux-wood of the desk. She'd be damned if she jinxed herself now.

She hastened to shove the newly-signed form into a folder and put it back with its proper stack, then she stood for the first time in probably two days. Her knees almost buckled at the now-foreign movement, but she forced them to hold her as she stepped back from the desk and turned to go out the office door. She'd have one of the guards (probably Ivan, since he was the only one who didn't regularly smoke questionable substances in the bathroom, and he was therefore probably coherent) put the paperwork away in her filing cabinets or something later. It wasn't her problem anymore- she'd done her job by signing them.

She checked her watch and snorted a little in amusement- it was five o'clock. She didn't recall ever actually going to a bar for "happy hour", but it felt supremely appropriate to be getting her first drink in weeks *now.*

She had to walk past the infirmary to get to her hidden study, so she decided to look in and make sure Jefferson was still alive. He was, in fact, awake. *Finally.* Normally the thought of having to deal with him again would have annoyed her, but she was honestly in too good a mood to let it bother her. This year, the stupid paperwork had forced her to miss out on the New Year's Eve tradition she'd started when she began living on her own. That was probably fitting, since it was born out of her desire to get shitfaced and forget that her mother was dead, so now that she knew that Caeda was alive, it would be symbolic to end the tradition. Still, it didn't stop her from wanting to get drunk on elven wine and ring in the new year by setting off enchanted roman candles.

She could practically taste the bittersweet mix of vanilla and cherry that would linger for hours after she'd gotten to drink the charmed bourbon mix she kept in her cabinet for special occasions.

All of the inmates were in the dining hall for dinner, so she didn't have to worry about anyone seeing her go into her study. As soon as she got there, she made a beeline for the hidden drawer in the bottom of her desk that served as her liquor cabinet. She sifted through several half-full bottles of wine and whiskey before finding the object of her affections- an ornately decorated bottle of bourbon. The glass of the bottle was a deep red, and there were runes painted on in gold filigree to say the name and year of its distillation. Those were half-faded now, but the embossed enchantment sigils were still clearly legible, and that was the important part. Without the enchantments, the bourbon would be *considerably* less fun to drink.

She grabbed a dusty glass from the bookshelf beside her desk, blew into it and wiped it with her sleeve, then uncorked the bottle with a smile. She held it up to her nose for a few seconds, taking in the scent of the vintage. She closed her eyes and listened to the clink of the bottle hitting the glass, the sloshing of the alcohol going into it, and then the soft thump as she set the bottle down flat on the table again. She opened her eyes to look at the dark liquor, swirling it around in the bottom of the glass gently. There were traces of something shimmery in it, which she found annoying when she first acquired it, but now she'd come to find the faint shine pretty, in a strange way. She wasn't sure if the sparkle was from some unknown ingredient, or if it was just a byproduct of the magic infused in the bourbon, but she didn't really care either way, since the bottle was centuries old at this point so there was no real way of finding out.

The alcohol was smooth and warm (from being locked in a room-temperature drawer for gods knew how long) as it ran over her tongue, and she let the nostalgia of wintertime drinking memories fill her mind. She drained her glass and poured herself another, then carefully put the cork back in the bottle. She finished her second drink before long as well, then decided to pour one last one, for old time's sake. It had been a very long time since she'd gotten to have any of this particular vintage. Satisfied with herself, she picked up her glass, her vision already heavily hazing over at the edges. Human alcohol was very rarely strong enough to get an elf drunk on its own, so it was customary for elves to enchant it if they wanted to have any fun. This bottle was... particularly well-enchanted.

She made her way over to her armchair and curled up into it, careful not to spill any of her drink on herself. She intended to sleep off her stupor in her study so as not to let anyone know that she'd been drinking, so it would be very counterintuitive to make herself smell like alcohol.

She continued to sip her drink, mostly keeping her eyes closed as she did. Her neck and shoulders were so tense from her most recent front office nap that she couldn't really turn her head very well, but the alcohol would likely take that edge off soon. So, she fumbled beside the chair for the blanket that she usually left on the floor there so she would have something to curl up under when she inevitably fell asleep.

She felt the softness of the blanket lying on the floor by her weapons chest, and she reached further down to grab it. In doing so, she felt her wrist brush up against the lock of the chest. She thought nothing of it, her mind clouded over with drink and the desire to sleep in a position that wasn't *awful,* and she pulled the knitted blanket up towards herself.

When the blanket came up off of the floor, she felt it catch on something and heard the angry *thunk* of the lid of her weapons chest crashing open. Startled, she let go of the blanket and drained the last tail end of her drink, setting the glass on the floor on the other side of the chair as she sat up. She leaned over the side of the chair and peered down at the offending chest suspiciously.

*Who the hell unlocked my weapons chest? I know **I** didn't do it, and Caeda wouldn't have done it, and my door's been locked since she left after healing me... Hasn't it?*

She was both worried and unable to fully care, drunk as she was. Whatever had happened to her study was *probably* not life threatening, so she could *most likely* survive sleeping off her drunkenness before investigating it further. She looked around the room in an attempt to catch anything else out of place, but her efforts weren't really fruitful, considering the fact that she was almost totally unable to see straight. Satisfied with her attempts at investigation, she leaned back in her chair again and let her eyes drift back closed. A warm, pleasant weight seemed to settle in her chest and stomach, and she fell asleep after a few seconds.

She woke back up sometime late the next morning with a headache and a vague sense of impending doom that told her that, for once, she'd had a dream the night before. She didn't really remember any of it, but the longer she sat in her chair, the more she got the feeling that it wasn't a natural kind of dream. There was a distinct aura of magic around where she was sitting that couldn't have come from her drink the night before.

Quickly, she stood up and crossed the room to the door, inspecting the knob carefully.

Someone used magic on the lock. It looks vaguely singed, like whoever it was did it in a hurry.

She let out a colorful stream of curses in German and elvish, then moved back over to the chest. She could see that it had clearly been tampered with, though she had to admit that the culprit had done an admirable job of trying to make it look like it hadn't been touched. The guns had all clearly been shuffled around (and it had been left unlocked) and someone had even had the audacity to *take one of her knives out* and *play with it.* Fury boiled up in the pit of her stomach, and she quickly slammed the lid shut. She spun on her heel, making a beeline for her desk. The papers there had been moved too, and a couple of the books from the well-cataloged mess on the floor beside it had been stolen.

Furious, she rummaged around in her desk, praying that the crystal that Caeda had given her was still there. Thankfully it was, and she picked it up and spun it in her palm. She vaguely remembered the spell Caeda had taught her (that she'd used when she first came to the Ark in order to make the pocket dimension her study sat in) which would allow her to move her study to a more secure location. She paused in the middle to look at the map of the Ark that was hanging behind her security camera monitor, then pointed at an empty room in the basement of the building. She felt the crystal go blindingly hot in her hand, then the whole room shuddered. The floor rolled like the deck of a ship in a storm, and several books fell out of place on their shelves. The bottle of bourbon from the night before tipped dangerously over the edge of the table, but Linda managed to lunge forward and catch it with her free hand before it could hit the ground or break.

The crystal started to float (saving her palm from being burned anymore by it) and glow a bright, pale pink. A loud hum vibrated through the room, and then everything stopped. Linda put away the crystal and the bourbon and straightened the things that had fallen when the localized earthquake hit.

Who the fuck broke into my study?

She looked at the door, loathe to leave now that she knew someone had gotten into her things but aware of all the things that could be going wrong while she wasn't upstairs to supervise. She noticed, upon second glance, that there was something off about the way her coats were hanging in front of her dartboard. It was as if someone had moved them to put something on it.

She walked briskly over to the door and pulled down the four coats hanging on it, revealing her dartboard. On top of the expected pieces of parchment with scribbled names and the crudely-drawn photo of Roger with a stick up his ass that she expected to see there, there was a white sheet of paper with two sigils written on it in green ink. One looked like a strange compass with a fancy cursive letter in the center of it, and the other looked like a cartoonish cloud with lines in the middle. Written in a ring around the symbols, a line of text in looping cursive read:

"We know you are not loyal to the council you work for. We are not your enemy. We can set you free."

She threw the note on the floor, seething, and made her way up to the main floor of the prison. Linda spent the next few hours carefully watching all of the guards, thinking that one of them might be disloyal to her. When it quickly became obvious that none of them had done it, she began to suspect the inmates. She stood in the front office, pretending to listen to the guards give a report on the new inmates as she did mental back flips trying to figure out who could've broken into her study, and how.

None of the newbies could've done it- judging by the new layer of dust on the things that had been moved, the break-in would've had to have happened before a lot of them arrived. She highly doubted many of the other inmates were magically talented or energetically strong enough to break past her protective barriers without exhausting themselves.

Wait. Energetic exhaustion.

Hazy, sick memories came flooding back to her. Laying in her armchair, delirious with pain. Blood all over the place, then Caeda's cool hand on her forehead. **Caeda helping her into the main office**. Randy being there...growing plants to heal her with. Caeda holding her up, using her magic to help them both. Passing out, then waking up with him sitting next to her on the floor of the office.

Jefferson was in the front office when he used his magic that night. Caeda was giving him the energy he needed to grow her healing herbs. He didn't exhaust himself doing that, and I checked the violin after the concert. He didn't tune it with magic, either. **That son of a bitch used the talent show as a break-in opportunity.**

Startled sounds erupted from the assembled guards and whichever one had been speaking jumped back in alarm as she suddenly threw her coffee cup across the room. It shattered like a porcelain bomb, and left a giant mess of gritty instant coffee, cold water, and disgustingly sweet creamer trailing down the wall above a pile of broken shards on the floor.

"I know who broke into my study."

None of the guards knew that her study had been broken into at all, so hearing her say she'd figured out who did it was quite a shock. Immediately, a round of murmurs started up, and she didn't bother to shut them down.

She stormed out of the front office and down the main hallway to the common room, betting that Jefferson would be in there with his little accomplice friends. She was right, finding him sitting with Von Fer, O'Connell and one of the new inmates.

Stern. The one who worked with him, who tried to intimidate me over the phone.

None of them seemed to notice her, and as she got closer, she could see that Jefferson was speaking animatedly and holding a book in his hands.

That's one of the ones that were taken from my fucking study. This little bitch is telling his friends about how he stole from me.

Every instinct told her that she should punish all of them—whether with death or something worse she couldn't decide. Still, something kept her hand from reaching for the knife on her hip.

Jefferson left that note on my dartboard. However he charmed everyone at the talent show, if he did it for long enough to break into the study, he would've also had ample time to kill me too, if he wanted to. Either he's playing mind games, or he actually wants to help.

What if he's one of the people with the bounty out on Roger's head? What were those symbols? What did he mean, he could help me? Who else is working with him?

She stood for awhile, glaring at the group and listening to whatever parts of the story she could catch. Jefferson was telling the others about her...security cameras.

Oh yeah, those. He doesn't seem to realize what they are, at least, which is nice.

Now he was talking about... something he and Stern knew about? And Von Fer? He was saying names she didn't recognize, then he mentioned something about the new prisoners. Before she could hear much else of their conversation, someone tapped her on the shoulder.

In a flurry of motion, she spun around and grabbed their wrist. She twisted around quickly, hooking her leg around their ankle and bringing them down to the floor. She pressed their wrist into the hollow at the base of their shoulder blades. They were coughing and trying to fight her off, and yelling something about being "on her side."

After a second of digging her knee into the person's back, she recognized the dark blue uniform jacket and pressed slacks of one of the male guards- Felix, to be exact. She immediately let go of him and got off of his back, and she muttered an apology while helping him stand.

"What do you want?" she asked, letting him take a moment to catch his breath.

The only good thing about all of us officially having to wear uniforms 24/7 is that it's a hell of a lot easier to recognize your own.

"I came to inform you that someone called the front office for you. Same last name as Roger," Felix replied, gently inspecting the newly- forming bruises on his wrist. Linda looked thoughtful for a moment, then he continued, "it was a woman."

Her head snapped up to attention and she thanked him for the information. She pointed to the group she'd been observing, who had stopped talking at the sound of the commotion she'd caused.

"Take them to solitary."

~~~~~~~~~~~~

"Cindy, he broke into my fucking study!" Linda exclaimed, slamming her hand on the front office desk. She'd locked herself in and soundproofed it with a spell, expecting to be answering a call for help from *Caeda*. Instead, she was met with a cordial check-in call from "Mrs. Callsworth" on behalf of her husband, who was very busy at a town hall summit and wouldn't be able to check in with her himself. Such calls would henceforth be a weekly occurrence. Once they'd each covertly reassured the other that the line wasn't bugged and they had no eavesdroppers, Cindy dropped her facade of council grandeur. She'd asked Linda how things were going, *really*, and Linda began going *off* about her study. Linda could practically hear the wince in her mother's voice when she yelled into the phone.
~~~~~~~~~~~~

"Language!" Cindy chided. She'd never cared before whether Linda cursed, but hearing swear words yelled in her ear at 11 in the morning was evidently where she would draw the line. Her voice was even as she continued, "You said yourself that he left a note-what did it say again?"

Linda crossed her arms over her chest and slumped back in her seat, pouting like a petulant human child.

"...we are not your enemy..." she muttered under her breath. The older immortal seemed unamused.

"What was that, dear?" she asked in a tone that Linda could have mistaken for nonchalance, if she weren't able to picture the exact facial expression that went along with it. She knew too well the well-hidden, sickeningly sweetened anger that hid in Cindy's calm smile.

"He wrote 'we are not your enemy' next to some weird symbol shit."

"Symbols? What kind of symbols?" Cindy responded quickly. Linda described them to her as best she could, from memory.

"Wait. What is this inmate's full name?" the demigoddess seemed frantic now.

"Uh, his full name is Randoloph Arthiticus "Randy" Jefferson. He's the one who grew those plants for you, remember? When you healed me?" Linda replied, confused as to why Cindy was so interested in him.

"Linda, you know how I'm... associated with people who share our hatred of Roger? Who knew there were dark things going on in Kacapa county? One of the people I worked closest with was the mayor, Marlene Fitzgerald. She was the leader of a society of magic users in Dufferton that believed magic should be used only for good, but kept a secret from quotidians unless absolutely necessary. She found me just before she was taken by the council, and I explained everything to her.

"She told me she was going to spread that information like wildfire with all of her allies, including the leader of another organization that thinks everyone -quotidians included- should have access to magic. She only managed to talk to her own followers before... you know. Anyway, it hardly matters. The important thing is that *the leader of the second organization is named 'Randy Jefferson.'*

I didn't recognize him that night because I was far too busy making sure you lived to give a damn about learning his backstory or to remember what she'd told me, but now it all makes sense. Both of the societies have sigils associated with them. I've seen them both- they look exactly like what you described.

They're *definitely* your allies, Linda. The leader of the Twalnaverra broke into your study. *Take him up on his offer of help.*"

~~~~

Once Cindy ended the call, Linda had Randy, Quin, Mitchell, and Abigail brought into the front office. The younger two inmates looked afraid, Randy looked bored and pale, and Abigail looked...

Abigail looked *furious.*

Before anyone could attempt to maul her, Linda held up a hand. She pulled up chairs around her desk, and motioned for them all to sit. When they did, she opened her mouth to speak.

"I only had you put in solitary because I didn't know who you were, yet. Jef-*Randy.* Yeah, that's right, I used your real name, shocker. Randy, I know who you are now. I know Cindy, an ally of Marlene. She explained your little secret society business to me. I know you broke into my study, and I read your note. I know that you took some of my books, *and touched some of my knives,* and I know that you mean me no harm. I had you all brought here because I know you're all very powerful. Even if you choose not to or don't know how to use them, you've all got a lot of power. I assume you're all members of the societies?"

None of them interrupted her, only nodded their heads.

"That's what I thought. Randy, in your note you said that you could help me. "We can set you free" and all that. What exactly do you propose?"
~~~~

She folded her hands on top of her desk, waiting patiently for his reply. He pushed up his glasses and looked her up and down before seeming to chose his next words carefully.

"You have to join one of the two societies, then we can offer you collective protection and an army of allies to fight against Roger and the council. You know they'll kill you when (not if, when) they find out you're not loyal. Join us, and we can help you fight them. We can help you bring Roger down." He paused, letting her contemplate his offer. She was about to retort that she was fine on her own, but he continued, "it's what Cindy chose to do, anyway, by contacting Marlene. She's part of the Marmara now."

Linda thought about the deal for a long time, before finally making her choice.

"I guess I'm joining the Marmara too, then."

CHAPTER 17: FIRE, FLOOD, AND ESCAPE

The day was uneventful. Randy had begun holding meetings of the two societies, having Abigail and Linda join him in explaining what they were up against. Abigail seemed... antsy, and she didn't want to trust Linda at *all*. Three months after she'd join the Marmara, Linda still hadn't really opened up about who she was. She was helping Randy plan for an overthrow of the council from the inside, though, so she was proving herself to be quite a useful ally.

The council conducted 5 more "random check-ins" and everyone now knew why they had to cooperate. They would all act like they'd been converted so they could get out, "join" the council, and then when they were supposed to fight with them against the quotidians, they would turn and take them out from the inside. Everyone seemed to either endorse the plan or begrudgingly go along with it.

Their plans seemed to be coming along nicely as the wintry snow of the mountain slowed its rapid fall. They'd had a bit of respite for New Years', but a blizzard hit in mid February that left snowdrifts five feet high in some places across the plateau and an icy slick down the unsalted mountain road. Now, the snow had stopped falling and was beginning to thaw, just a little, across the plateau. It *was* nearly April, after all.

It was late afternoon, and Randy was curled up in the courtyard with a handful of Linda's books in a sunny patch of grass. Linda had begun letting people practice their magic in the front office and, once Randy figured out how to reroute energy from the sun to use for magic (thanks in large part to the books in Linda's study that she'd begrudgingly let him read and his own extensive knowledge of plantlike magic) they all started practicing outside. Mitchell was beginning to get better at controlling his abilities, and he'd cleared the snow from the courtyard.

Now, Randy was trying to teach himself as many defensive spells as he could that would work specifically against Roger's powers. As he sat engrossed in his reading, he felt the sun become hidden behind a cloud, then someone sprint behind him across the grass, heading toward the far fence of the courtyard. He didn't really pay them any attention, assuming they were practicing some sort of training exercise. He just kept reading until he heard a loud ZAP! Followed by stream of heavy cursing. He looked up from his research in time to see Mitchell chastising Abigail for swearing.

"Abigail? What were you doing over there? Did you think Linda was kidding when she said she had Lilac amplify the current in the fence to make it more powerful?" Randy snorted, looking at his newly- singed friend.

She shot him a glare and backed farther into the shadows as the sun began to come back out. She picked her way back to the court-yard doors, using patches of shade and the shadow of the building to protect her. There had been no way for Linda to get her a new sun shield talisman, so she was forced to try her best to stay as much out of the sun as possible.

Randy found her behavior odd, but didn't really have time to be concerned about it. He went back to his research, staring at the dusty pages in his hands until his eyes burned and chills began to run down his arms from staying too still in the cold. He took off his glasses and squeezed his eyes shut for a few seconds, hoping to stop the feeling of fire behind his eyelids.

When he felt a little less like he was going to go blind, he sighed and started picking up the books around him. The sun was starting to set a little later now that it was beginning to be spring, but it still began to hang low in the sky around the time that the dinner "bell" rang at the Ark. Making his way inside, he dropped off his research at his cell before meeting with the others in the dining hall.

To his surprise, Abigail was nowhere to be seen. While she didn't usually eat what everyone else did, Linda did have a supply of magically-synthetic blood for her, so she usually had *something* at mealtimes. For her to be missing completely was... suspicious, at best. He asked Quin from across the table if she'd seen her room-mate since she'd shocked herself, and so learned that Quin was un-aware that she *had* shocked herself. No one at their table had seen her since Mitchell had told her off, and apparently that had been almost five hours ago.

Suddenly, he heard a loud peal of laughter from a few tables down, and when he looked towards the noise he saw Abigail sitting next to Lilac and Marissa, joking about something. He huffed, re-lieved that Abigail was accounted for, but (though he would *never* admit it) jealous that she'd abandoned him. He wondered why ex-actly she'd decided to leave the seat at his right hand empty, just to pull up a chair at the end of an over-crowded table that she'd complained about before, saying it was too noisy. He tried not to let it bother him, and if Mitchell or Quin noticed that he wasn't as talkative as usual, they didn't say anything. He finished eating faster than normal and excused himself, meaning to go back to his cell and try to do more research. Or maybe he would try to catch Linda and see if she wanted to know any of his findings. Or maybe he would just go to bed early.

He decided on the former, returning to his cell and pulling the cover from his bed over him. He'd been storing some energy while he was outside, photosynthesizing it like a plant, and now he was using it so that he could create a ball of light that he could use as a flashlight while he hid under the blanket with his books.

Time passed quickly and he heard Mitchell come back, then the lights out bell, then nothing for awhile. Then, he began to smell something... dangerous. He lifted the edge of the blanket and the smell grew much, much stronger. The air was hot and thick, and as soon as Randy let his light illuminate the room, he found out the source of the smell. It was smoke, pouring off of Mitchell. His bed was engulfed in flames that seemed to be emanating from him, but he... wasn't burning? It took a moment for things to click in Randy's head- he was using his powers in his sleep!

Randy scrambled up, coughing as he breathed in the dense smoke. He yelled Mitchell's name and kicked his books across the room, dashing to the door. Linda had stopped locking everyone in when they'd all agreed to work together on the "acting brainwashed" plan, so as soon as he got the door open, he swept all of his research out with him and then waited for the smoke alarms to detect his roommate's unconscious pyrotechnic act. Within seconds, the sound was blaring, everyone was awake, and several guards were rushing down the hall towards him.

Then, someone was behind him, telling him to pick up his research. He did, and then a hissing, bubbling noise came from inside the room. Mitchell was awake now, and shouting some kind of conversation at everyone else, and then he yelped as the room began to flood. Randy then realized that Ivan- the one guard he'd ever felt uncomfortable around, and even then, only because it's always awkward when first interacting with an ex- was using his magical abilities to douse the flames. And drench the entire room. And the hallway outside of it.

This is going to be a long night.

Randy tried to continue his research in the common room, but he could barely focus. He was exhausted, and a strange sense of impending doom was settling on his shoulders that he couldn't quite place.

On the one hand- he couldn't help but feel a little hopeless when he thought about how few of his allies were walking free. And Abigail- she'd been getting quieter and quieter at meetings, and the more he thought about her behavior, the less he liked its implications.

First, she sprints full tilt at a magical electric fence like she's trying to escape. Then, she leaves her place at our table- with no warning or explanation- to sit by the girl in charge of our power grid. Something's... wrong there.

On the other hand, though, Randy had to be careful. He'd stayed up for days doing research before and it always made him paranoid- not to mention the fact that Linda had given him a can of *Creature* (™) energy drink so he could stay awake while researching after Mitchell drove him from their room. It was having some... *weird* side effects. He felt energetic and sleepy all at once, and now that he was sitting in the common room, a not-too-small part of him was burning with a fury that he hadn't had fifteen minutes ago at the fact that he'd had to move at all.

He was trying to put his feelings aside so he could work by the light of the overhead common room lamp when he heard a high pitched buzz, followed by a loud *ZAP!* sound. Then, everything went completely pitch black.

Somewhere, generator-powered alarms were blaring and he looked frantically out the nearest window, trying to see in the pitch black outside. Vaguely, he saw... someone sprinting through the leftover snowdrifts, off towards the woods that lay far beyond the Ark. It looked like...

Abigail!

He pushed his mind away from himself, desperately searching for her in the prison. He found her, fleetingly, rushing away into the night outside. He began to hyperventilate when he was hit by a wave of the emotion- anger, sadness, hurt, something more- that burned in her. The instant she noticed him, she pushed him away, cutting off their connection. Then, someone was near him, yelling at him. Linda was there, *furious.* **Betrayed.**

"What the fuck Jefferson??! I thought your vampire bitch was our ally!" she spat at him, grabbing his shoulder and spinning him around quickly, giving him a poisonous death glare. She kept yelling, saying something about how they were all going to die, because now Roger's suspicions would be confirmed, and he would know *immediately*- probably already did know- that she'd escaped, so now they were all fucked over...

"*I never should have trusted you, you fucking idiot.* **And here I thought you could help light our way out of this mess.**"

At that, at hearing the words of his father from the mouth of someone else, something in Randy- some coil of memories he'd spent *so long* trying to forget- snapped. He was no longer there, in the dark common room of the council's prison. He was back in his father's house. *Back in the basement.*

He was back in **that** *darkness.*

He didn't hear Linda yelling anymore, no, he heard *his father*. He heard the same anger that earned him fists to the teeth and palms to the cheek. The couches and rug of the common room became the cold concrete of the hell hole his father had kept him in for *six months* following his sister's death.

"*I deserved it,*" he told himself, uncaring whether Linda or anyone else could hear him. Tears started to slip down his cheeks and his vision grew dark around the edges. The others (Mitchell and Quin were there now, trying to get Linda to calm down enough to eliminate the possibility of her actually hitting him) were drawn out of their argument. They looked over at him, saw him losing control of his composure and powers. Mitchell recognized the nervous energy surrounding Randy as the same that he had when he was having a nightmare. Quin recognized the absent, terrified look in his eyes and the rapid, shallow breaths that he was taking as the same ones she'd seen in her friends at school during unannounced lock down drills or when bad teachers got violent over missing work. The teens looked at each other and came to the same conclusion at the same time.

"*Linda, shut up he's having a panic attack and you're making it worse.*"

The words cut through the horrible haze in Randy's head and the swarming sickness in his stomach and chest began to ease, just a little.

Panic attack. That's what this is.

Just because he recognized what was happening, it didn't make it any easier to stop it. His breathing stayed rapid, but his eyes cleared a little. The dark walls of the basement faded back to the dark surroundings of the common room and Linda's voice became less like...

She was being strong- armed out of the room by Quin. Mitchell's hand was on his back. His head was between his knees.

Breathe in for one. Two. three. Four.

He counted his breaths. Mitchell told him he was safe. Quin reminded him he was in control.

Hold your breath for one. Two. three. Four. five. Six. seven.

Quin asked him how old he was. He held up two fingers, then five.

Breathe out for one. Two. three. Four. five. Six. seven. Eight.

Mitchell asked him if it was too dark. He nodded. Mitchell asked... why he didn't use his powers to light up the room. Tears slipped down his cheeks and he shook his head, hard.

"Because I-I couldn't...I couldn't save her? He said... Dad said I couldn't ever glow again. He'll hit me again if I do, don't you remember?"

Randy's voice was impossibly small.

"Randy? You can glow. He can't hit you anymore. Not ever again, do you hear me?"

Quin's voice shattered the frosted glass that seemed to cover his mind. He gasped, then blinked several times, coming out of the flashback slowly.

Dad's not around anymore.

He looked in Quin's face.

I'm not with him.

His eyes flicked to Mitchell, who felt safe and familiar.

I'm here.

He recognized the room he was in, and ran his hands along the seat beneath him.

I'm safe.

A spark of light appeared in his palm.

CHAPTER 18: GO TO HELL, DEAR.

"You insidious bitch!!!" Roger screamed when he found Cindy in the pantry, picking up some fruit and baking ingredients off of a shelf.

"Roger! What on earth are you upset about?" she feigned innocence, then gasped as he grabbed her by the neck and lifted her off of the ground. There was something dangerous and wild in his eyes- the same thing she'd seen every other time that she'd defied or questioned him, but this time a million times worse. He leaned in close to her, baring his too-white teeth in a snarl.

"You. know." He was mere millimeters from her ear, but she almost couldn't hear him over the sound of her blood rushing in her head. Though she was older than Lake Tamory and the entirety of the country around it, she still had a pulse and he was still choking her. "Why did you leave the meeting early, darling?" he growled, emphasizing his words by tightening his grip on her throat.

Her voice was barely more than a whisper, but she managed to breathily choke out, "because I left a c-cake in th-the oven for our anniv....ersary and I didn't want to burn the house down." She sputtered and coughed as he suddenly dropped her on her back, stepping over her and readjusting the cuffs of his sleeves.

"Really, darling? Well then, where are the smoking remains of your mistake? The house doesn't smell of fire, or burned cake," his eyes glimmered darkly as he circled the kitchen island, running his fingers along the marble counter tops as if he were checking for dust or flour. As he rounded the corner of the island again, he swooped down and grabbed her by the wrists, this time pulling her up so that her back was to him. He pinned her arms across her chest as he finished, "or the air freshener you would've used to get rid of those smells. I should've *known. You're one of **them**, aren't you?*"

In a flash of movement that neither of them had anticipated, Cindy flipped him over her body and threw him against the pantry door, her eyes flaming with the fury of a mother bear fighting hunters away from her cubs.

"Yes. I am. I have been for awhile, now. I'm a little surprised, you didn't think it suspicious that I rose through the ranks so quickly?" She dodged him easily as he sprang up to chase her. She had nothing left to lose, and knew that she would die tonight either way, so she let herself be angry.

"I could put up with your horseshit when it was just me, Roger. But you hurt my child, after I'd just got her back. For that, no matter what happens to me, *you will **pay.**"*

She saw realization flash across his face at the mention of Linda, but it was quickly replaced by his anger at her.

She dodged another swing, this time catching his arm. She crushed his wrist in a vice-like grip until she heard the bone crunching, pushing him down onto the floor. Roger bellowed and let his aura fully surround him. His eyes turned black as pitch, and swirling spikes of poisonous energy shot off of him. All around Caeda's body, shields that seemed to be made of the night sky blocked the attacks, and she let him go.

They fought for what seemed like hours, circling each other and grappling. Roger got in a few good hits, and Caeda lifted the fridge and threw it at him. He retaliated by throwing a knife at her, which grazed her side and caught her off guard by actually making contact. She gasped and he took his opportunity to tackle her while she was distracted.

He threw himself on top of her and began pummeling her, beating her as she lay on the floor, trapped under him. She managed to get a hold of the knife and slash at his back, and he let out a pained screech. She laughed through her teeth, flecks of blood spattering on his face as she did.

"*Go to hell, dear.*" She said, plunging the knife into his side. He writhed and grabbed her hair, pulling her head up and then slamming it down onto the kitchen floor. Caeda let out a scream of pain and her ears rang loudly, as if a tea kettle were whistling directly into her ear drums. She lay limply on the floor, dazed and no longer able to fight Roger. He got off of her and staggered to the side, pulling out the knife with a yell that she barely heard and fleeing the scene completely.

As he left, Caeda heard his last words to her:

"Happy anniversary, darling."

~~~~

As the room around her dimmed, she felt blood dripping down the back of her head from one of her ears, and she knew that a dark blue puddle of aether was forming under her. Her physical form was, her father had told her when she asked a thousand years ago, nothing more than skin and bone stretched over and holding up *the night sky incarnate.* Her protective wards had never let her skin be cut this deep, so she'd never seen the cosmos spill out before. In a very sad, violent way, it was almost beautiful.

She closed her eyes and thought of Aemenora. She remembered, long ago, when she went into the forest, and sang for three nights as stardust and wind and water and earth converged to bring her
~~~~

daughter to life. She remembered all of the times, when her baby was still young, that she took her out to dance in the moonlight and talk to the fairies, so as to teach her never to let herself become tricked by their games. She remembered leaving, when she was told that her daughter was dead.

She remembered finding her, again. Seeing her across the room at that fateful council meeting, older, and angrier, and so good at pretending. She remembered their conversation in the parking lot, and the furry grandchildren she got to meet.

She remembered driving home, and letting Aemenora see the mess she'd gotten herself into in the name of spying on the council. She remembered Aemenora's new name, but didn't pay it any mind now.

She remembered healing her daughter after that wretched monster hurt her. She remembered the kindness of the prisoner who'd helped her neutralize the poison in Aemenora's veins. She remembered promising her daughter that she would do everything she could to see the destruction of the man who hurt her.

As the room grew darker, and her bleeding, broken limbs grew heavier, she remembered hearing of the vampire's escape, and seeing her husband's anger rise. She remembered trying her best to convince him to find the vampire first, and let his warden punish the other prisoners. She remembered the sting of his palm across her face for her insolence.

She remembered the meeting, earlier that day, when it was decided that "Linda" was next to die. She remembered the panic, and then the hard knot of resolution in her. She remembered taking things into her own hands.

As her mind floated away from its physical bonds, up and away to rejoin her father in his kingdom amongst the stars, it replayed the afternoon for her one last time, as if to prove to itself that it did the right thing.

~~~~~
~~~~~

Cindy's heart pounded as she stepped out of her car and closed the driver's side door. It was one of the few times she hadn't taken a cab to a council meeting- Roger finally bought her some gas to fill the tank. She clutched her handbag in gloved hands and shivered in the brisk early spring air.

She walked into the hotel and down the back stairs, taking her new place in the *fourth* row of the audience. Other people began to fill in the seats around her, someone deemed "more important" took her old chair, and soon the Elders filed in to take their places at the front of the room.

She knew what was coming- she'd seen the fury in Roger's eyes after he'd heard of the escape at the Ark. Her pleas for Roger to focus on catching the escapee first had fallen on deaf ears and only seemed to make him more determined to call a meeting of the council to discuss Linda's punishment.

Roger stood up once everyone had taken their places and raised his hand for silence. His black cloud of an aura was visible even in the low light of the basement, and everyone immediately shut up. Most of the new recruits were missing, Cindy noticed, and Linda was nowhere in the crowd.

"As I'm sure you all already know," Roger began, his voice deeper than it should have been, "One of the disgusting Quotidian-sympathizers in our rehabilitation facility has escaped. Though it deeply saddens me to inform you all of this, myself and the other Elders have conducted a thorough review of the facility, and we have come to the conclusion that the person at fault for this failure is none other than the elf we put in charge. She clearly was not fit to guard such powerful prisoners, and her conversion methods were not effective enough to save her from being corrupted herself by the insidious whispers of this Twalnaverra and Marmara." His words were a carefully controlled growl that sent shocks of terror through her. She could almost taste the venom of his voice, and she could feel the violent vibration of his aura. Snakelike tendrils were branching off of him and traveling through the crowd, making people's hair stand on end in the front row.

The crowd was in an uproar, and several people began chanting at once behind her, calling for Linda's death. Roger seemed pleased by the violent outbursts, and let them go on for a while before he raised his hand again for silence.

"She will be dealt with accordingly, do not worry. I will break her mind myself, and our lost sheep will be brought back into the fold. As for her prisoners- those who are still worth the council's time will have their minds broken immediately, and those who are not will be killed. Does anyone have any questions?"

He paused for a moment, and no one moved. Then, from the sixth row, a man lifted his hand above his head and Roger nodded for him to speak.

"What about the Marmaran leaders, sir? Should we dispose of them too? The Alpha Werewolf is alive, but barely able to fight for us in his current condition, considering he's missing his dominant leg. Should we bother to keep and convert him? And what of the mayor? She-"

Roger hissed, and the man immediately stopped stuttering through his question. Cindy flinched at the malicious, faux-innocence in his tone as he practically purred his reply.

"I understand your concern. It is certainly a waste of our resources and energy to keep people we don't plan to convert alive, so allow me to put your mind at ease. We will be breaking their minds soon, and when we do that, we will necromantically replace the werewolf's leg. He will fight for us, as will the mayor, and we will use them to destroy our enemies. The Alpha will take back his pack, including his sister, and that loss alone will be a substantial hit to our enemies. The mayor can- and will- destroy our enemy's infrastructure. And, when our dear Linda has returned to us, she will fight for us too. She was right about one thing- the more people we can convert- by logic or by force- the better."

The hairs on the back of Cindy's neck stood on end, and she knew she had to warn her daughter of the coming storm. Roger kept talking, undoubtedly stirring up the bloodthirst of the homicidal fanatics around her. She waited for a moment when no one would notice that she'd left- someone said something and the whole crowd of believers jumped up from their seats to applaud. Then, she slipped from her seat and into the shadows of the basement and made her way to the far back of the room, praying to her father and her mother that no one would see her leaving.

She looked back once, as she mounted the stairs to the exit, and saw Roger looking directly at her. He said nothing, but his flinty gaze pierced her skin and weighed her down with its toxic venom. He knew she was going to warn them. She knew that she didn't fear him anymore.

~~~

She got in her car and sped back to her house as fast as she could, taking every back road and shortcut she knew. Rain was starting to fall, and she could see a massive storm on the horizon which made her hurry even more. Once she was inside, she made her way to the kitchen pantry and pulled a rope that hung from the ceiling there. A trapdoor to the attic opened, and she pulled herself up with the aid of an almost-empty shelf. She was careful not to knock down any of the cans of peas, overly ripe fruit, or old, broken cookware that Roger refused to let her throw away.

She closed the trapdoor behind her, pulling up the rope so that he couldn't corner her if he managed to get home before she was done with what she had to do. Crossing the bare wooden floor, she touched the knob of a small door recessed into the far shadows beneath the eaves.

Cindy's hand trembled with sadness and adrenaline, but she did not let that stop her from opening her mouth and murmuring "Home. I want to go home."

When the door swung open and she stepped through it, she was no longer in the attic of the Callsworth residence. As if she'd walked
~~~

straight into a period drama, everything shifted. Her mind fluttered with thoughts of now-antiquated traditions, and she felt like she was back in the home she'd lived in before she'd had to worry about the problems of mortals. She was once again herself, Caeda.

She sat for a long time at the old elm wood writing desk, brushing her fingertips over the ancient parchment before her. She began to softly sing a song in Old High German, one that had been lost to humanity for centuries.

The butterflies of night are flying,
upon their wings I soar.
The night binds us together
as we fly to distant shores.

She opened a bottle of dark green ink and poured a few drops of it out across the top of the parchment. It spread down, moving in spiderwebs of meaning along the veins of the paper, running to voice her melancholy thoughts.

The fire of the sunny world
has fin'ly burn'd away,

There were instruments playing somewhere. They played along to the tune of her song, softly lamenting with her. She began to forget the words. The ink was forming itself into its own words, writing a warning to the only child that Caeda had ever cared for.

And soon, the stars will go,
ne'ermore the moon will shine
Dear Aemenora
but dear one, please remember
this is not goodbye

The page was trembling on the desk now. The wind outside rattled the attic in bursts, battering the house with enough force to shake the desk. More ink splashed itself onto the parchment, another line of sorrow painting its way across its surface. She wished with all her heart that she did not have to write this warning.

Deep green letters continued to scrawl of their own accord as Caeda drew a small box from her desk drawer, now only humming her song's melody. Opening it, she pulled out a heavy wooden wax seal and a spoon to melt her wax into. As the letter finished writing itself, she set her sealing supplies to the side and gingerly picked up the freshly-written message.

Aemenora always liked it when I folded my letters into stars.

She shook the parchment dry, gently shaping it into a 5-pointed masterpiece. She took an amber-colored candle from on top of the desk's lid, lighting it with a snap of her fingers. The snap seemed as loud as a thunderclap, with a force strong enough to shake birds from their nests on the other side of the mountain. The candle lit itself, and she held it over the bowl of the spoon. The wax dripped like frozen molasses into the silvery bowl of the spoon. When it was full, she tipped it over and poured the wax onto the center of the star, where the ends of the parchment met.

In the same instant, she blew out the candle and picked up the seal, which seemed to weigh a hundred tons. She made sure that it was right-side-up, then stuck it down in the wax and held it until everything was cool. Her hands dropped afterward, staying down at her sides. The seal extricated itself from the wax, leaving behind tiny ridges that made a picture of a constellation. An arcing, gold-dipped ox-bow now took the seal's place within the wax. Her personal crest. Her life's purpose.

Caeda touched the letter to her lips, giving her daughter a blessing of hope and protection. She would not let the man she didn't love hurt her. Her eyes fluttered closed and she stood, walking across the floor. She left her sanctuary, taking up her title as Mrs. Cindy Callsworth once more. She didn't watch the door melt away behind her, for she was busy opening one of the attic windows. Far below and away from her, she saw the headlights of Roger's car turning down their excessively long driveway. The wind rushed around her and she held out the star, letting it be swept out of her hands like a blade of grass.

She knew the moon would see to it that her last goodbye reached Aemenora in time for it to be of help. She was closing the attic window when she heard the front door slam open, and heavy, furious footsteps pounding toward the trap door.

~~~~

Later that night, far away from the scene of the murder, the silence of the night was shattered by the wind blowing the doors of the Ark open. Linda, gun drawn, was ready to call for all of her guards when a single, crumpled sheet of paper swirled into her line of sight. It settled itself gently on the lobby floor, almost as though someone had placed it at her feet, and then the wind died away completely. The doors shut with a crashing finality that made Linda flinch.

She picked up the paper and unfolded it carefully, hoping it wasn't full of anthrax or glitter. Her vision ran over the familiar handwriting and elegant runes, taking in a letter from Cindy. When she got to the middle of the message, her heart stopped. Her eyes widened, then brimmed with tears for the first time in nearly 5 centuries. She opened her mouth and let out a heart-wrenching shriek that could have shattered the windows of a normal building.

Linda's screams could be heard from the base of Two Peak mountain, and every guard came running to the entrance, where they found her on her knees, crying furiously over a note written with words of a language none of them knew and in scrawls of the most beautiful gibberish anyone had ever read.

Dear Aemenora,

I'm afraid I haven't nearly enough time to tell you all that I wish I could. I'm so proud of you for keeping up the fight and protecting the good and light of this world from those who would plunge everything into darkness. My father and his kinsmen truly blessed me when they chose you, my brave, wonderful girl, to be the daughter I sang into the world.

You and I both know the nature of rebellion far too well to pretend that this war will have no casualties, so I will come right out and say that I may be the first. Roger knows of our deception and has placed your name on his list of traitors. I know he saw me leave the council meeting early so that I
~~~~

could do what I could to help you. This letter is enchanted with wards to protect you from the treachery of the council.

Fight well, Lady Light-Bringer, and do not forget me. The stars will shine for you always.

Forever your mother,

Caeda

CHAPTER 19: CONTROL

Searing pain, blinding and horrible, cut across Roger's hip. The demigoddess- for that is what he'd finally realized she was, as she lay in a pool of her own aether-blood- had almost definitely dislocated it slightly when she threw the refrigerator at him. He hadn't noticed in the fury of the fight, but his knife wounds weakened him enough to feel the pain. He leaned heavily on one arm, the other curled instinctively around his side as he knelt on the floor of the master bathroom. His weight was all on his uninjured hip, and his aura whipped around him as his body tried to heal itself. He drew in a labored breath and then unleashed a howling, static-filled shriek as he pulled the knife with one hand and used a dark cloud of energy to push his hip and leg back into the proper place. For miles around the Callsworth residence, lights came on and frightened quotidians barred their doors and didn't go out looking for the monster they'd heard screaming into the void behind their houses.

The world blackened for an indeterminate amount of time, but at some point, Roger's vision cleared. The infuriating agony in his hip was now just a dull ache, and the stab wound in his chest was fully healed. He staggered to a standing position and tentatively tried to walk. It was less painful than he'd been prepared to endure.

He slowly made his way out to the kitchen, where Cindy's body now lay- cold and rigid. The pools of aether were still forming, and they looked like beautifully violent reminders of his power. It was as if he'd opened a portal into the void under his wife's corpse.

Something glittered at her neck, and he slowly bent to look at it closer. A tiny bottle of blue-violet liquid hung around her neck, suspended by a silver chain. It rested on her chest, haloed by a very faint silver light produced by tiny silver specks inside the bottle. He pulled it away from her neck, and found it sealed impossibly tight with a magic not even the fires of infinity could break. As he held it in his hand, he curiously pushed his mind out towards it, and was stunned as a flood of memory and energy coursed through him. Flashes of scenes he couldn't hold on to cut across his vision, then he drew his mind away.

Roger looked at the necklace closer and a vicious smile cracked across his face.

"This will make me as powerful as a god."

Every member of the council had a part to play in the overthrow of the quotidians, and now it was Roger's time to play his. Felicia sat in the passenger seat of his black sedan, a megaphone sitting in her lap and a wicked grin on her face. A taser was strapped to the outside of her pants leg, and as Roger drove, he could feel his seat belt press against the knife at his waist. They were going up the mountain to the Ark of Light, just as the rest of his agents were busy preparing themselves for the battle against the quotidians.

It was obvious that there would be a fight- the escaped vampire had by now been given enough time to gather up the remaining Marmarans and Twalneres. They would try to face his council, so Roger had sent half the remaining council members to try to gather weapons and energy stores to prepare for battle, and the other half were to begin work on attacking quotidians. His plans to enslave humanity were, in his definitely-not-biased-at-all eyes, foolproof.

The bare trees and rocky surroundings of the barely paved road to the prison flew past the car at a blinding speed, and several times, Roger's aura actually made the car float for a few seconds in order to keep them from flying off the side of a cliff. Roger made it up the mountain in record time, turning onto the Devil's Bed Plateau just as the sun rose over the sky high horizon.

The reinforced front doors of the Ark exploded open, spraying shards of glass so fast across the front lobby that the fragments became embedded an inch into the walls. The guards and a few inmates came running at the sound, and startled screams were heard from deeper in the building. Roger's aura drew up and flung itself outward in long tendrils, sending the guards flying back like rag dolls thrown into the engine of an airplane. He braced himself and his aura cut out his hearing for a second as he saw Felicia part her lips from the corner of his eye and she let out a deafening scream that knocked the remaining witnesses unconscious.

Roger put his hand on the bottle he'd taken from Cindy and blinked. When his eyes opened, they'd gone from silver-grey to a complete black abyss. He snapped his fingers and the guards' bodies vanished in a cloud of black smoke, sure to reappear locked in the solitary confinement cells he'd keep them in until he could break their minds.

He took Felicia's hand and they stepped over the unconscious inmates, making their way through the prison. They found the inmates all cowering in the dining hall, pitifully attempting to barricade the door and keep them out. Roger's aura nearly tore down half the wall taking the doors off their hinges and exposing the inmates inside.

Like finding a nest of roaches in the wall.

"Where. is. Linda. Bernard?"

The sniveling, quotidian-loving group of inmates cowered before him on the floor of the dining hall as he stood at the front of the room. As he watched, Felicia crossed the ruined threshold of the dining hall, dragging Linda behind her by the hair. Her eyes were veiled in a slick of emotion that Roger couldn't read, then they locked onto the bottle in his hand. They widened, filling with a far-off anger that Roger found...amusing. Felicia threw her forward into the chair in front of him when they got across the room, and Roger let out a deep chuckle.

She'll be fun to break.

He turned his attention to the room, conducting himself in a more cruel parody of the way he did during a council meeting. He blinked away the black haze over his eyes and his voice normalized to something slightly closer to human.

"I expect that you all know by now the true purpose of this facility. You know who I am and the cause I serve. Who among you wish to escape severe punishment and join me?"

No one moved. A large part of Roger was irritated at the lost time, money, and work that had been put into the prison, but then another piped up, reminding him of how much *fun* he would have, breaking their minds. He sighed loudly and waved his hand, turning his face away from the crowd.

"Well, I suppose that's your mistake then."

He looked down at Linda. Her attention hadn't left the bottle, but tears were forming in the corners of her eyes. He opened his mouth to say something, but before he could, she whispered some-thing and an unhinged shine filled his eye.

"You took it.

Why?"

He laughed, startling the crowd.

"Why? Why did I take *the soul of the demigoddess* **I killed?**

Because.

I.

Could."

A violent grin spread across his face, and he drew back his hand. Linda's eyes were burning with hatred for him, and the small rebel-lion he saw in her otherwise-catatonic mind was enough to push him over the edge.

The back of his hand crashed against her head, striking across her face from temple to jawbone. She cried out and tried instinc-tively to fight back, but before she could move, Felicia moved in and grabbed the taser from its clip. She unceremoniously brought it down on the side of Linda's neck, turning it quickly onto its highest setting and leaving it there until the elf stopped screaming and went limp. Then, she let Linda's unconscious body slide off the chair and onto the floor. She looked up at Roger for approval, and he smiled horribly at her, nodding with pride.

He looked back at the crowd, which sat in stunned silence. No one seemed to even breathe, and most looked as though they were going to be sick. He straightened and smiled hysterically at them.

"And so you see what happens to those who defy my will."

He let the darkness consume him completely again, teleporting Linda's body to the trunk of his car and leaving a burning kiss on Felicia's lips. She raised the megaphone to incapacitate the remain-ing inmates as Roger walked out of the prison. Though, he didn't see, because his back was turned as he walked out the door of the Ark, that one inmate was left standing when Felicia finished her demon call. He could not tell, from as far away as he was, that she was deaf, and therefore immune to his mistress' screams. He didn't even hear Felicia scream his name for his help, as 50 thousand volts shot through her body.

Because his mind was too consumed by the thought of conquest.

CHAPTER 20: OUT OF HERE

The first thing that Quin became aware of was the high-pitched note in the back of her head, layering over a roar of static. She coughed and whined, next becoming aware of the cold tile beneath her as she curled into herself, pressing her hands over her ears.

Someone was standing over her. Quin looked up and locked eyes with Lilac, who was signing something at her, slowly spelling out the message in simple letters.

"Can you hear anything?"

Her hands were shaky as she responded, *"just. Ringing."*

Lilac gently took her head in her hands and presumably muttered something into her ear, and then the ringing stopped. Quin's head instantly stopped hurting, so she tentatively uncurled and hugged the human spark plug.

"Thank you," she breathed into Lilac's shoulder, not expecting to be able to hear.

"Don't mention it," she replied, helping the younger girl up. "I used to do this kind of thing all the time for my coworkers. Working in a loud factory's dangerous when your supervisors don't wanna pay for auditory safety equipment."

She stopped to help the next inmate, showing Quin how to do the same spell that she had done. The two worked their way around the crowd of people, shaking some awake and shushing others who were trying to yell over their hearing damage to ask what had happened. When everyone was alert and able to listen, Randy spoke up, "Someone better get the guards!"

"We need to find Linda, Abigail, and all of our other allies. Lilac's attack on Felicia cut out the power up here, so all the barriers are down. There's weapons and information we could use in Linda's study-she gave me a temporary key to use in case of emergencies. If a few people could help me carry the weapons upstairs, and find the guards while we are at it. Then, we can start down the mountain."

A few people, Mitchell included, stood up to join him, and he looked over at Quin.

"We need more fighters. I'm gonna go try and find my pack so they can help us. Where should we meet you guys? Is it safe in town?"

She was already itching to transform and get out of the prison. Randy looked thoughtful for a second before lifting his palm to the air before him. He muttered something and a ghostly image of an old mansion appeared.

"This is where I live. I told the spell- and it's a show-me spell, which is one of the few that it's impossible to lie with- to show me if anyone was hiding out or watching the building. I don't see any-one, so I think that means this is a safe place to rendezvous. Plus, Abigail said she'd been accumulating weapons there too, so I'd lay down money that she went back there to wait for us. It's right on the edge of the highway at the base of Wapetona. The mini bus that brought all of us up here can technically hold 16 of us "safely", but if we're willing to cram together 3 to a seat and count the driver, we can fit 25 in." He furrowed his brow for a minute in concentration, letting the picture of his house disappear while he tried to count something out on his fingers.

"And then, the five cars that the guards and Linda came up here in would hold another 25 of us including whoever drives the car, so counting the guards, the 52 of us could all get down there like that, if Quin runs with her pack," he rushed out breathlessly, looking out at the crowd for their approval of his math skills. Quin thought about it for a second, then frowned at him.

"That's only 51. Someone would have to run with me, because 25+25 is 50. Not 51."

An embarrassed flush crept up Randy's face as he realized she was right. He cleared his throat, and was thankfully saved from having to respond by Sidwell, the ghost Quin hadn't really gotten to know that well yet.

"I can fly pretty fast, since I'm a ghost. I'm a nomad by choice, so I'm used to traveling outside all the time anyway. I can fly along with Quin and help her get her pack together, and then we'll all meet up with you at the shop."

Quin quickly grew bored of the logistical talk, and she longed to stretch her legs and run. While the others were preparing to leave so they could gather everything to meet up later, she said goodbye to Mitchell. When the two parted, Quin walked out into the early spring air of the parking lot, taking a moment to stretch and take in the clean, wild scent of the mountains. No one at the Ark had eaten breakfast, so the smell of deer and rabbits was making her *ravenous*. She transformed and decided to hunt for a while. Sidwell could find her later.

~~~~~~~~~~

Crunch crunch crunch crack crash

Ow.

Quin was hunting, her pack running with her. They'd been chasing a herd of young deer along the bank of the Wapetona River, when their prey took a turn down the mountain into the woods. Quin was so focused on catching the deer that she didn't notice the tree branches smacking her sides until she ran headlong into a particularly big one, tripping and falling on the underbrush beneath the tree. Two of her packmates stopped to look at her while the rest managed to catch up to the herd and circle them. She shook herself and ran to the others, flinging herself at a doe.

When she'd eaten her fill, Quin looked up at the sky, trying to guess how much time she'd been hunting. It felt like only a few hours, but the sun was now noon-high.
~~~~~~~~~~

"We should start heading towards the bookshop" she thought to her packmates, leading the way towards the road to town.

I'm surprised it only took me half an hour to get across the lake. Thank god for the poor idiot who left his fishing boat up there over the winter. She laughed at herself. *I'll have to leave some gas or something for him.* She thought, feeling guilty she'd used almost all of his supply.

They followed the road for awhile, all 13 wolves alert and watching in case a council member or a car came up the road. Quin was thinking of the Speed-e-mart and how badly she wanted a slushy.

Just after the pack passed the sign that said "5 miles to Duf-t-n" (the one Quin had offered to repaint so the county didn't have to keep pretending it would), one of the other wolves let out a short bark. The group stopped and looked at the wolf, whose hackles were slightly raised as he looked across the road.

I don't remember a turn in the road there. Wait- there's a warehouse back there! When was that built?

Quin cautiously crossed the road and stepped onto two legs, resuming her human form. She shimmied up a nearby tree and looked down at the building, which looked more like a big garage now that she was close to it. A vile, rotting stench clung to the door, as if a corpse had been hung and left to fester there. Quin could smell it from nearly 50 yards away. She wrinkled her nose, her stomach turning at the memory of the last time she'd smelled it.

The creature that took Linda smelled like that. When he called himself Roger and looked like a quotidian, he smelled like cologne and malice. When he looked like that black-eyed demon thing, he smelled like a sewer full of dead animals. He must've been here.

Before she found the courage to get any closer to the building, she felt a hand on her shoulder. She screamed, almost falling out of the tree, and flailed to press her body down against the branch she was laying on. She turned her head to try and see who it was and growled when she realized that the person who'd scared her was Sidwell.

"What the hell, man! You might be able to fly so you don't fall out of a tree but I can't! I could've fallen to my death!" she covered the pounding in her chest by snapping at him angrily.

"Well *soooorry* wolf girl. That's payback for abandoning me at the prison. Nobody knew where you lived, so I've been flying around this mountain for the last 4 hours looking for you. I found this thing a little while ago, but until about half an hour ago there was a bunch of council members hanging around. I saw Roger's car pull up and he used that black cloud thing of his to throw someone inside and then I heard a big crash. He collapsed one of the walls inside so whoever he put in there would be trapped. I have a sneaking suspicion he put our dear warden in time out here," the ghostly cowboy bit back, watching as Quin slowly backed down out of the tree. He led her over to the door, rolling his eyes as she coughed dramatically and covered her nose. The scent was *so* much stronger now that she was near its source.

"I can float through the door and open it for you if you think you're strong enough to get the debris away from the place she is stuck, but I'll warn you, it smells even worse in here."

Quin nodded solemnly at him, covering her nose. He floated through the wall and got one of the huge doors open, and she held her breath, transforming so she could run through faster. She found the source of the crash- a crushed van laying on its side, in the back of the building. Someone was banging on the inside, and Quin recognized Linda's voice through the metal.

She closed her eyes and thought of her siblings. She pictured Vei Vei trapped in the van, crying for their mama to come get her. She was flooded with the memory of her parents, of their own car crash. She'd seen the police photos and she remembered being filled with an awful sense of inadequacy.

I couldn't dig them out. I couldn't... **I have to get Linda out. I won't let her follow them.**

She transformed back to have opposable thumbs then threw herself at the van, startling both Sidwell and Linda. Adrenaline and inhuman strength filled her and she managed to pull the side of the van away from the wall enough to expose the back doors. She kicked at the locks on them until they broke off, and then Linda was pushing them open. She grabbed her and pulled her free the rest of the way. Linda insisted on getting outside as fast as possible, and the others agreed. Even while probably concussed and definitely injured, Linda could still relatively keep up with the wolves as they ran towards the Pocket Watch. Linda had overheard a *lot* while she was stuck in Roger's car, and Sidwell and Quin both agreed that everyone else needed to hear what she had to say, ASAP.

CHAPTER 21: THE COMING STORM

The tea room and main floor of the Pocket Watch were absolutely packed. Randy and Abigail were upstairs, yelling so loudly at each other that Mitchell could hear them over the crowds of magic users in front of him.

Quin was sitting on a couch, looking shell-shocked and tired. When she had arrived at the mansion with Linda and Sidwell, she'd stayed transformed into a wolf for over an hour, pacing in circles around the greenhouse until someone had called her inside. Introductions had been happening between everyone who'd been at the Ark and everyone who'd managed to stay free on the outside since the bus pulled into the parking lot, and by the time she'd been dragged inside, Linda was trusted enough to share her story without risk of disbelief.

"The Marmaran leaders, Marlene and Maurice, are alive," Linda began. Gasps rose up around him, and Mitchell's eyes widened, flicking over to Quin. Instead of seeming happy, she just balled herself up tighter into the corner of the couch. Clearly, she'd found things out on the way down the mountain.

"They have them both hidden. They didn't say *where* they were hidden, but they were talking about breaking their minds soon. Roger said he wanted to break mine first, because" -here Linda shuddered, pulling a disgusted face- "I would be the most *fun*. They thought I was unconscious, so they talked a lot about their plans for destroying the Quotidians, and I'm proud to say, we've got them beat on one thing. They didn't think Quin would be as smart or strong as she is, so they didn't plan on her taking the leadership of her Pack from her brother. They think the wolves are wandering aimlessly right now. Unfortunately, they need to heal Maurice, because in the process of capturing him by hitting him with a truck" -disgusted cries rang through the building at this, and Linda had to wait a moment before she could finish. Mitchell saw Quin's eyes well up with tears.

"His leg was badly broken," Linda continued. "It would've been fine, but because they didn't treat it until a few days ago, so it had to be amputated. From what I heard, Marlene's better off than he is, because they had to heal her first. In the process of faking her death, she lost three pints of blood in the name of "making her 'murder' more realistic", so they had to heal her and give her a blood transfusion in the back of the kidnapping van. Until now, the two of them have just been locked up somewhere."

Mitchell stopped listening.

No wonder Quin's so sad. She can't heal him until we find him, and he's so hurt...

By now, Randy and Abigail had come downstairs to try to direct the crowd, and everyone started to talk at once. Mitchell made his way over to Quin. He put his hand out, catching her attention. She wiped at her eyes and reached out, taking it and pulling him down to sit beside her on the floor. He stayed with her there for awhile, providing quiet support as groups of Marmarans and Twalneres began to file out of the building. Randy came over at some point to tell them that everyone else was going to go collect supplies and spread rumors around town about an upcoming storm. That way, Quotidians would start to vacate the area.

No one will question big groups of people stocking up on water, food, and bandages before a storm, and a few more cars than normal going up the mountains will get overlooked.

"Linda said the council's got about 200 members, all really good at black magic and, for the most part, pretentious to a fault.

They're all focusing on building up spells to attack the minds of the Quotidians, but very few of them were actually tasked with "paying attention to what's going on in town". They're almost all out at a group of farms in the valley that they have control of. As long as everyone avoids the cops, we shouldn't be noticed too much. You two are going to stay here with me and guard the weapons we've started stockpiling here."

What were they fighting about so loud?

Mitchell voiced the question, and Randy sighed heavily.

"I was mad at her for not trusting Linda and not telling anyone about her dumbass plan to go rogue. She almost got all of us *killed. She got Linda kidnapped.* I'm not being unreasonable, am I?"

Mitchell frowned.

*I hadn't really thought about it, in the rush after the blackout and the stuff that happened this morning, but yeah. This plan change totally **was** her fault.*

The more he thought about it, the angrier he got, and he didn't notice until Quin pushed him away from the couch that his hair was actually starting to smolder. He made an effort to calm down, and gratefully accepted Randy's offer of hot chocolate. The three moved to the tea room for something to eat and drink, and then they took up positions around the house to protect the rebels' hoard.

~~~~~~~~~~

My feet hurt.

When he'd volunteered to help guard people's quotidian loved ones on the way to the caves that the Marmara and Twalnaverra had mapped out as safe house areas, Mitchell really hadn't thought about how much *hiking* that would entail. Even taking cars to the start of the trails, everyone had to hike for two or three miles before they would hit any of the caves that they were all going to hide in. At least, he mused, he wasn't listening to more of Randy's relationship stories, though his old roommate seemed kinda hurt when both Quin and Mitchell had left to go with Abigail.
~~~~~~~~~~

He'd been a little nervous to knock on the door of the mayor's fiancee, but when the scary business lady who opened the door heard that her partner *wasn't* dead, he'd realized that one can only be *so* scary when one is crying from relief. She'd immediately begun organizing groups of the Marmara's Quotidian allies, who she'd been in charge of for Marlene, to round up vulnerable family and friends, ones who were close enough to local cryptids and wizard-like entities that even the conservative rules of the Marmara were lax for them. She'd been the one to remind Randy and the others about the safe house caves in the first place.

Compared to everyone else I've ever ridden with, Konna "Not-Fitzgerald-yet-but-I-don't-know-her-real-name" is the safest driver I've ever met.

Something rustled in the newly-growing underbrush and Mitchell's head whipped around, eyes scanning the woods for any sign of anything. It was getting late, and there were dark, dangerous clouds forming in the sky. By the time that they'd reached the caves, bulbous drops of rain were falling on their heads, and they'd had to create weirlights and get out flashlights to be able to see.

Konna herded elderly Marmaran family members who couldn't fight and children too small to be of help into the caves first, and Abigail did the same for the Twalneres. Quin's brothers, Titus and Theo, held onto their sister's shirt while Vasha wailed in her arms, begging not to be put down. By the time that they'd finally let her say goodbye, everyone else was already bundled up into the safety of the caverns, and tents and stakes had been set up for protection against intruders. A few of the prison escapees stayed behind to keep watch over everyone, and Mitchell, Quin, and Abigail began their trek back down the mountain, past the hidden cars parked where no one would notice them.

~~~~

They'd been fighting the gale for almost half an hour, making their way down to the highway again. Abigail had picked him up and ran with him on her back for a little while, and her speed matched with Quin's transformation got them back to the base of
~~~~

the mountain much faster than he'd expected. Still, the torrential downpour was enough to make him feel physically sick.

There they are.

"What?!" Mitchell called over the wind, frightened by the unmistakably *internal* voice he'd just heard.

We can get them. NOW!

He let out a cry that caught Quin's attention just before she ran headfirst into a line of 5 council members wearing dark cloaks and bloody smiles. She snarled and barked a threat, her hackles rising dangerously. Abigail dropped him to the ground and grabbed at a silver knife she had hanging on her hip. Mitchell rolled over and screamed, just missing an axe thrown by a councilmember who had the head of a bear.

You will die today, prisoner.

Hearing his heart pounding in his ears, he stood and let his instinct take over, summoning a ball of fire in his palm and throwing it towards the monster. It roared at him and retreated, and he looked back at Quin to see her tearing at the arm of a council member. Abigail was pinned to a tree by two others, a fourth raising a stake over his head. A crack of lightning struck nearby and momentarily stopped the action, and Mitchell took that as his cue to try what he'd never attempted before. He drew in an immense breath and screamed, spitting flames toward his enemies.

Stay away from my friends, you buttheads.

The tree and the council members holding Abigail to it went up in flames just as Quin managed to pull the vampire out of the line of fire, and the two called for him to follow them as they escaped down the rest of the mountain. But he couldn't move anymore, vision going black as the last uninjured council member watched him fall to his knees in the mud.

You're ours now.

He didn't have the energy to even think anymore, as five minds converged inside of his. A shrieking pain filled his head, and his lungs stopped filling with air. An agony that lasted an eternity and a half coursed through him, and then.

He knew no more.

CHAPTER 22: SAFE AND SOUND

"I did it! Guys, I know where they are!"

Abigail's voice rang out down the attic stairs, undoubtedly catching Randy's attention on its way down to the others. She shot down the stairs a few seconds later, holding a book of runes and a map.

When everyone had chosen their tasks to prepare for the "final battle" they were going to spark, she'd volunteered to go over the new map Linda had stolen from in the trunk of Roger's car and try to decode it to find the others.

Randy hasn't said more than four words to me at a time since that night.

Memory flashed across her mind- Randy screaming, his first question wasn't *"how could you betray us?"* It wasn't *"why don't you trust my judgment?"* She'd been prepared for an argument about those. When the first thing that came off his tongue was, "you could've gotten yourself killed", she was left entirely without a defensive argument to make.

"I didn't think you'd care," she'd said. *"You were too busy with your research for the blonde bitch, I'm surprised you weren't incinerated by your roommate before I broke out."*

The words left her mouth before her brain could comprehend them. He'd swallowed hard and gotten a dangerous edge. They'd argued for a long time, her rebuttals only half as smug and effective as she'd hoped to make them.

She'd been forced, by the virtue of the memory-sharing she'd had to do with Linda, to learn how wrong she'd been to go off on her own.

I hope this show of faith is enough to prove to him that I deserve another chance with his trust.

Lilac and Quin met her at the bottom of the stairs, and they swarmed her as she stepped off the stairs. Randy followed behind her, looking quietly hopeful.

"Linda's memories and my code-cracking hobby combined quite nicely, I'd say. See that mark? They only use it twice, hidden inside other runes. It means "under here" or "under ground". I've heard of lots of farmers who keep sub levels in their barns around here to protect them as a shelter-in-place in case of earthquakes. They usually keep some animal-keeping supplies there, so they can hold their prized farm animals down there if need be. I'll bet anything that Maurice and Marlene are being kept there, and Mitchel's probably there too."

Linda sucked in a breath, barely detectable past Quin's excited squeal. Abigail looked over, reaching out with her mind to her new friend.

"Will we find Caeda there, too?"

Before Abigail had time to make the mental connection between "their ally who warned them all and kept Linda alive" and "this name she just said," Randy piped up.

"We have to go get them!"

~~~~~~~~~

There's no one here?

There was a very suspicious *complete lack of council members* at the farm. Abigail's questions were answered when the group cautiously rounded the side of the farmhouse and almost ran into the back of a cloaked figure who sat guarding a line of cars.

The storm, which had been raging for the better part of a week since they'd orchestrated the "Great Escape" (as Randy had dubbed it), was giving them cover now. The creaking of the wooden porch and the sounds of their feet in the underbrush by the buildings was completely covered by the rain and wind.

Thank god there are Twalneres who can manipulate the weather.
~~~~~~~~~

Everyone in the group shrank back, thankful that the sentry was paying attention to the book in his hands and not to anything else. Abigail thought quickly, trying to find a spell to strengthen the killing force of the knife at her hip.

"Steady hand, fast and true,
this kiss of death I give to you.
The darkest shades of night shall frame
Your soul now for the void to claim."

Abigail snuck up behind him and hissed the curse into his ear, plunging her stiletto into his heart. Dark red blossomed across his back, visible dimly against the black fabric as a spreading stain. He let out a gurgling cry that was (thankfully) covered by the shrieking wind.

*"Tornadoes don't happen in the mountains" my ass. At least it's giving us some cover, even though it **sucks** to have to walk through woods and farmland in this bullshit.*

Once the guard at the farmhouse was down, Abigail motioned over her shoulder, hooking a finger at the others. She started inching around the porch, mud squelching under her boots.

Linda, Randy, Quin, and Lilac all followed behind her, trying to dodge raindrops (in Lilac's case) and stay hunched over so the house's 6-foot-high window sills didn't brush the tops of their heads (in Quin's case). They made it across the front lawn, and then they scattered out among the cars, ducking and slinking through them so as not to be seen by any council members who might be looking out a window.

There has to be at least a hundred cars here, with footprints at both front doors.

They were up against *way* more members of this army than they'd prepared for.

They got to the barn and were met by two sentries, both looking to be young and probably new to the council. They let out startled yells and lunged at the group, but Lilac caught one by the wrist. She snarled defiantly and sent a shock through him that brought him, twitching and thoughtless, to the soaking wet ground. The other tried to turn and run to warn his elders in the farmhouse, but Linda overtook him almost instantly and nearly crushed his throat with her arm.

"*Where are they?? Where are your prisoners?* **Where is Cindy Callsworth's body?**"

The guard trembled and tried to use a spell on her, but Linda squeezed his throat tighter, wrapping her other arm around his head in a nasty choke.

"*Answer the questions or I pull your hell-fucked head off, you piece of shit,*" she growled in his ear, just loud enough to be heard by her victim and by Abigail, who was standing closest to the pair.

"Wolf a-nd m-mayor in s-storm cell-lar, un-der th' la-ast stall," he choked out past her arm, desperately trying to gasp for breath.

"And the body?" Linda urged, grabbing a fistful of his hair and rewarding his meager cooperation by letting him take in a gulp of air.

"Never told who they were. Just put them out in a hole by the silo. That's where Elder Callsworth said all the traitors go. His ugly wife would be no exception."

There was a bite in his tone that Abigail *almost* pitied him for.

Aw, you dumbass. You shouldn't have said that.

Suddenly, she had to jump and pull Quin farther back as Linda howled furiously and jerked her arms, unceremoniously ripping the sentry's head off of his shoulders and throwing it at the outer wall of the barn. She dropped his body and spat on it, then looked over at Abigail with a *terrifying* glint in her eyes, not noticing how the others shrank away from her or how Randy turned away to retch onto the ground. After a second's pause, she motioned to the unguarded barn door and silo with both of her bloody hands.

"*Let's go.*"

~~~~~~~~~~

They'd decided to split up so Linda could find Cindy's body. Randy pulled open the trap door and walked down the crumbling
~~~~~~~~~~

concrete steps, and Abigail followed close behind him. Quin took up the rear, casting a glance up at Lilac's retreating form.

She's gonna see some fucked up shit, Abigail thought, imagining how Linda would react, seeing her mother's body thrown into a pile.

They followed a narrow corridor, cautiously calling, "Maurice? Marlene?" into the darkness. They got no audible answer. This continued for awhile, the passage leading them farther across the property than it should have. They passed dozens of makeshift stone cells, obviously meant for overflow prisoners. The Ark had been almost at capacity when she'd broken out, so the council would have no doubt started bringing people here too, if need be.

Many of the cells were crumbling, rusted doors betraying how long the council had been planning this for.

This must've been built around the same time the prison was, or else the council didn't know it existed until after they'd started carting every-one up the mountain. There isn't any waterproofing, so it makes sense stuff is breaking down.

The damp passageway ended, and yet, there was no sign of the Marmaran leaders.

"Were we lied to?" Randy wondered aloud hotly, shooting her a suspicious glance.

"W...what if they've already taken him away to have his mind broken?" Quin fretted, a tear threatening to roll down her cheek.

Abigail said nothing, her eyes scanning the dark passageway. There were single, dusty bulbs that dimly lit the hall every hundred feet or so, but they barely did anything for the oppressive darkness that hung in the air.

Suddenly, out of the corner of her eye, a flicker of light caught Abigail's attention. One of the cells, which had almost been hidden by a pile of stones across most of the door, drew her forward. She pointed it out to the others and they all rushed over.

"It's Marlene!" Randy exclaimed.

She was waving a...glowing antler? Abigail thought for a minute, then remembered the luck charm he'd made her shortly before her disappearance.

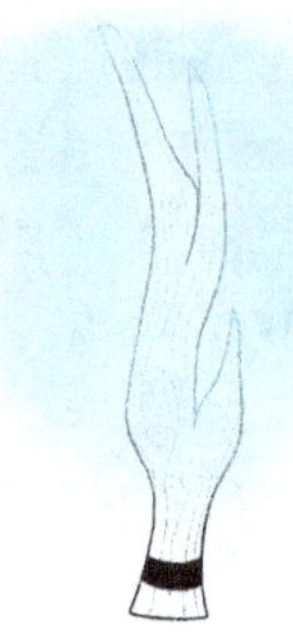

She was waving that and straining against the chain that tethered her to the far wall of the cell. She looked like she was yelling something, but Abigail soon realized that she couldn't hear her because of a silencing hex on the walled-off door.

"Help me get this stuff away from the door." Quin picked up the stones two at a time and flung them at the opposite wall. As soon as they got the door open, they all rushed in and Abigail broke the chain on Marlene's wrist. When they'd helped her out into the hallway, Marlene threw herself at Randy.

"Your luck charm saved my life! They didn't find it when they kidnapped me and they didn't bother to take my clothes or anything, so I've had it hidden on me this whole time. I genuinely didn't think you'd find me because of the dark and the silence hex, but you did, thanks to the charm and Abigail's good eyesight. Maurice is two cells down. They just brought him back...last night? I think. I don't exactly have a clock but it was a little while and they said something about him "waking up thankful in the morning." They healed his leg using necromantic prosthesis, but they couldn't mess with his mind until after the effects of the procedure wore off. Something about "undermining the integrity of the magic" or something."

*That's a **horrible** process, damn. I hope he wasn't awake for it.*

Marlene led them to his cell and cracked her knuckles, murmuring at the metal. It cracked and screamed in protest as she bent it down into a rusted pile using her powers, then fell back heavily to try to regain her strength.

They must've had the stones and silencing spells there to keep her from breaking herself out. I think she's the reason there wasn't a lock on her cell door anymore.

Quin pushed past the mayor, squeezing through the bars as soon as she physically could. Everyone gave her a moment alone, watching as she shook her older brother awake. He flinched away, his eyes glossy and distant, before he recognized her. He burst into tears, and Abigail turned away uncomfortably. While the two embraced, she motioned to Randy and he looked at her quizzically before following her a little ways down the passage. When she had his undivided attention, Abigail found herself fumbling for her words.

"Listen, Ran, I... I wanted to tell you I'm sorry. I didn't listen to you, and I gave you a panic attack, and I forced our hand, and... I never apologized. I acted like I didn't care about you, and I acted like a total asshole." She fidgeted with the hem of her raincoat, looking away as soon as she'd said her piece. She waited for his reply.

"I forgive you. I'm sorry I ignored your input in all the plan meetings- you were right. They *would* have broken us anyway." He looked down and lowered his voice, as if only half of him wanted her to hear him.

"I was far more upset by the thought of losing you."

He looked up and caught her eye, giving her a look that told her everything she didn't know she needed to hear. He let her feel his emotion for a moment, and she could feel an unfamiliar, but deeply appreciated feeling spread through her chest.

Abigail's mind sort of went... blank. All of the things she'd refused to think about, the feelings of emptiness without him, the jealous pangs she tried to deny, rushed at her all at once as he reached out and took her hand, brushing his fingers over her knuckles.

"I spent... more time than I'd care to admit rewatching that hologram of you," she mumbled. "I watched it until it stopped playing. I..." she met his gaze and interlocked her fingers with his, letting him feel her mind back.

"I really missed you."

Something told her to lean towards him, and she listened to it. Their noses touched, his hot breath tickled her upper lip, then...Quin was yelling at them. Randy let out a small laugh, and pulled away from her face, refusing to let go of her hand.

"You two can suck face later!! We have to go, before anyone finds those sentries!"

CHAPTER 23: THE LAST BATTLE

"What do you mean, "you didn't find him?" You had time to drag a corpse back here, but not to look for Mitchell?" The Marmaran in front of her looked Linda up and down, seeming not to notice the dirty tear stains on her cheeks or the way she clutched Cindy's body close to her. The corpse was freezing cold, but somehow, the rain and hailstones weren't hitting it on the way back to their ride.

"*She* is the reason I *lived* to help you find Marlene and Maurice. Ca-*Cindy* was your ally too, or have you forgotten that?" There was an acidic bite on her tongue as she snapped back at the person barring her way, who thankfully didn't question the slip-up.

They huffed and let her pass, and she could tell that after a moment, they wanted to offer t o help her carry the body. The group of rescuers and rescued had scryed the others, telling everyone to meet at Lake Wapetona's cabin-filled campgrounds. The council had talked about fighting there before, as Linda had told everyone, and it was decided that it would be wise to cut off as many of the council's advantages as possible.

There were already several large groups of people who'd been assigned tasks- some were digging spike pits, some were putting up barriers using magic, and Marlene and Maurice were working together on...something. They'd taken a bit to recover and she'd replenished their magical energy, and now they were getting accustomed to free life again. The rain and storm had stayed in the valley, and as people arrived at the camp with weapons and supplies from their homes in Dufferton, they brought with them reports of a cloud of dark fog, as purple as a bruise and as thick as the smoke from a house fire.

They've put the quotidians to sleep, then. Here's hoping that killing the spell caster stops the spells.

Linda took the body to a repurposed fishing cabin that everyone was calling "the healers' area," and found the Marmaran that Marlene had told her about.

I'm surprised my mother bothered to make friends with any mortals, but at least I'm not the only one mourning her.

If the sorcerer who took the body out of her numb arms was surprised by how intact it was, aside from the injuries themselves, he didn't say anything. Marlene had assured her, upon hearing of Cindy's death, that her coffin would be spectacular. Linda trusted her word, because she didn't really have any other choice.

When she'd gotten cleaned up, she went out to try to be useful. She found Quin and her pack milling around, and the pack was... *much* bigger than it had been 6 hours ago. Linda's dogs (and some strays), wild wolves, and even a few feral cats all clustered around, waiting for an order from the teenager. Quin told her where to find Maurice and Marlene, and she decided to pay them a visit.

"Ah, Linda!" Marlene exclaimed from somewhere under a giant hunk of metal that probably used to be an abandoned car. Maurice was sitting at a picnic table nearby, running his hand up and down his leg. The skin had a greyish tint, and it was much thinner than his other leg, but from what she'd seen before, it was strong enough to hold his weight already. For all their horrible intentions, Linda had to admit that the council's healers were some of the best in history. Marlene had already built a mechanized brace for him, and she seemed to be tightening the last bolts from the install as Linda arrived. The mayor pushed herself out from under it and took Maurice's offered hand, knocking on the front of the metal sculpture three times.

A light inside whirred to life and the thing purred as it stood up. It was a giant mech suit, shaped like a bear, which loomed over Linda's head. Panels of glass revealed the compartment where Marlene would sit.

"What do you think? Pretty, isn't she?" Marlene looked at her creation lovingly before turning to Linda for approval. The elf nodded, impressed.

"Oh wait, that's right. I was hoping I'd see you. I think I know who your mark is going to be, when this battle comes, and I know you're going to need a weapon. So, I made you these."

She motioned for Maurice to move and let Linda see something, then Linda gasped. Behind him on a picnic table sat a pair of clawed metal gauntlets, inlaid with protection and strength runes and crowned with barbs along the knuckles and at each fingertip. She stepped forward, repeating thank-you's as she pulled one on, stunned to find that they were *perfectly* her size. Somehow, the clunky-looking metal felt weightless, like nothing was there. If she closed her eyes, they were just the skin of her hands.

I'm gonna do so much damage with these.

~~~~~~~~~~~~~~~~~

Mitchell was back in the fold. It was almost midnight, and he'd been found by two of the wolves, soaking wet and wandering the side of the mountain.

They wouldn't let him go like that. This is a trap.

Linda tried to warn the others, but all her protests were drowned out by the excitement of having him back. No one else seemed to notice the far-off look in his eyes, or the way he stared at people's weapons and vulnerable spots just a *little* too long. Before she could get the others to listen to her, they all heard *it*.

The first sound of war. The cry of "council!!!" from a sentry on the edge of the camp. They readied themselves as they saw 200 black-robed council members advancing across the plains next to Lake Tamory, coming at them from the Two Peaks side of the plateau. Linda snorted, picking up a bottle of gin someone had thought to bring with the supplies and downing a quarter of it.
~~~~~~~~~~~~~~~~~

*This is going to be absolute hell, but as the gods are my witness, I will make them all pay for what they've done. For what **he** did. To me.*

To her.

The battle was fought in fits and spurts, stretching across several days. Linda spent most of her time breaking curses put on her friends by council members, but she did a fair bit of fighting as well. She was one of a handful of actual doctors, so everyone came to *her* when they broke something or got something cut off instead of the entire tent of healers. She found that when she was fighting, her gauntlets were excellent for wielding knives. Marlene had built some kind of magnet into the palm that kept the weapons from getting stuck in anyone and ripped out of her grasp, *and* they had a bit of energy stored up so she could sling spells at people. Most of her friends only fought by daylight, but she and the wolves didn't need as much light to attack, so they antagonized council sentries. Even the opposing army was wary of fighting at night, when the temperature dropped sharply and there was nothing to draw energy from but yourself. The council didn't think they were going to be up against such a bold little army, so both sides needed the time after dark to lick their wounds. The breaks meant that the council was no longer confident in their ability to overpower anyone by sheer number, their main advantage. They were almost double the size of the Marmaran and Twalnaverran forces, and yet, the two sides were even. For awhile.

At some point, however, Linda was proven right. Mitchell lit an ally on fire and let himself be taken by the council, and everyone who asked Linda (who had been near him when it happened) about it got the same response.

"I fucking told all of you!"

Gradually, the balance shifted. The council began winning, dominating the psychic and physical fights they engaged in. They beat back their foes slowly, and as Linda clawed apart an older recruit she'd seen at meetings glaring at her, she realized something.

Roger isn't here.

As if on cue, she spotted him. A jet-black shadow silhouette of a man, with burning red eyes and bone-white teeth stood across the battlefield on a high outcropping of rocks at the shore of the lake. He seemed to see her too, and he smiled maniacally, lashing out towards her friends with his aura. She knew, then, exactly how she was going to destroy him.

I'm going to tear your fucking heart out, you damn demon bastard

CHAPTER 24: BUT THE SUN REMAINS THE SAME

It was day five of the fighting, and Randy was really getting the hang of tearing people apart with poison ivy. The councilmembers almost seemed to be multiplying, with their original 200 coming back again and again to fight even when they'd been killed. Mitchell had turned on them all, going to fight with the council and lighting a Marmaran on fire.

A wicked, bone chilling cackle rang out across the battlefield, the sound no doubt riding down the sides of the mountains to fill the valley below. Randy could see Roger standing at the head of his troop, a disgusting grin splitting his face, full of blood lust and the false promise of glory. Bile rose in his stomach at sound and sight of the repulsive creature, making him want to be as far from him as possible. His own allies surrounded him, each with determination in their eyes, ready to do what it took to end this.

Randy watched as people began to part, and soon he spotted Linda running ahead, straight towards Roger. He saw her tear through a swarm of Council of Blight members like they were sidewalk grime and she was a power washer. The elven woman stopped in front of him, making everyone watching freeze in their tracks, afraid of what was to come. Roger laughed at her, his voice ringing out across the field, everyone hearing his words.

"So we meet again, Linda. Think you've come to avenge your mother? *Think you can kill me?*" His voice was manic and horrible, like nails on a chalkboard, and loud enough for Randy to hear from almost a quarter of a mile away. Randy realized that he must be able to hear so clearly thanks to an amplification spell.

"No, I know I can, you sick son of a bitch!" she yelled, thrusting her fist forward, gauntlet flashing in the light above them as she punched through his chest. The sound of his ribs breaking echoed across the field. The stunned onlookers, council and non, were all horrified as they watched her pull his heart from his chest, black and still beating in her hand. She looked him in the obsidian eye and tore the muscle in half.

"And it's Aemenora," she growled, her voice still projecting through the silent stillness of the stunned battlefield.

Randy felt like he was going to throw up.

~~~~~~~~~~~

The pause in action gave the Marmarans and Twalneres enough time to overpower the council members that had frozen in shock. Many of them had begun to bleed and die from wounds that Roger had healed for them, and down in the valley Randy could see that the purple fog that the council had conjured was starting to dissipate. Out of the hundreds of people who had stopped dead to watch their leader get himself killed, several dozen crumbled immediately to piles of gore. Randy pushed off a man who had previously advanced on him, tying him down and turning to go help others, when he caught a flash of red hair out of the corner of his eye. Before he knew what was happening his back hit the ground, the air in his lungs leaving him from the force of his fall.

Above him, Mitchell's eyes were hollow, as if he was looking at everything from the corner of his vision, empty of their usual light. He held him down, hand lifting in the air, palm glowing as he prepared a spike of flame. It didn't take long for Randy to realize that his former friend was going to burn him alive. Mitchell moved to drive the spike into his chest, but he was able to stop him, his fingers tight around the pyrokinetic's wrist, their eyes meeting, Randy silently pleading with him to stop.
~~~~~~~~~~~

For a few, horrible seconds, the only thing Mitchell did was push harder against Randy's life-saving hold on his arm. Then, he moved his other arm to wrap his hand around Randy's neck. The older man sputtered, trying to gasp for air. Just as he was about to let go of Mitchell's arm and succumb to his death, something flew at the side of his attacker's head, bouncing off of it with a soft *thunk* and distracting him.

"Get off of him, you asshole!"

Abigail was throwing rocks at him, and Mitchell growled at her angrily, beginning to turn toward her with more fiery force than he'd been ready to hurl at Randy. Then, Randy thrust out a hand and caught Mitchell's wrist, turning him to look into his eyes.

Something clicked, and Mitchell faltered. His eyes cleared, and he shook his head, extinguishing his flames. He fell to his knees, clutching his head and babbling about "the voices" for a moment, before seeming to relax, as if he'd had a swarm of bees trapped in his head and they'd just all flown out and left him alone. Cautiously, Randy put out a hand and pressed it into Mitchell's back.

The teen drew back, frightened, then looked up at Randy with long-awaited recognition. Tears sprang into his eyes at the realization of what he'd almost done, and he shot up off of the ground to hug Randy close, apologizing between hiccuping sobs. Randy rubbed his back as Abigail came over, waiting for the right time to butt in. When Mitchell was calmed down he began heading toward the rest of the Marmarans and Twalneres, who were by now almost done rounding up the leader-less council members that hadn't managed to escape, and she was alone with him.

The first thing Randy noticed was the sun, bursting through the clouds for the first time since Roger came to the Ark, in celebration of their victory. The second thing he noticed was that there was a new sun-protection talisman around Abigail's neck, keeping her from burning. The third thing he noticed were how soft her lips felt against his, and how protective her arms felt around him. How safe she made him feel. How...hopeful. He smiled against her lips, holding her back.

They'd won.

CHAPTER 25: IN WHICH WE SAY GOODBYE

The pines shifted and creaked over the heads of the survivors, bowing low as if they, too, were mourning. The night was clear and cold, but there was not a star in the sky. Even the moon was muted; a waning gibbous frowned down over the earth. Every face in the small crowd was somber as 200 eyes tried to stay dry.

They stood at the base of the mountain in a quiet clearing. It was the early morning after the battle, so no one had time to change into proper funeral clothes, and they'd all been too busy seeing healers and contacting their families to even think about a shower. The air was thick with the scents of sap and the coppery tang of blood and sweat. At the head of the clearing, a picnic table had been brought down to be a makeshift podium.

Aemenora stepped up to it first, looking out at the faces below her. She was chosen as the first to speak in honor of her mother's sacrifice. She drew in a breath of the mournful mountain air and, for the first time in centuries, she was afraid that she would cry where someone else could see. She took another breath to steady herself, then opened her mouth to speak.

"None of you knew her in her younger years like I did. This isn't" -she swallowed the lump in her throat with a dry cough- "*wasn't* the first enemy we've fought together." she coughed again, then bit back a curse as a single, uncontrolled tear slid down her cheek.

"I guess you all expect me to say the old clichés. You expect me to remind you that she was an excellent warrior, protector, healer, friend. I-" she choked on her words, audibly sniffling. "I'm not gonna do that. Sure, she'd want to be remembered for that protective, motherly nature of hers, but the spells she wove and the things she made were just as big a part of her. She wouldn't want us to only remember her as a double agent, either. In fact, she would want us to forget the council and the bastard in charge of it entirely. She would want us to celebrate our victory, not focus on hatred for our enemies."

Aemenora reminded herself to take a breath, letting a few more tears slide down her cheeks.

"So that is why I'm speaking to all of you. You, who did not know her as anything but Cindy Callsworth, the villain's wife. She was so much more than that."

She gave a small nod to someone in the crowd, who gently carried a box to the podium and handed it to her. The sound of glass clinking together made her cringe as he placed the box beside her hand. She turned her attention back to the crowd as he took his seat once more.

"My mother's true name was not Cindy. It was Caeda. She was the daughter of the elven god of the moon and an elf who gave her life to become a star by her lover's side. Caeda was born of the sky, and nearly everything about her reflected that fact."

Aemenora gently lifted something out of the box, holding it up for everyone to see. It was a vial of pale purple powder that sparkled and glowed, even in the dim light of the forest. As soon as she held it up, the moon began to peek through the clouds to shine on the mourners.

"For example, did you all know that she used to bottle galaxies like it was an art form? As long as I can remember, she kept one of them on a cord around her neck, so that it was with her always."

She held the vial higher, towards the moon, and its glow seemed to intensify.

"She spun moonbeams like cotton candy, and she drank starlight like it was fine wine. She treasured beauty like dragons treasure gold and diamonds."

The elf murmured a word and beakers, vials, mason jars, and many other glass containers of various sizes and shapes floated up out of the box to rest on the podium in front of her.

"I always thought that she was eccentric, with her bottled sunshine and condensed horizons, but now I really wish that I had listened when she was telling me how she made them. If I have one regret in life, it is that I wish I could catch a falling star and keep it in a fish tank. She did that once, y'know. Offered to let me keep it, but I was too worried I'd kill the poor thing so I told her to take care of him for me."

Aemenora sniffed again, wiping her eyes with a pale blue handkerchief that she pulled out of the box. She studiously avoided getting anything on the embroidered "C" in the bottom right corner. She smiled when she looked at it, then let out a small laugh.

"She always said that someday she'd give me this handkerchief. She got it in the early 1300s, right after they were invented. I told her, in no uncertain terms, that I was totally uninterested in inheriting her old snot rag and that I'd never use it. I guess I was wrong."

The solemn mood of the crowd shifted a bit. Five or six faces smiled a little at their friend's dry sense of humor, and one or two snorts of guilty laughter were heard (Aemenora would later deny one of them was from her).

"She told me once, when I was drunk on something she made out of wildflowers and stardust, that she was the daughter of the moon. I thought she was full of shit, but then she waved her hands and pointed at the sky and did something that looked like some sort of seizure, and then I watched the stars move into a whole new constellation. She couldn't sustain it for a long time, but- oh, look. I guess she's decided to make it again for us."

She pointed out over the treetops and everyone turned to see a huge swath of stars shifting and dancing as they repositioned themselves. When they stopped, a huge crescent-shaped ox-bow was stretching across the sky below the moon. A sweet, wildflower scent floated past the mourners on the breeze, and several stars twinkled as if they were eyes blinking down on the world. A woeful smile touched the corners of Aemenora's lips as she looked at the sky.

I just got you back, mother. I can't believe you're already gone again. What am I supposed to do now?

If Aemenora's voice shook more than before, no one in the crowd noticed. She drew a breath and continued with her eulogy, no longer caring if anyone saw her cry.

"She was a better mother than anyone else I've ever met, and losing her feels like a knife in my heart, but I know that now she's safe from the worst of this world. She's with the others we've lost. She is in her rightful domain, ruling the kingdom of the sky. As much as I will miss her" -she dabbed at her eyes with Caeda's handkerchief again- "I know that she is where she belongs. Finally, after 7,000 years, Caeda has gone home."

Silence fell across the clearing at the finality and profound sadness in Aemenora's shaking voice. They all watched as she stepped down from the podium and made her way to the back of the crowd, in full view of the night sky, to stand by the side of Caeda's coffin. It was made of luxurious rosewood and carved with runes and intricate knots, made by several of the warriors before the battle started. She ran a hand along the lid, delicately brushing fallen leaves off of the top and away from a small indentation in the wood.

Aemenora pulled on a cord around her neck, releasing the knot that held it in her shirt. She held out a tiny vial of dark, glimmering liquid, then carefully pulled it off of the string and held it up above her head.

You vowed to keep it with you always, and now I'll help you keep your promise.

She placed the vial into the indentation and it fit in perfectly with a soft *click*. She slid a carved glass panel over it and muttered a spell of sealing and protection, then she stepped back from the side of the coffin. She raised her voice, looking up at the sky as she shouted,

"May you forever shine, Caeda."

A chorus of voices echoed her words, and gasps were heard from the crowd. High in the air, filling the sky with trails of shimmering starlight, a hundred thousand shooting stars blazed across the night sky.

EPILOGUE: GUARDIANS

The hot, early-August air ruffled Marlene's hair as she walked out of her town hall office for the last time until September. There was a small crowd of reporters standing outside, and she wasn't sure if they were reporting for the local tabloids about her personal life, or if they wanted to know how the Marmaran-Twalnaverran merger talks were going.

Though she and the rest of the Marmara had been, at first, resistant to the change, Randy had very sensibly pointed out that there was absolutely no point in acting like magic could stay hidden from the Quotidians forever, because "purple fog and a demon creature walking down main street attacking people and caught on film" were not things that Quotidians would just...forget on their own.

Ever so slowly, magic became normalized. The first places to use it were the hospitals and libraries of Kacapa county. Local news stations *loved* Randy, with his interesting (and mostly harmless) magic and his charming personality. They'd also been eager to talk to her, when they'd found out about the Marmara and Twalnaverra, because they trusted her leadership and wanted to know how new or uninformed magic users might join.

Thankfully, they'd accepted the explanations that they'd been given, that the evildoers who'd imprisoned many of the upstanding citizens of Dufferton were insane (which they no doubt were) and no longer a threat. This part was untrue, as many of the most powerful had escaped, but the Quotidians did *not* need to know that unless absolutely necessary. They also didn't need to find out that Mitchell had shared some concerning information about *Roger summoning something, to be bound to him and set loose upon his death.*

The idea of merging the Twalnaverra and Marmara was brought up by a quotidian, then it gained traction. Marmarans didn't condone frivolous use of magic, but they no longer thought it prudent to hide. Twalneres condoned frivolous magic, because sometimes frivolity can mean the difference between happiness and total despair. Both sides of the issue got along fine, for the most part, so they decided to put it aside and merge. It was to be led by Marlene, Maurice, Randy, and Abigail equally, though Linda had been the one to choose the name in honor of their greatest ally, Caeda. The official merge of the Twalnaverra and Marmara into The Guardians would happen in the fall, once Marlene and Konna got back from their honeymoon. They chose their new name in honor of what Caeda had called them when she had been convincing Aemenora to trust them so long ago.

~~~~~~~~~~~

"...And do you, Marlene, take this woman to be your lawfully wedded wife, to hold and to have, in health and in sickness, to treasure and to cherish, in the light and in the darkness, until the void does take you?"

She held Konna's hands tight, the silky pink ribbon tied around her wrist sliding just slightly as she turned to look away from her partner's face and at the officiant, then back at Konna.

"By my deepest honor and with all my now-beating heart, I swear by all the kings and queens and goddesses and gods, I do."

"Then, by the powers vested in me, I now declare you wife and wife. You two may now each kiss your bride."

They leaned into each other, pushing back each others' veils and cupping each others cheeks, and did just that in front of a crowd of all their friends, family, and several of the tabloid news cameras.
~~~~~~~~~~~

They then both threw their bouquets into the assembled, laughing when Randy caught them both and looked at Abigail with a grin.

The entire crowd was so ecstatic for the happy couple that every single guest failed to notice the dark, looming thunderheads gathering far in the distance above the devil's bed plateau.

ACKNOWLEDGEMENTS

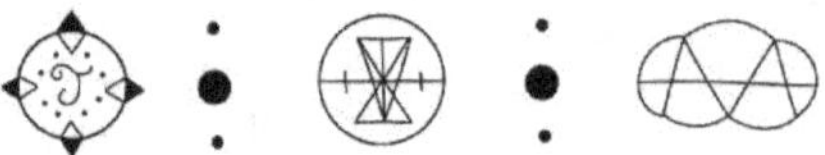

From the very start of this journey, there have been a few very special people who have inspired, supported, and helped me create this story. Starting with nothing more than an inside joke and some nicknames, The Ark of Light has grown so much in the last several years into the story it is today. The people who inspired the characters in this book are some of my very favorite people in the world, and I am so thankful to them for their influence.

Thank you to KC, for her beautiful art and her amazing personality, who inspired my vision for Quin. Thank you to Maria, whose strength, death stare, and late-night brainstorm help brought Linda to life and helped me deepen the lore of the story. Thank you to Marrion, the inspiration behind Mitchell, for your amazing sense of humor and for being excited with me at every milestone. Thank all of you.

Your support through all of my writing process, your willingness to listen to me rant, your input on character development, and even your generous donation of your floor as a writing space truly shaped me into the author I am today. I am so, so honored to be able to call you my friends.

Thank you to everyone who made the audio drama of this book possible, too. You each inspire me every day, and your unique perspectives helped me make the story better. Thank you to Emily, of www.fantasynamegenerators.com, whose incredible website is a treasure trove for writers who can't figure out what to name stuff. Thank you to Audrey, the prompt wizard on Tumblr who inspired

Caeda's death. Thank you to Kenaz and Rowan, Maria and KC, for your contributions to the wonderful illustrations in this book.

Thank you to my family, who have always supported me as a storyteller and a person. I love you guys so much.

Thank you to everyone who's shared this journey with me, from Madeira, where I learned and grew as an author and a person and gained my confidence and love of writing, to college and beyond. I am who I am today because of all of you.

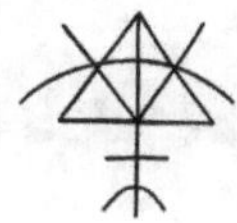

About the Author

Katherine Gardner is an up-and-coming young author from Virginia who started writing *The Ark of Light* in 2017, during her sophomore year of high school. She graduated from the Madeira School in 2019, and is now pursuing a bachelor's degree in creative writing at Shepherd University. When she's not telling stories, she enjoys listening to music, hiking, crafting, and spending time with loved ones.